THE COMING OF THE FAE

A CONTEMPORARY SCIENCE FANTASY

RETURN OF THE FAE
BOOK ONE

MARTY C. LEE

Bookaholics Press

Book design, cover, and publication by Bookaholics Press LLC
Edited by Martha Rasmussen
Author photograph by Melissa C. Baxter

ISBN-13: 978-1-950230-32-7 (epub)
978-1-950230-33-4 (paperback)
978-1-950230-34-1 (large print)
978-1-950230-35-8 (hardback)
978-1-950230-65-5 (audio)

Published by Bookaholics Press LLC
Provo, Utah bookaholicspress@gmail.com

Contact the author at MCLeeBooks.com

For Kylia, who gave me the idea for this series, too,
and for Tad, who told me how to fix this book. (It's his fault people die.)

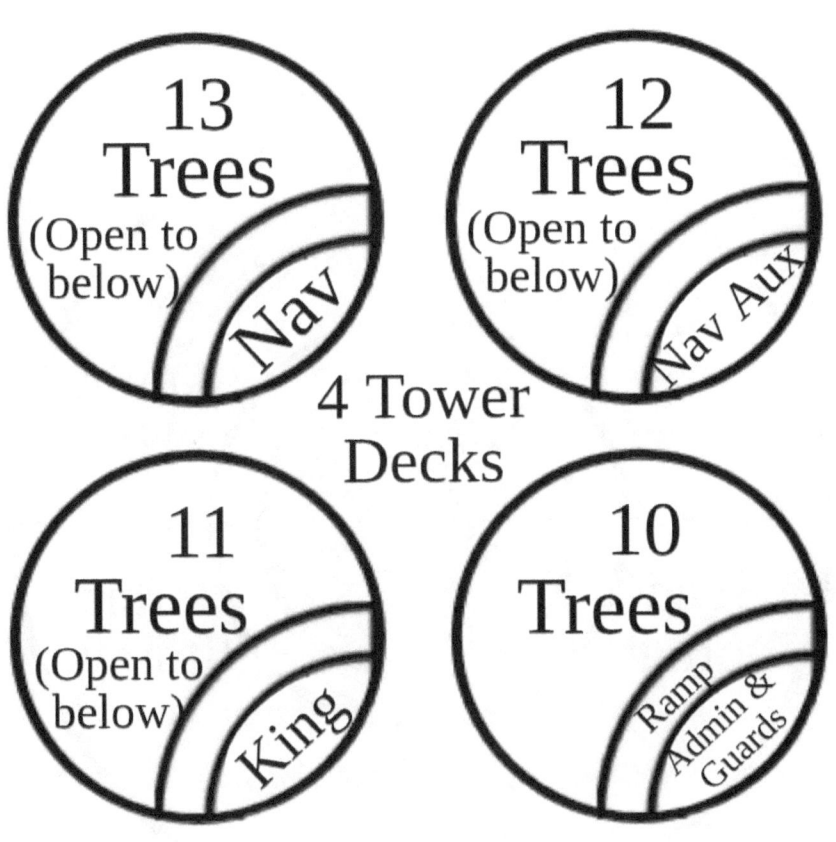

13
Trees
(Open to
below)
Nav

12
Trees
(Open to
below)
Nav Aux

4 Tower
Decks

11
Trees
(Open to
below)
King

10
Trees
Ramp
Admin &
Guards

Population: 10,000
Animals: 500
Dragons: 3

Exterior
View

New Kunisu

Living Decks
3rd, 5th, 7th, 9th

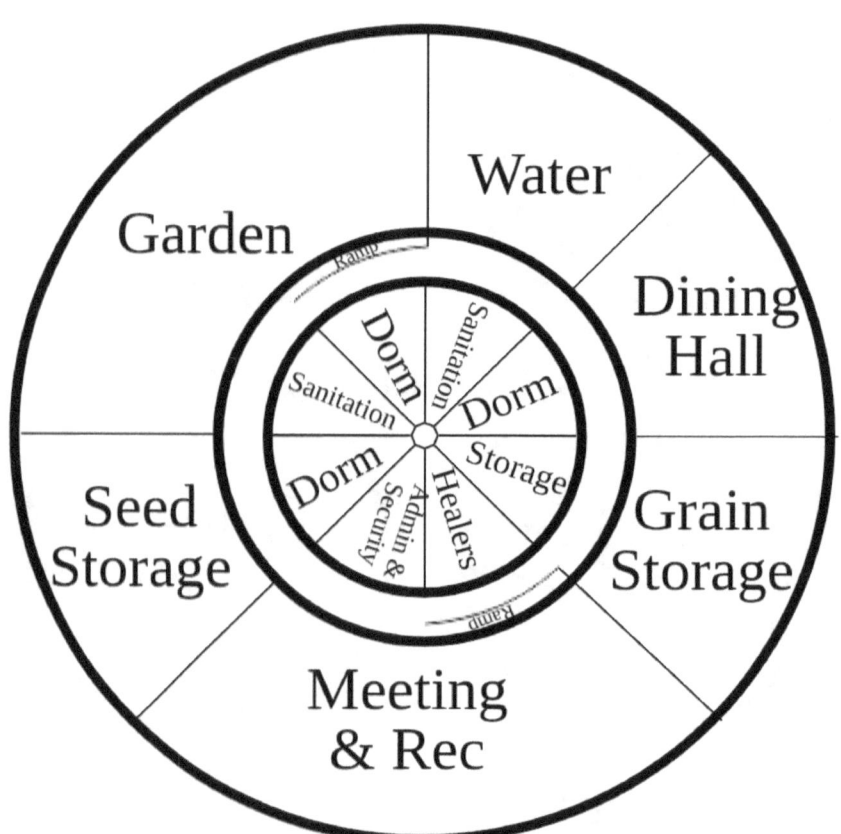

9 full-size decks:
4 living/storage, 3 garden,
1 animal, 1 hold/dragons' den

Author's Note

While I have been meticulous to real life detail and science in some places, in others I could not find information, or changed things for the sake of the story or to protect real people, or simply made mistakes. Most of all, please remember this is a work of fiction. The characters are completely imaginary.

PROLOGUE

WISH ON A STAR

MAY 5, 2021, OAHU, HAWAII, UNITED STATES, EARTH

THE MYSTERIES of the universe shone in the sky. While the other teens and their adult chaperones took turns using the telescopes, Alexandria Fitch flopped onto the sand and looked at the dark sky with her bare eyes. Above her, meteors fell from Aquarius, zipping between the stars as if they were late for dinner.

"This was a great idea, Alexandria," Lindsay gushed as she took her turn after Ian. "So much more fun than cake decorating."

Chad scoffed. "You just like staying up late. My turn."

One by one, all the teens in their church group peeked at the meteor shower through Alexandria's telescope or the one borrowed from the library, then lined up for another turn.

She'd seen it all many times before with her grandfather, so she stayed where she was. As the next star fell, she closed her eyes and wished for her perfect life to stay exactly the same. She had her family back together again, a clear sky of stars, and all her plans were on track.

In the darkness, Ian lay on the sand and put his head onto her shoulder. Her twelve-year-old brother tended not to say much in the group, but at least he had come this time.

"One of these days," Alexandria whispered to him, "I'll get to explore space with an even bigger telescope."

"Yep," Ian said.

"Pan-STARRS has the biggest telescopes," she said, "and they're just three islands over, but who knows what will be available by the time I get through college."

"LS-whatever should be up in a few more years," Ian agreed. "And James Webb before that."

Alexandria laughed. "LSST. Have I been lecturing you too often?"

"Mm-hm."

"Sorry?"

Ian snorted. "No you're not. But I'll get even."

"Oh, no," Alexandria said with mock-horror. "Are you going to read ancient Greek to me again?"

"Better believe it."

She chuckled, and they lay quietly under the stars until someone asked about the Institute for Astronomy. Alexandria popped up to combat their ignorance, leaving Ian in the sand.

"They're doing a sky survey with two wide-field telescopes," she explained. "They snap several pictures each hour, then use computers to look for differences that would mean a moving object."

"Like meteors?" Chad asked.

"Sure, or asteroids, or space debris. There's a lot of stuff out there. A lot of movement between pictures usually means fast or close."

"Yikes," Lindsay said. "Like something that could hit Earth?"

"Not likely," Alexandria assured her. "But if there's any possibility, the info is sent to the Minor Planet Center, and Pan-STARRS keeps watching to identify the orbit. And not just the fast objects, either. Something that looks very slow might actually be a rock coming straight at Earth."

"Does that happen often?" said the new girl whose name she hadn't caught. She'd ask someone on Sunday, if she didn't figure it out before then.

"When was the last time you heard the White House say you should worry?" Alexandria asked.

"Um, never?"

"Yep, that's about right. NASA and the president will tell everyone if they ever find a real problem."

She lay back on the beach, and Ian whispered, "Lecture mode activated. You're getting Greek all day tomorrow."

"Hush, you, or I'll tickle you."

Ian giggled but said nothing more, and they watched the meteors until the adults announced four a.m. and hurried them into the cars. Alexandria was the last to get in because she had to pack up her telescope, and by the time she slid into the backseat with Ian, the other cars had left.

In the front seat, Lindsay chatted with her mother.

"Everything is perfect," Alexandria said softly to her brother. "Hawaii is fabulous, and I slayed freshman year."

Ian leaned against the window. "Mm-hm."

"I get to learn to drive, and Dad is home. How much better could it get?"

"Mm." Ian twitched.

"Hey, don't you have any faith in my driving?"

"Haven't seen it yet. You might be scary." Ian paused for a long moment. "Does Dad seem different to you?"

She sighed. "Mom says it will take a while for him to readjust from Afghanistan. Just be good and don't make loud noises around him, okay?"

"I'm always good," Ian muttered.

She reached across the empty middle seat and took his hand. "It will be okay."

Lindsay's mom dropped them off and waited until they went inside. Alexandria closed the door quietly and texted her mom.

Home safe.

She and Ian tiptoed down the hall to their bedrooms. She was asleep in minutes, dreaming of the stars.

In the morning, Dad woke them much too early and dragged them out for fresh pancakes.

"I've got great news," he said briskly. "Here's the syrup, Alex. Ian, stop poking your food."

Alexandria smothered her pancakes with syrup, too tired to remind Dad again that she no longer liked the old nickname.

"What news?" Mom asked. "Did I know about this?"

Dad didn't look at her. "Probate on my parents' house finally went through."

"Oh, good," Mom said. "The money from the sale should cover the college fund for both kids."

Mouth full, Alexandria nodded. She only had three years left to go, and her babysitting money didn't add up to much. If they set aside enough now, she could spend her time studying instead of working.

Dad grunted. "Even better. I got a transfer to Colorado Springs, and we're going to live in it."

Alexandria dropped her fork. "No! Not again! You promised we'd stay here until I graduated high school."

If they moved, she'd have to make new friends again, and maybe she hadn't taken the right classes for another school. She'd have to drive in the snow, and did Colorado Springs even have an observatory?

Mom took a deep breath. "Honey, don't you think we should talk about this first?"

"It's my house," Dad said.

Ian jerked upright. "If we're getting a house, can we get a dog?"

"I don't want to move," Alexandria said. "What the—"

"No swearing," Mom barked.

"We're going," Dad said. "But no dog."

Ian slumped and poked at his pancakes again.

Alexandria pushed away her plate and ran for her room.

So much for wishing on a star. Why did Dad have to ruin everything?

CHAPTER 1

In Which Good News is Heard

149 CONJUNCTIONS AFTER DEPARTURE, *New Kunisu*, SOMEWHERE between constellations

A LOW BELL rang twice through the ship. Gil moved his brother's arm and rolled out of bed, flipping in midair so his feet pointed toward the pale green that shone even in the dim light, then waited. In another moment, weight gradually returned, pulling him to the newly oriented floor.

All around him on *New Kunisu*, hundreds of people did the same. The remaining sleepers grunted a little and pulled blankets over their ears. Only a few pixies glowed on the walls to show the way between the rows of bunks. The gentle whisper of giant wings flapping echoed from the roc or phoenix or gryphon on air circulation duty.

Gil flexed his knees gently, testing his heavier body. When he was little, the ship had spent more time accelerating, so walking felt normal. Now the pilots pushed them only on alternate shifts, so weight would still strengthen bones and muscles and allow certain tasks to be accomplished more easily.

And speaking of tasks, he only had four hours to clean and feed the animals, so he had better hurry. He used to work with the animals infrequently, like everybody else, except when he volunteered for extra shifts. But the old keeper didn't like the job, so when Gil grew enough and still preferred it, the king's secretary reassigned him permanently, and the housekeeper sang all his new duties into his mind. His family had been assigned berths on the third deck to be closer to his charges.

He grabbed an apple from the barrel by the door and hurried through the crowd in the circular hall with the painted dark red sky above him. The inner wall was painted like Old Kunisu and its neighboring worlds. The female half of the Starry Lovers had been a lowborn seer, and the outer wall was painted with her vision of their new home — Ki — and the worlds that surrounded it. Pictures on the doors marked their purpose, since only the highborn could read. And a few select commoners, like Grandsire and the secretary. Grandsire had promised to teach Gil once they landed and could live apart from the lords.

Once down the ramp to the zoo below, Gil wound through the crowd of workers waiting for him to unlock the door, greeting everyone.

Zak pulled on his elbow, his pointed ears flushed bright green with excitement. "We're only a few conjunctions from Ki," the short gremlin whispered. "The fleet will slow more, so there will be more weighted shifts."

Gil nodded and squeezed the older boy's shoulder. "I appreciate the time to plan."

As a navigation contriver, Zak frequently had useful gossip. In this case, the news meant Gil must start exercising the animals more to strengthen them for when they landed. Even the weight from the ship's acceleration was less than their home world or the new colony, or so the adults all said. Gil had never known anything different, though he loved Grandsire's stories.

Gil pulled off his necklace to access the key hung next to his silver family crest. "All right, I need half of you to clean and half to bring food and water or escort animals next door to graze. As soon as all the animals have eaten, we'll walk them around."

He swung open the door and let everyone file through while he replaced the key around his neck.

The noisy room was partitioned into cells just large enough for their occupants, who bleated or neighed or otherwise called for attention and food. Above the stalls, the walls and ceiling were lined with cupboards full of harnesses and tools strapped firmly into place.

As Gil fed his apple core to the closest hydra, some of the workers tried to linger by the door or pretend they were busy, so Gil unstrapped shovels from the wall and handed them to the dawdlers.

"Shovel the dung into the barrels," he said, as he always did, pitching his voice to carry over the din, "and carry it across the hall to the compost heap."

Scraping the mess from the floor was a thousand times easier than collecting it while it floated in midair. Keeping it contained was the reason the room was always locked during weightless shifts.

Larger fae started with the aisle floor while winged people attacked the cupboard doors with trowels and rags. One or two at a time, the animals were led out so their stalls could be cleaned. One team ferried grain, while a second carried buckets of water. Zak led a third crew taking animals through the back door into the garden to graze. He worked with Gil frequently enough to know some tasks by heart, even without a memory song.

As each stall was cleaned and re-occupied, the proper food was added to each trough, and the noise level gradually diminished. Most of his workers ignored the animals, but Gil gave each one a pat or head rub along with a quick word. Occasionally, he nudged someone into work again.

When he found a golden-haired highborn mocking a much shorter pukel, he sent both to opposite sides of the room. The pukel slipped away with relief evident on his face, and once safely out of reach, obediently returned to work.

"At least that flying pest isn't here," the highborn muttered as she stomped off.

"Miknon knows how to feed a unicorn without annoying it," Gil said. "She's a valuable help in the zoo."

In fact, his adopted sister worked with him often enough to be trusted supervising workers. Sadly, this was one of her sleep shifts.

"Stupid pixie," he thought he heard, but he chose to ignore it. Miknon wasn't stupid.

Like the other children raised on the ship, Gil was used to living in close quarters with fae of all kinds. The older generations, however, had lived in very different circumstances, both physical and social. Working side by side with those they considered their inferiors — even *working* instead of being served — was a difficult adjustment for the highborn fae. Or so Mother claimed. Gil thought other people were fascinating, and working was more fun than floating around doing nothing.

He sent some of his more experienced workers to check hooves and assigned novices to brush coats and sweep up spilled grain. Finally, the basic chores were complete.

"Everyone taller than my waist should choose an animal and walk them in the aisles," Gil ordered, opening the closest cupboard of bridles. "Make a line and stay orderly."

He chose the crankiest kelpie and kept one hand in its black mane. "Come on, let's walk."

The green kelpie neighed at him and tapped a hoof on the newly clean floor.

"I know," Gil said, "it hurts your feet. It will hurt more if you don't get the exercise. Come on."

The kelpie snorted into Gil's hair and started walking. With everyone helping, they got every animal up and down the aisle at least twice, then retrieved the grazers before the shift bell rang, once this time, for no change in weight. They tethered every beast and filed through the door.

Gil waved at the animals and locked the door behind him. Fortunately, without sunlight to eat, the dragons slept for conjunctions at a time and needed little care. He dropped the key around his neck and headed to the third floor's grain hold. For the next four hours, he would shelve crates or carry whatever his troll supervisor ordered. If nothing else, Grandsire said lifting during a weighted shift was good exercise for his muscles and bones, and as the king's best warrior, he should know.

Everyone worked for two shifts and ate and visited for one, but the order varied, as did the number of sleeping shifts. He didn't envy the king's secretary and housekeeper keeping the schedule for all the different races on board. And though his next favorite task was unskilled labor in the garden where Mother worked, he didn't mind lifting.

As usual, he crossed paths with a friend, and the two of them chatted happily. Most supervisors didn't mind talking as long as the work got done, and Gil always worked as hard as he played.

The time passed quickly, and the double bell rang before he expected it. He strapped the last crate onto a shelf as his feet floated off the floor. With both of his work shifts finished, it was time to eat with his family. It would be the first time he had seen Grandsire in a couple of days.

Gil pushed off the wall, shoving again to build up speed. Lucky Miknon, who could always fly instead of only floating half the time. But as he reached the dining hall next door, a golden-haired highborn approached from the other direction. Behind him came more off-duty fae. No more flying, then.

Gil tucked himself into a ball and rolled, grabbing for a safety bar. He pivoted around his grip, swinging until he crashed into the wall and bounced to a stop.

What was a highborn doing on the third deck if he wasn't on a duty rotation? Most of them lived on deck nine, though some overflowed onto seven and a few of lower rank chose housing with the commoners.

The lord sniffed and tried to smooth his embroidered tunic, which did little good when the fabric drifted. Even the jewels along the hem couldn't pull it down. The lord's fancy hairstyle floated in odd gold waves, unlike Gil's pinned braids.

"You go first," Gil offered, waving a hand toward the door.

The lord's eyes widened, and he turned up his nose. "Of course," he said. "I merely stopped to remind you to keep one hand on the safety bar at all times. Be dignified, if such control is possible for a whelp like you, and have a care for your betters. If you had bumped into me, I would have a word with the king." Without waiting for a response, he swept through the door.

"Ooh, a word with the king," Gil repeated. "I don't suppose that word would be 'fun.' I bet he doesn't know who my Grandsire is."

A kobolos waiting to enter the dining hall shook her head, waggling her long ears. "Be careful, youngling. You don't want to cross a lord. They have ways of getting even."

Gil tipped his head to the side and grinned. "They're always telling me to settle down and be boring. I'm not worried."

"You should be, unless you like your lungs filled with water or your blood turned to fire." She swam through the doorway.

Such a doomsayer. Nobody knew how to enjoy themselves. Gil floated through an opening in the crowd, looking for his family. Mother and his brother and Grandsire were already in line for the meal, almost to the front. Gil squeezed in beside them and hugged Mother.

The room was filled with tables and chairs bolted to the floor, and the ceiling and walls were lined with straps attached to bars. With so many people on the ship, diners had to eat whether they had weight during that shift or not.

"How many?" a bored huldrekin droned. He turned to grab the next box, revealing a hollow back and cow tail.

Grandsire looked at Gil, who nodded. Miknon would join them as soon as she shook off sleep. Her duty shifts came afterward, and if she ate with them, she didn't have to settle for the scraps left at the end of the meal.

"Four and a half," Grandsire said.

The huldrekin grabbed three more boxes and a small bag and handed them to the head of the family.

The four of them made their way to a corner and buckled straps around their waists to keep them still while they ate, then Grandsire passed out the small boxes of fruits, vegetables, nuts, and mushrooms as Miknon fluttered through the crowd on rapid blue wings.

"Greetings, Miknon," Grandsire said. Mouths full, Mother and Ram merely nodded.

"Greetings," Miknon replied. Instead of using a much-too-large strap, she anchored herself by holding on to Gil's necklace, as usual.

Grandsire passed her the bag, which held the same foods in smaller quantities. Upon discovering the fruit of the day was a plum, Gil slipped it to Miknon, who loved them.

"I saw that," Mother said.

Miknon quickly gobbled half the plum and handed the rest back to Gil. Reluctantly, Gil ate the nasty thing. He'd have to be sure Mother wasn't watching next time. He slid the pit back into the box, closing it to keep the remains from drifting away.

Ram chuckled and tapped Gil with a clawed nail. "Nice try, little brother."

Gil scowled at him. Ram was only two minutes older, but he never let his twin forget his seniority. And he always acted so perfect. His kilt was clean and unwrinkled, and his braids wrapped smoothly around his head. His pale blue eyes shone with mischief, though, and Gil thought of a million retorts.

Instead of replying and starting a fight that Grandsire would break up before it got interesting, Gil split his attention between his meal and the mural on the wall. Every room not filled with shelves or cupboards was painted with some kind of story. This room showed the evacuation treaty. Unsurprisingly, King Arishaka stood with his lords, flanked by his guards. Grandsire looked ferocious behind the king, even though he wasn't the tallest of the Companions.

The remarkable part of the mural, compared to other paintings on the ship, was the number of common fae pictured. The king's secretary was a pukel, chest-high to the sirin housekeeper with knee-length hair, next to an even shorter gnome and a sharp-eared female gremlin who bore a striking resemblance to Gil's friend Zak. As she ought, since Zak was her grandson. Behind them was a long line of pilots and navigation contrivers of many races. Most of them were so important and protected that everyone knew their use-names, though politeness still dictated not using them.

And in the background, a small, dark-haired girl stood with her back to the audience, staring at a picture of the colony world. Her raised hand held a paintbrush.

"Look at all the heroes," Gil said dreamily. "We're so lucky most of them are on this ship with us."

"And the treaty has improved all our lives," Ram said. "Praise the king."

Grandsire snorted. "We did what we had to do. That doesn't make us heroes."

Gil winked at him. Sure it did. Grandsire was the biggest hero he knew.

"I think it was luck," Ram said. "What were the chances the gremlin would find a new way to fly a ship at the same time the mapmaker found a path?"

"The gremlin is dead," Gil said, "but we could ask the mapmaker, if we knew who she was. I don't understand why the king has never revealed her identity."

Mother made a face. "Maybe she didn't want to be famous."

"Maybe it was to keep her safe," Grandsire grumbled. "The highborn didn't appreciate the treaty."

"Well, it would still be fun to know who she is," Gil said. "This is my favorite story. Imagine how exciting it would have been to be there when everything was happening."

Grandsire lightly cuffed him. "Excitement is not always good. Even now, our survival is uncertain."

"It would help if everyone would grow up and take our situation seriously," Ram said with a significant look at Gil.

Gil ignored him. Ram was always harping about responsibility. How could they be twins if Ram didn't even know how to have fun?

"But we're alive now," Gil said. "Do you think Old Kunisu is destroyed yet?"

Mother turned her head away. "There's no way to know how long it lasted after we left. Focus on the present instead of old stories."

"I still think it's exciting that we're following the Starry Lovers," Gil said, ignoring Mother's advice. "And Zak said we're getting close. Imagine, soon we'll be on a whole new world, with real grass under our feet, like the garden room, except we can walk on it. We can plant a new garden, twice as big as the entire ship."

Grandsire laughed. "Much, much bigger."

Gil whistled. How could something be that big?

"No more food rationing." Ram crammed the last of his meal into his mouth.

"You aren't starving," Mother said gently. "Nobody is starving."

But never quite full. Gil rubbed his belly thoughtfully. The older he got and the faster he grew, the less his meal ration seemed to be enough.

And he never got enough to eat to be able to shapeshift. As soon as he grew old enough to control his shifting on purpose, Mother had made him stop. By now, he wasn't entirely sure he remembered how.

To distract himself from his belly and his confined shape, he daydreamed about flying over an impossibly endless expanse of grass.

No, on the new world, he wouldn't be able to fly. He would always have weight. How strange. Run, then. He could run over the grass while Miknon flew over his head.

And trees. His gardener friends said they would plant hundreds of trees in the new world. Thousands, maybe. Would there be enough room for thousands?

They would have to build new homes, of course. And they would spread out across the world instead of living altogether. They might be a whole league apart! Grandsire could retire and let someone else protect the king so Gil's family and all his friends would stay near him.

And speaking of his friends...

"I'll be back in time for bed," he promised Mother, then swam toward the closest friend he could see in the crowd.

Miknon let go of his necklace and flapped her wings. "I'll see you at work."

He waved and kept swimming. He only had a few hours to talk and play, and he intended to make the most of it.

GIL ARRIVED at the dormitory just as the shift bell rang. He swam to Mother and his brother and strapped himself with them into one of the many-layered bunks that lined the wall. Grandsire had a work shift with the king this time, as he frequently did. Poor Grandsire, alone so often.

"Sleep well," Mother murmured, already on the edge of sleep.

Ram didn't answer, but his snores rumbled in Gil's ear. The room echoed softly with the sleepy breathing of hundreds of people.

Gil smiled to himself and pulled the blanket to his chin. In four hours, he would be refreshed and ready for more fun. Always more fun.

But sometime later, not long enough for a full rest, the emergency alarm clanged, all the notes in a discordant clash.

The ship jerked, throwing Gil against his sleep restraints. He howled in pain and tried to steady himself. All around him, people cried out.

"Ram, Gil." Mother clutched them to her.

"I'm fine," Ram said breathlessly.

Gil fumbled at the straps. "I have to check the animals."

The ship stopped shaking, and the alarm bell turned off. The all-clear sounded, so those assigned to emergency cleanup stations struggled from their beds while everyone else went back to sleep.

By the time they crowded out the door into the hall, rumors were already flying.

Something had hit the ship.

CHAPTER 2

NEW SCHOOL

AUGUST 16, 2021, COLORADO SPRINGS, UNITED STATES OF AMERICA, Earth

NIKOS SHOVED his sunglasses higher up his nose and bent to see his host mother through the car window. "Thank you, Mrs. Moss. I'll catch the bus home."

He'd have caught it this morning if he'd been awake five minutes earlier. Stupid jet lag.

"Oh, you're welcome, dear. You remember which bus?" She smiled under her cloud of white hair.

He patted his backpack. "I've got the schedule."

All the schedules, all the information. He rubbed his forehead. Stupid headache making it hard to remember anything. He would review his class schedule and the building map again to refresh his memory.

"Okay, dear," she said. "Have a nice day at school."

When he backed up, Mrs. Moss slowly pulled away from the curb and slipped into the line of departing cars.

Nikos turned around and stared at the American high school in front of him. Students already streamed into the large brick building, chattering and laughing and hurrying along. As he should be, if he didn't want to be late and disappoint his new school on the first day. Presumably, the front doors would lead to the office where he was to report. If not, he could ask a student. He straightened his collar and headed inside.

The office was clearly labeled right inside the front door, and even through the crowd, it was no trouble to find. He went inside and stood at the back of the short line, listening to the frazzled secretary deal with students needing lunch tickets and locker combinations. Even with his sunglasses, the fluorescent lights were uncomfortably bright, and the American chatter was so different than Greek.

Finally, it was his turn. "I'm Nikolaos Antonakis. I was told to report here before classes?"

"Oh, yes! Our foreign exchange student. Welcome to Colorado." She shuffled through a stack of papers, then sighed. "You were supposed to come in for school pictures last week."

"My apologies," he said. "My flight was bumped several times because of Covid restrictions. I only arrived last night."

He rubbed his head again. Jet lag and too little sleep. His parents had driven him to the Heraklion airport early yesterday morning, but he'd been alone among strangers for three hours in Munich and two in Denver.

"Well, you'll have to do retakes next week so we can get your school ID. In the meantime, use this." She handed him a paper printout with his name and student number. "Here's your locker number and combo, and your school schedule."

He already had the schedule they'd emailed him, but he took everything. Better too much than to miss something he needed.

A loud bell vibrated through the halls.

"Better hurry to your first class," the teacher warned.

Nikos glanced at the schedule in his hand, which was at least more accessible than the one in his bag. Trigonometry, down the hall and around the corner.

Only when he arrived, the room number didn't match. His stomach roiled with nausea, and he took a deep breath to calm his nerves. Rubbing his head, he turned the map upside down and tried again.

Just as he opened the door to the correct classroom, another bell rang.

"You're late, mister," the teacher snapped. She stopped writing on the whiteboard long enough to glare at him.

"I'm sorry. I won't be again." He'd memorize the school layout today, headache or not.

"Well, hurry and take a seat."

Light streamed through the windows all along the far wall, and Nikos winced at the sun's enthusiasm. A little more sleep would have made today easier. He found an empty desk in the back row and sat, tucking his backpack under his desk and turning his face away from the window. The front was better, but he could switch tomorrow.

All around him, students whispered and chewed gum, blatantly disrespectful to their teacher.

"Welcome, students," the teacher drawled. "I'm Ms. Blackwell, and this is Trigonometry. If you are in the wrong class, you may leave now." She looked around rather hopefully, but nobody left. "In my class, we have assigned seats, and I don't want to hear complaining about it. When I call your name, come get a math book and then take your seat."

The first student called was assigned the front row next to the window. The second got the desk behind him. Nikos was third.

"Nicholas Anton-akiss."

"Nikolaos Antonakis," he corrected, raising his hand.

"Just say 'here.'" She pointed to the third row by the window, and he took a book from the pile and reluctantly moved into the bright light.

As she continued the roll, Nikos tried to match names with faces, but she spoke quickly, and the sunlight dazzled his eyes, making it hard to see. If only his plane had gotten in a little earlier last night. By the time he called his parents to say he'd arrived, it was early morning for them. He tried shading his face, but it didn't help much.

Eventually, everyone was assigned seats. The girl two seats over from him squinted at him, almost a glare. She was tall and skinny, with her brown hair pulled up in a ponytail, and the overenthusiastic sunlight made her green eyes glow. He wavered a smile, then ignored her and concentrated on calming his stomach. He should have accepted Mrs. Moss's offer of something to eat in the car on the way to school.

"All right." Ms. Blackwell clapped her hands. "Attention, please. Let's start in chapter one." She stopped and looked at Nikos. "Nicholas, take off your sunglasses. They aren't allowed in class. And I'd better not see the rest of you with gum tomorrow. Now, chapter one."

She kept talking, and Nikos reluctantly took off his sunglasses and tucked them into his bag. When he sat up again, the sunlight hit him full in the face. His sleep-deprivation headache rebelled, and so did his empty stomach. With no warning, he vomited onto the shiny school floor.

Students screamed, and Ms. Blackwell stopped lecturing. "Emilio, go find a janitor."

A young man bolted for the door while everyone else scooted away from Nikos.

"Nicholas, you may go to the nurse's office. And next time, don't come to school when you're sick."

He tried to explain on his way out, but his stomach swirled again, and he hurried for the exit. Throwing up on his teacher would be a terrible apology. As he turned to close the door behind himself, the skinny girl across from his seat marched to the teacher's desk. She glared at him, then smiled at the teacher.

Oh, great. Now his teacher *and* his fellow students hated him. With half-closed eyes and one hand on his stomach, he pulled out his map and headed for the office again. When he called his parents, maybe he would edit this story. Not lie, just omit a little. Like being tardy and sick and an embarrassment. They hadn't been too confident of his plan in the first place, and he didn't want to worry them.

The nurse's office was a small room off the main office, with a narrow cot and a couple of chairs and a locked cupboard on the wall. The nurse took his temperature and asked about symptoms.

"No cough or sneeze?" she double-checked.

"I'm fine," Nikos mumbled. "I had a very long airplane flight yesterday, got to bed late, and woke up too late for breakfast. I just have a sleep-deprivation headache."

"Mmm." The nurse gave him a knowing look. "I imagine nerves are no good on an empty stomach, either."

Nikos shrugged and tried to smile. He'd be fine once he learned his way around and mastered expectations.

The nurse rummaged through a box and handed him a pudding cup. "Eat this, and you can take a nap on the cot. If you're still nauseated, try one of these mint candies. I'll write you a note for class when you get up."

She left, and Nikos ate the pudding in three bites, then popped a mint into his mouth and turned off the light. With no windows, the room was dark as soon as he closed the door. Within a minute, he was asleep.

As expected, his headache was gone when he woke. Sleep was always the cure for exhaustion. He emerged from the back room and discovered he'd missed all his morning classes.

"Don't worry," the secretary said, "we sent a note to all your teachers. Go ahead to lunch. Better luck for the rest of the day, eh?"

He nodded ruefully and pulled out his map again. This time, he found his destination with little trouble, in part because half the school was streaming down the halls in the same direction.

The cafeteria was noisy, extremely noisy, and he blessed the nurse for the end of his headache. Now all he needed was food in his empty and protesting stomach. By copying the other students, he managed to get his lunch successfully. Cheese pizza was an easy no, and there was little fresh fruit. He debated the hamburger before taking a chicken sandwich with carrots, fries, and applesauce. Greek food was definitely better, even if it wasn't Mama's cooking.

He smothered a pang of homesickness and searched the tables for an empty place to sit. Apparently eating outside wasn't common here, either.

He approached a table, and someone shouted, "Don't sit by me, vomit boy!"

The other students erupted in raucous laughter, and Nikos sighed and turned aside. But the next two tables said the same thing, and he stood in the aisle with nowhere to go. Had he already ruined his reputation at this school?

"Hey, Nikolaos," a girl called.

He turned in a circle until he saw her waving and smiling at him. Slowly, he approached. Why would a total stranger call to him or even know his name? Maybe it was a mistake, though she had pronounced his name correctly.

Nikos slid his tray into the last empty spot at the table and waited to be told it was only a joke. All the students at this table were laughing and talking together, and though they didn't greet him, they didn't mock him or send him away. Taking advantage of the respite, Nikos gobbled his sandwich. Finally, his stomach stopped protesting. When he moved to his fries, the girl next to him turned.

"I'm Alexandria Fitch," she said.

The tall, skinny girl had brown hair in a ponytail, and he suddenly recognized her from Trig. But her face looked completely different with a smile instead of a scowl, and the eyes that had been green in the sunlight were now definitely hazel. She made introductions for everyone at the table, though Nikos couldn't possibly remember everyone yet.

"Now that you've had a chance to eat," she said, "why don't you tell all of us something about you?"

"I'm Nikolaos Antonakis, exchange student from Crete," he said.

"Where's Crete?" a boy whispered.

"What's something you've noticed that's different here than from *Greece*?" Alexandria subtly emphasized, winking at the boy who had asked.

"The food," Nikos admitted, diplomatically not mentioning his opinion of their diet. "And no mandatory military training. I knew about the compulsory schooling to age eighteen."

"When do Greeks stop school?" Alexandria leaned on one elbow and focused her full attention on him.

"Fifteen, if we don't want to go to university, but most of us do."

The table erupted in exclamations, mostly "No way!" and "Lucky!"

"Then why are you here?" the geographically challenged boy asked. "You look older than fifteen."

"I'm senior," Nikos explained, "but I want to go to an American university."

He'd made all his plans based on that, including which visa to get, but it had taken him a full year to talk his parents into it. They'd had a fit when they realized how little they would get to see him for five years. Instead, he promised to faithfully call or email every week, and they were already planning to visit him next year.

"Man, only if I get a sports scholarship," the boy groaned.

All the students started talking about their favorite sports teams, and Nikos concentrated on his vegetables. Alexandria made a few laughing comments, then relaxed and listened.

After waiting to make sure he wouldn't be interrupting, Nikos leaned toward her. "Thank you for inviting me to your table," he said softly. "I didn't want to intrude into your group."

Alexandria shrugged. "No worries; I met them today."

"Really?" Nikos glanced down the table. She knew all their names and interacted so comfortably, and she had just met them?

"Sure. In the military, we make friends fast. If we wait, we lose out." She stole one of his fries and wiggled her eyebrows at him.

"Okay, but I have English next," a girl blurted. Apparently the conversation had shifted.

"Me, too," someone else said.

All up and down the table, students pulled out their schedules and started comparing.

"American History next for me," Nikos volunteered. "It's junior class, apparently?"

"Don't feel bad." Alexandria huffed. "I've got Social Studies 9 because Hawaii does things differently."

"They're making you take that as senior? They didn't make me." He paused. "But they did assign me to freshman Health."

She laughed. "I'm sure they had to choose what they thought was most important. I'm only a sophomore. They figure they have plenty of time to torture me."

He stared at her in confusion. "But you are in Trig with me? My apologies if I confused you with your older sister."

"Oh, no," she said, "I'm in Trig. And my only sibling is a younger brother."

He tried again. "Trig as sophomore?"

He and his parents had scoured the class requirements to make sure he was taking the best options, and he was sure Trig was normally taken by juniors and seniors.

She frowned and glared at him, and her eyes lightened to a piercing sage green. "Yeah, so? My dad's an engineer, and my grandpa's a physicist."

And that was definitely the glare he recognized from Trig. "Okay, see you in math tomorrow?"

She pulled his schedule closer. "Actually, I might see you during the last period. We have different PE classes, but they're in the same gym."

The bell rang, and everyone grabbed their trays and headed for the door. Alexandria dumped her garbage and pulled Nikos to the hallway.

"Look," she said in a low voice, "you don't have to take my advice, but if you want to fit in more, ditch the fancy black shirt. It looks like a work uniform. Get jeans and either t-shirts or polos, in colors. And don't button the collar. See you later." And then she disappeared into the crowd.

Nikos glanced at his pressed slacks and button-up shirt. Didn't American schools use uniforms? At least he hadn't vomited on himself. As he wound through the halls to his next class, he examined the other students, who wore jeans and casual shirts, just like in Greece. At least something was similar, even if the food wasn't great.

He slid into an empty desk before the bell rang. Might as well take his new friend's advice, even if she was a bossy thing. Maybe Mr. or Mrs. Moss would take him shopping tonight. If not, he could at least unbutton his collar until the weekend. The teacher started taking roll, and Nikos sat up straight.

American History and World Literature went quickly, with more time spent on assigning seats and handing out books than on learning, though the syllabi assured him that would change tomorrow. Sadly, with only seven minutes between the last bell and the bus for home, he wouldn't have time to collect books and syllabi for his missed morning classes. He'd just have to make up the homework.

For his last class, he stashed his backpack in his locker, finally, and made his way to the gymnasium. Yet again, most of the time was taken by introductions, rules, and distributing equipment, though in this case it was ugly uniforms in the school colors.

Nikos did wave at Alexandria across the main gymnasium before heading into the smaller weights room to learn about the different machines and hear the safety rules. He was familiar with it all from his personal weight-lifting, but he still listened. Considering how little the other students paid attention to the teacher, he wouldn't be surprised if they hurt themselves during the semester.

After class, he grabbed his backpack and dashed for the bus stop. The kids pushed and shoved their way on board, and Nikos let them go first. By the time he finally got on, there was only one place left.

Alexandria smiled and patted the seat. "I don't bite, Nikolaos. Nice collar. What's that around your neck?"

Nikos fingered the blue eye he wore on a chain. "Protection against the evil eye." Papa insisted he wear it all the time while he was gone, just in case.

"Hmm," Alexandria said. "Want me to give you the trig homework?"

"Yes, please." Nikos flopped down as the bus took off. "And you can call me Nikos, or even Nik."

Alexandria chuckled. "Gotcha. So, we're taking the pretest in chapter one to make sure we're all ready for the class."

She pulled out the book and showed him the page, and he dutifully wrote it down.

"Too bad you aren't in my other morning classes," he said. "I'll have ton of homework to make up tomorrow."

"Which ones?" she promptly asked.

"Speech, Health, and German. Why?"

She stood up. "Hey, everybody. I have a new student here who needs help. Does anybody know today's homework for Speech, Health, and German..." She raised an eyebrow at him.

"Three." During his Munich layover, it had helped him order food and talk to other travelers.

"Ooh, German III. Be nice and welcoming to the new guy, will ya? Anybody, anybody?"

The students laughed.

"Speech is a two-minute introduction of yourself," someone shouted.

"I can email you the health assignment and the pages you need to read," a pretty girl offered, blushing.

Alexandria pumped her fist. "You're all wonderful. How about German III? German, going once, going twice? Nope, no German." She sat down and shrugged. "Sorry. Two out of three's not bad. I imagine your German class will probably have the fewest students in the lot. Most kids take the required two years of language and then quit."

A note moved down the aisle until it landed in his lap with the email address for the girl with the health homework.

Nikos tucked it into his pocket. "Well, you're a lifesaver, anyway. One extra class of homework is bad enough. Four is not fun."

She winked at him. "No prob."

The bus squealed and stopped, and Nikos recognized his new neighborhood. A couple of kids stood, and he followed them. When he got off, he discovered Alexandria was behind him.

"See you tomorrow," he said.

She waved. "See ya."

He headed home, and her footsteps followed. At the corner, he turned. So did she.

Nikos whirled. "Why are you following me?"

"Uh, no. I live there." She pointed past him. "The white house."

"What, really?"

"Of course really. Why?"

"I live there. In the yellow house." He pointed at the house next to hers.

Alexandria burst into laughter and passed him. "Tomorrow, bus. I won't be following you."

Nikos was still laughing when he walked in the door of his host home.

"Did you have a nice day, then, dear?" Mrs. Moss offered him a fresh peach.

"Thanks. Yes, I think I did."

"That's good." She smiled and returned to dinner preparations, and he headed to his room to do his homework.

The next day, Nikos and Alexandria sat together on the bus. With twenty minutes before classes started, she helped him find his other classrooms and collect his books.

Firmly gripping his schedule instead of giving it back, she pointed to a certain line. "You missed advisory yesterday, too, so you probably don't know that when they don't have something to talk to us about, it works like a short study hall. Half an hour to work on German?"

"Thank goodness," he muttered in Greek.

She raised an eyebrow at the foreign words, but didn't ask for an interpretation. "Okay, off to Trig. I have something to show you." She towed him down the hall, ignoring his questions.

In the classroom, Ms. Blackwell was writing on the board, but only a few students had arrived.

"Oh, good," the teacher said. "Alexandra, are you showing Nicholas his new seat?" She scowled a little at Nikos.

"Yep, I've got it." Alexandria towed him to the back of the room. "Sorry, I think she will mispronounce your name all year. And mine. Nobody ever gets mine right, but you should tell people to call you Nik. It will be less miserable."

He sighed. "Yeah. What are we doing back here?"

She pushed him into a seat in the darkest corner and plopped into the seat next to him.

"This is your new desk!" She waved her hands over it as if it were the best present.

Nikos pinched his nose. "Am I being banished because I threw up in class? Would it help if I apologize?"

"No, silly," she said. "I told Ms. Blackwell that being out of direct sunlight will reduce your migraines and thus prevent you from being sick again. Good idea, right? She said I should sit by you and make sure you're okay."

"I don't get migraines." Nikos squinted at her in confusion.

Alexandria shook her head. "Duh. Killer headache, right? Nausea, light sensitivity, maybe some funny visual effects? Migraine!"

"It wasn't that bad," he lied. "I just didn't get enough sleep and didn't eat breakfast, and maybe I was little nervous." He held his fingers a millimeter apart.

"Sure," she agreed. "And what did the nurse do for you?"

"Pudding, mint candy, and nap. That's it. Sleep and food."

She nodded. "In the dark nurse's office, right?"

"Yes."

She raised her eyebrow. "Uh-huh. Totally a migraine, just like my little brother gets. He always has to take a nap in a dark room to feel better, even if he takes medicine."

Nikos pondered the idea. He did get a lot of headaches, though he always had an excuse for them. And they did frequently create a glare in his vision. He particularly wouldn't mind not humiliating himself in front of fellow students or disrespecting his teachers.

He sat back. "Then I guess dark corners will make me a better student, yeah?"

The bell rang, and Ms. Blackwell called the class to order. The students swapped pretests to grade them, and Alexandria got a perfect score. Nikos watched her all through class. Even when she didn't raise her hand, she almost always knew the answer.

After the end bell, he followed her to the hall. "Know what else would make me a better student? Good study partner. You interested, neighbor?"

She raised her eyebrow. "Sure thing. See you at lunch?"

"You bet." He darted left and hurried to his next class.

By the end of the day, he'd have the map memorized and be caught up on his homework. It would be easy after that, except for missing his parents. Next year, university.

CHAPTER 3

IN WHICH AN ACCIDENT OCCURS

MIKNON LET GO of Gil's necklace and flapped her wings. "I'll see you at work."

He waved and headed to his friends in the meal room, and she flew to find one of her usual hiding places to wait for her first work shift. Her adopted brother was so friendly it made her teeth ache. She hated crowds. Everyone pressing around, everyone arguing and talking in loud voices.

Her second shift was in the zoo with Gil, and that was tolerable because nobody liked her telling them what to do anyway, so they avoided her. She and Gil always had one work shift together each rotation, but not always the same one, since she needed more sleep and was on a six-shift pattern instead of his four. And even when they shared a sleep time, she avoided the dormitories, preferring one of her hidden spots where no one would accidentally lie on her when the shifts changed.

All too soon, the single shift bell rang. Time to get back to work.

Miknon sighed and headed for the parts storeroom for two bags of air filters. She could fly herself at any time, but she always changed the filters during a weightless shift so the bags would float. Otherwise, she could never move even one, since it was bigger than she was. When they weighed nothing, dragging two was only unwieldy instead of impossible.

Each shift rotation, she changed the filters in a few sections. The entire circuit took her most of a conjunction. Not that there were conjunctions on board, but until they reached their new home, the traditional measures of time continued. Days had twelve shifts of four hours, weeks had nine days, and a conjunction covered two weeks. As if anything other than the shifts mattered. Nothing changed from day to day or week to week. Nothing had changed for well over a hundred conjunctions on the ship, and she had to assume the rest of the fleet was equally boring.

Today her assignment was in the water room and grain storage. As she pulled the filters past the pixies serving their time lighting the hallway, they waved from their perches in the corners of the ceiling. None of them understood why she would rather do physical labor than sit quietly and glow. As if staying in the same place for hours wasn't as boring as watching grass grow. Besides, the lights were in full view of everyone on the ship, all ten thousand of them. Ten thousand sets of eyes staring at her as they went by. Miknon shuddered. Even just the two or three thousand on any floor were bad enough.

But someone had to do the work in tiny spaces, and there were never enough volunteers for the hard labor. Getting assigned to the filters had been easy, and she didn't even have to glow for the job.

She didn't move as quickly as her carelessly bouncy brother, but she reached the rain-painted door soon enough. She hung one bag of filters on the closest light sconce, ignoring the pixie inside the glass. This one glowed pink, edging to rose.

After unlatching the grille that covered the small maintenance tunnel by the door, Miknon backed in, dragging the other bag behind her. The filters still weighed nothing, but the fit was tight, and she had to yank hard to move them through the wall. Fortunately, the tunnel had occasional safety grips for leverage.

On both sides of the wall, dozens of closely woven filters fit into holes that allowed air circulated by the winged creatures in the public rooms to carry through the walls into the storage rooms. Periodic grilles allowed multiple workers access in case of an emergency, but for scheduled replacement, one was sufficient and easier.

At each filter hole, she removed the old filter and replaced it with a new one, locking it into place. Once her bag was empty enough to leave a gap between the tunnel walls, she pushed the used filters past the sack, toward the hallway. When she left, she would collect them and take them to the garden for compost.

Steadily, she worked her way down the entire tunnel, then returned to the outside, pushing the old filters ahead of her. By the time she reached the exit, she had to hold on to the safety bars and kick to dislodge the stacked-up filters. They finally popped into the hallway, and Miknon crawled after them.

"Right on time," the light pixie volunteered. "The shift is half over."

Miknon nodded but said nothing. Of course she was right on time. She had been doing this same job for dozens of conjunctions and had the timing memorized.

Now free of the tunnel, she chased down the floating discards and stuffed them into her empty sack. After hanging that on the light and retrieving the other bag of new filters, she moved to the wheat-painted store room next door.

Yet again, she tugged the full bag through the narrow tunnel. One by one, she replaced the old filters in the wall with new, making sure they were completely settled into place.

Halfway through her task, the door to the store room opened and shut. Miknon kept working. Gil and the rest of her family were sleeping, and she had no other friends, so it made no difference who it was. They wouldn't see her in here, and they weren't likely to care. Few people cared about the nobodies who did the invisible work of keeping the ship running.

"This way, Sire," Dagan said.

Sire? Though the Companion guards sometimes worked in regular jobs for a shift, the king was always busy with leadership tasks. What were he and Grandsire doing here? Miknon dropped the air filter and fluttered to the next grille exiting into the store room.

The room was filled with boxes and bags, either strapped to the walls and ceiling or to the many shelves bolted between floor and ceiling. After more than one hundred and forty conjunctions, many of the crates on the right side of the room were now empty. But if rumor was correct, and Gil usually knew all the best rumors, they would soon reach their new home. On a whole new world, the diminishing supplies wouldn't matter. They would replenish their food in a growing season.

From her position by the door, she could see down half the aisles, including where the king himself and his chief bodyguard floated, staring at crates along the left wall. The king wore a plain tunic, though it was cleaner than most people could manage on the ship with no servants, little spare time, and water floating for half the day. His golden hair was practically braided tight against his head instead of in an elaborate style. Dagan wore his usual linen cuirass over his kilt and had his long dagger and his sling tucked into his belt.

"This is the lot the boy mentioned." Dagan tapped the label on a box.

"Very well, let's take it down and have a look." The king pried off the lid and slid it a few thumb-lengths, just enough to look carefully into the box. "That dryad helping the cook was right. Nobody can eat this." He replaced the lid, unbuckled the strap, and pulled down the entire crate.

Dagan pointed to the wall. "There's the problem, Sire. Water is leaking into the stored grain and causing the fungus."

Oh, no. Miknon pressed closer to the grille, trying to see more. Something must have been barely leaking for nobody to notice, but for a long time in order to ruin the grain.

The king rubbed his chin. "How bad is the leak? Can we quietly dispose of the infected grain, or do we have to take bigger measures?"

"That depends how far the leak goes." Dagan pushed himself a few crates away and moved another box.

Even from the tunnel, the discolored wall was obvious.

Dagan repeated the process several more times, moving farther and farther along the wall, across the ceiling, and down the opposite wall. All the boxes had water stains behind them.

Miknon leaned her head against the grille and squeezed her eyes shut. This was terrible.

"It's the whole room, Sire." Dagan rubbed his chin. "It looks like the shielding water between the walls is leaking, so that's why we didn't notice the water storage levels falling. We'll have to dispose of all the grain touching the walls, find the leak, and repair the walls. We need to check the storage room two decks above, too, since the water is just as likely to go up during weightless shifts."

He looked toward the ceiling and frowned, calculating. "If we lost a quarter of the grain in each room, that's an eighth of our entire supply. Possibly more, depending where full and empty crates were stored. There's no way to keep this quiet. Besides, everyone will certainly notice when they get less to eat."

"Very well. We will tell everyone today." The king opened the door and poked his head outside. "Companions, go collect as many workers as you can find. We'll carry the boxes to the barge room and purge them into space. And tell Nik and Shalla we'll need to discuss new rationing, and schedule an announcement for shift change."

Miknon bit her lip. They would wait for Gil to wake before taking the boxes into the barge room, in case the dragon woke and needed to be calmed. But enough crates were infected that they must move them soon. And then what? Corral them in the stairwell until shift change? Probably.

"There's more, Sire," Dagan continued.

The king groaned. "What else?"

"We might have lost a large amount of water, also. If we can't reclaim it from the walls, we'll have to refill the shields from storage, and the gardens will suffer. That will hit rations, too."

"Then Zaidu had better investigate soon," the king said. "He can do some actual work for once. Assign him a team to inspect every water tank on the ship." The king unstrapped another box and pushed it closer to the door.

"Sire," Dagan protested, "you should wait until others arrive to move the crates."

The king laughed.

Dagan sighed and unfastened another crate. "I know, I know, that's not how you do things. I'll help you."

The king moved to the next box, working slowly but steadily.

Despite the continued bad attitude of the highborn, the king had kept his promises of equality among the classes, as much as possible. Even the small, like Miknon, could share their opinions with him, and jobs were divided fairly according to abilities rather than by rank. The lords were limited to cruel words instead of the random punishments she heard the older generations talk about, though even that was enough for Miknon to maintain her strategy of staying hidden.

Her place in Gil's family, unofficial though it was, served as some protection, particularly with Dagan's skills and position. She didn't care to discover how much she could risk under that protection, no matter what the king said about equality. He couldn't be everywhere, though he and his staff tried.

Certainly, the upcoming change in rationing would be applied evenly across the races. Nobody would eat better than anyone else. Even the king and his son ate the same meals in the same amounts as anyone else their size. And the prince ate in the dining hall instead of in his father's quarters.

To be fair, Miknon was pretty sure the king ate in his quarters so he could keep working through the meal, rather than to avoid the lesser fae. She had once flown by, late for her own meal, and glimpsed him talking to his secretary while they ate.

The king and his guard kept releasing crates and pushing them gently down the aisle.

They had their work, and Miknon had hers. If she didn't finish, the air would grow stale, and people would get sick. She turned to retrieve the next air filter.

The ship jerked, and the hull rang like a giant bell. Miknon was thrown against the grille, and she frantically grabbed the bars and held on.

Inside the store room, boxes flew through the air. Dagan grabbed the king and dove out of the way.

The alarm bell clanged noisily. Miknon's own weight grabbed her and pulled. The pilots must be attempting an emergency maneuver, and the sudden acceleration returned heaviness to everything in the ship.

The king and his Companion dropped a few hand-lengths to the floor. The crates of grain plummeted from the ceiling.

Pressed against the grille, Miknon shouted a useless warning. Dagan had already seen the danger and yanked the king sideways, rolling toward the door.

Too late, and not far enough.

The heavy boxes hit both of them, even as Dagan pushed the king farther away. A pool of red seeped from under the debris, and Miknon cried out again.

The alarm stopped clanging, and the all-clear tinkled happily. The door opened, and more guards poured in. But were they too late?

"Grab the king!" an ogre shouted. "Move those crates!"

They threw the first box aside just as the weight vanished again. Blood droplets floated lazily through the air, though the red stain remained on the floor. Someone was still bleeding, but Miknon couldn't tell who under the pile of crates. She stayed pressed against the grille. Not only was it safer if the ship made another maneuver, but she couldn't tear her gaze away from the store room. If the king was injured, the whole fleet would be affected, but she loved Dagan more.

Now that the boxes weighed nothing, the Companions tossed them aside like feathers, digging through the pile to reach the king and Dagan.

The king moaned and turned his head. Dagan lay still.

Miknon pressed a hand to her mouth. *Oh please oh please. Dagan, wake up!*

"You four, take the king straight to the bloodworkers," the ogre shouted. "Try not to jostle him."

Obediently, four guards rushed the king out the door. Shouts and chaos echoed in from the hallway.

"You four, take Dagan."

Another four grabbed their chief, rearranging their grip when Dagan bent oddly. They exchanged grim looks but floated out the door with their bleeding burden.

And still Dagan hadn't moved. Miknon pressed her fingers to her lips and blinked back tears.

The ogre winced, then inhaled. "All right, let's get this cleaned up."

"Do you think the king—"

"No talking," the ogre snapped. "We'll get a report when there is something to hear."

Miknon squeezed past the filters and rushed to the hall exit. She had to tell Gil. But when she stuck out her head, she almost got squished by someone smashing into the wall.

People filled the hall with their bodies and endless chatter. Even if their sleeping restraints kept them from noticing the thud, the alarm bell was designed to wake everyone no matter how soundly asleep. And, as trained, they were all rushing to their emergency stations. That didn't keep them from gossiping as they bounced off all four walls in their hurry.

"What happened?" everyone asked. "Why did the ship jerk?"

"The alarm already stopped, so what's the big deal? I'm sure someone just panicked."

"I know they rang the all-clear, but I wish they would send a runner to tell us what happened. Since we aren't *important* enough to deserve a thought mage on our deck."

"Ha! You won't catch a highborn down here! Look, check your assignment and see if anything needs to be cleaned up. I want to go back to bed."

"Hey, was that the king?"

Gossip flew like a phoenix, reborn every time it passed to a new person.

Miknon frantically looked for an opening between the ricocheting bodies, but it was several long moments before the hall cleared enough for her to move safely.

Dodging the last of the scurrying fae, she dove down the ramp, searching for the darkest colors in the crowd. As expected, Gil stood outside the livestock door, key in his hand and messy braids falling a little loose from sleep. He didn't look sad, just a little worried. He must not have heard the rumors or been able to see through the chaos in the hallways.

Miknon flew immediately to his shoulder and leaned toward his pointed ear. "Did you hear the news?"

"Yes, everyone is talking about the king. It's terrible, but the blood-workers will care for him. Do you know why there's no acceleration?

How can I check on the animals without letting the mess float into the rest of the ship?"

"No, not the king." Miknon drew in a shuddering breath. "Your Grandsire."

"What about him?"

She pushed the news past the lump in her throat. "He was with the king during the accident. I don't think he survived."

Chapter 4

New House

Alexandria closed her world history book and reached for Spanish. "Hey, Ian, is your homework finished? Will you help me with this?"

Her little brother nodded and put his fat Russian novel on top of his Japanese textbook and a copy of *The Iliad* in ancient Greek. "Sure, what do you need?"

"Verbs, of course. It's always verbs."

Ian laughed and scooted next to her, brushing his long blond bangs out of his eyes. While they worked through the tenses, Mom checked on dinner in the oven and added icing to the fresh, homemade cinnamon rolls before returning to her own studies.

With Ian's help, Alexandria's Spanish homework didn't take long, and he returned to his novel while she switched to biology. She worked steadily but quickly, typing the answers into her laptop, trying to finish before dinner so she'd be free after. Lucky Ian, homeschooled because of his migraines and with plenty of free time to explore his insane interest in languages. Poor Ian, who didn't have friends or school activities but did have frequent headaches.

Ian smiled at his book and swatted his bangs again, and Alexandria shook her head. Whatever. Ian didn't seem bothered as long as he had his books, and he seemed to like her friends well enough, especially Nikos.

And that was the end of her biology homework. She'd finished most of her trig when Nikos came over earlier, and Dad could help her with the last two problems when he got home.

As if Mom had read her mind, she looked at the clock. "Your dad will be home soon. Is everything clean and ready? Hurry and pick up your shoes and put your extra books away." She turned off her computer screen and hurried to the oven.

Ian clutched his books to his chest. "Mom, we've been here for several months, and we're almost all unpacked now. Can I ask Dad about getting a dog now?"

"Oh, honey," Mom said, "I don't think that's a good idea."

Ian bounced on his toes. "Please, please, please."

Alexandria closed her computer and took everything except her trig homework to her room. When she got back to the kitchen, Ian was still begging.

Mom sighed. "Let's see how his doctor appointment went today, okay? If he got cleared to fly again, he'll be in a good mood, and we can try. But honey, you know he doesn't like dogs."

Dirty, rowdy, and disobedient, Alexandria mentally chanted. Never mind that they could be trained to obey, and vacuums handled dog hair. Dad thought everybody should be as disciplined and tidy as his airmen. She stacked her trig homework out of the way and washed the table.

"I know," Ian said, "but I really want one. Please."

"We'll see. Go put your books away."

The key turned in the front door, and Ian fled.

Alexandria straightened the kitchen chairs, and Mom wiped a spot of icing off the counter.

Dad walked in. "Hey, Alex. Helen."

Despite the despised nickname, Alexandria smiled at him. Ian crept back in, and Dad scowled at him.

Mom hurried over to kiss Dad. "Welcome home. How was your appointment?"

"Fine," he said. "Wonderful. I'm hungry."

"Dinner's almost ready." Mom grabbed the hot pads and bent to the oven. "Oh, the base lawyer called about transferring the house deed to your name. I told him I'd check with you to see when we're both available."

Alexandria grabbed plates while Ian got silverware. Silently, they set the table, lining everything up perfectly.

"Oh, don't worry," Dad said. "I'll do it when I go in tomorrow."

Mom put the pan on top of the stove and removed the lid. "But honey, you'll need me there to sign."

"Eh, there's no need to bother you now. We can add you later. For now, I'll just get my parents' names off."

Alexandria slid napkins across the counter to Ian and grabbed four glasses.

Mom turned around to look at Dad. "Wouldn't it be easier to add both of us at the start?"

Dad slammed his fist on the counter. "Don't I have enough to deal with without you harassing me?"

Mom flinched. Silently, she carried the pan to the table and dished up the food. Both kids sat quickly, not moving until after Mom said the blessing on the food and Dad started eating.

Halfway through the meal, Alexandria cleared her throat. "Dad, can you help me with a couple of trig problems after dinner?"

He nodded. "Sure, and if you don't have judo tonight, I'll take you for a drive to get in some of your hours. You can use my car."

She let her shoulders relax. If only Mom wouldn't antagonize Dad, he wouldn't yell. Look how nice he was being now, even offering his car. He could make her drive in Mom's old Ford Escape, especially since Alexandria had only been in driver's ed since June.

"Sweet!" She shoveled her food into her mouth, only slowing when Mom raised an eyebrow.

Ian squared his shoulders. "Can I—"

Mom touched his hand and shook her head. Ian deflated and poked his food without eating it.

After dessert, Mom washed dishes while Dad helped Alexandria with her math homework.

When they finished, Dad dangled the keys. "Ready to go, Alex?"

"Yep!" She grabbed the keys and dashed outside to his new black Lexus GX with all the perks. While Dad got in the passenger side, she adjusted the seat and mirrors.

"Let's go left today," Dad said.

Alexandria carefully backed up and followed his patient directions through the neighborhood.

"Ease off the gas a bit," he said. "Good job." He drummed his fingers on the arm rest. "I don't know why your mother has to spoil your brother so much. No school, no discipline. And that haircut!"

Alexandria flickered a glance at him, then concentrated on the road. Ian knew, or was learning, four foreign languages. He'd picked up Russian from Dad, ancient Greek from Mom, and Japanese from hanging out with kids in Hawaii, and he was learning Spanish as fast as she was. Faster, actually, since he borrowed her textbook every weekend and had added Spanish to the practice app on his phone.

"Your mother has no discipline, either," Dad grumbled. "She doesn't do anything except clean the house, and she's not good at that. She doesn't work, doesn't help support the family, and then—" He pounded his fist on his knee and swore. "Then she grouches at *me*. Doesn't she see how I'm doing everything for this family? Where would she be without me? Nowhere, that's where! She hasn't even finished her degree."

Because she married and had a family, Alexandria thought, but she kept her mouth shut. Mom had almost had her PhD when she married Dad, and between housework and teaching Ian, she still puttered with attempts to translate Linear A.

Eventually, Dad stopped ranting. When he started humming, she relaxed her grip on the steering wheel.

"Hey, Dad?"

"Yeah, Alex?"

Alexandria. Why wouldn't he call her Alexandria?

She bit her lip. "You promised to take me to the Air Force planetarium this month. When would be a good day for you?"

"Oh, not now, Alex," he said. "I'm too busy for your little hobby. Maybe next month."

Next month. That's what he said last month. "Sure, Dad. Next month."

She mentally recited words she'd never dare say around her mother. When would he realize astronomy was her life's work, not a little hobby? Just because she didn't want to go into the military didn't mean she wasn't following him into a science field. Astronomy was all about physics, thank you very much. More physics than his engineering, even.

And when would he stop calling her Alex?

"Turn here and head home," Dad said.

Alexandria silently obeyed.

When she parked the car, she waved at Nikos, who was mowing the lawn next door while wearing wrap-around sunglasses that hid his thick eyebrows as well as his brown eyes. At least he'd taken her advice and gotten some jeans and t-shirts so he looked normal. Mostly normal, anyway. She suspected he ironed his t-shirts, and his black curls were gelled into submission.

"Who's that?" Dad said. "I don't want random boys sniffing around here without my approval."

He glared at Nikos as if his straight nose was a dog's muzzle. Thank goodness their neighbor had been coming over to study while Dad was still at work.

"Settle down, Dad. He's just a very polite kid from my trig class. I don't have a boyfriend." She rolled her eyes. "You know I'm not dating until I turn sixteen."

He snorted. "I was dating at fourteen."

And married before he graduated college. Not what she wanted, even if it wasn't a double standard.

She shrugged. "Gotta keep the peace and obey the parental units."

Dad grunted. "Your mother's rules are stupid."

Without comment, Alexandria returned his keys and ran into the house. Behind her, Dad's cell phone rang as he shut the door.

"Oh, this is my CO. Gotta take this." He remained in the entryway. "Yes, sir. No, sir. Oh, you got the results, sir."

Mom stepped into the living room and watched him. Alexandria hung around the corner and listened hard. Ian stayed at the kitchen table, though he seemed to listen just as much.

Dad's voice dropped lower. "No, sir. Yes, sir. I understand, sir." He hung up and blistered the air with curses.

"No swearing!" Mom said automatically, then cringed.

Dad barked in Russian for two whole minutes, and Ian blushed and covered his ears. Alexandria peeked around the corner. Mom folded her arms and waited.

"The stupid doc says my inner ear still hasn't healed," Dad bellowed. "And he recommended me for a PTSD eval! So my CO is leaving me at the stupid desk job. My ear is fine. I don't have PTSD. They can't do this to me!"

Outside, a car backfired, and Dad jumped and swore again, slapping for the gun he wasn't wearing.

Mom reached for him slowly. "Honey, I'm sure it will be fine. It's only temporary. You'll be back in the planes in no time."

Alexandria winced at Mom's courage. Sometimes Dad struck out in his panic. He always apologized, but that didn't heal the bruises.

Dad straightened and moved to the window to glare at the cars on the street. "I've been trapped behind a desk since we moved here, and I hate it. Ought to quit. My term is up soon, anyway."

"Oh, honey, you only have two years left to retirement. You can make it that long, even at a desk."

It was less time than Alexandria had left in high school. If she could do it, why couldn't he? Military retirement was worth it, especially with only two years left.

"Two years! Forget it." He swatted at Mom's hands and stomped into the kitchen for a glass of water.

Ian slid down in his chair, and Alexandria tried to look busy.

"Look," Mom said, "maybe your ears will get better in a couple of months. Give it some time."

Dad swore at her and grabbed another cinnamon roll. "I'm going to watch the football game. Nobody bother me." He stomped to his den.

Ian slowly straightened in his chair and swiped at his bangs.

Mom rubbed her forehead. "Try to stay out of his way for a while, kids. You might as well finish the cinnamon rolls, though."

"I guess I still can't ask about a dog?" Ian whispered.

"No, Ian, absolutely don't ask about a dog. I'm sorry." Mom handed two cinnamon rolls to each of them and took the last for herself. "You might want to stay in your rooms tonight."

Ian grabbed a napkin and bolted.

Alexandria helped Mom record her driving hours and then wandered to her own room. As the oldest, she got her choice of the three kid's bedrooms, and she'd chosen the second smallest because it had two windows and a walk-in closet and was closer to the bathroom. She hadn't bothered repainting the boring white, since her space posters covered most of the walls.

Both of her telescopes nestled between the desk and nightstand, and her few books sat in her bookcase headboard. At the foot of her bed, her cedar chest served as blanket storage and a hiding place. Grandma Ellison had made it for her when she was born, and her name was carved below the keyhole. Spelled correctly.

Her mother had a matching chest, which she had refused to let Dad replace with something "professional." That was ridiculous, anyway, since Grandma had been a professional carpenter. She'd made a bookcase for Ian instead of a cedar chest, saying she had a feeling about him. Ian actually had three bookcases in his smaller room now, and he still piled books on the top layer of his bunk bed.

Mom had asked for the last bedroom for an office, but Dad said she could use her laptop in the kitchen. He deserved a private den to unwind from his stressful job. He'd installed a big screen tv, a comfy recliner, and a mini-fridge, and that was the end of the discussion. Now he watched his shows by himself, instead of joining the family like he used to.

Alexandria flopped onto her bed and nibbled at the pastries. Ian was right about Dad; he wasn't the same as he'd been before Afghanistan. Sure, he'd always been picky about a clean house, but he didn't yell about it before. And he used to buy her random presents and keep his promises. Where was the Dad that used to think she'd make a great astronomer? The one that bought her a second telescope to look at the stars when he found out Grandpa's was only good for the moon.

She missed that Dad.

IN THE MORNING, Alexandria showed up for breakfast with a determined smile. After a day to cool down, Dad should be back to normal.

But Dad grabbed muffins and left the house without a word. Mom watched him go, lips tight, but didn't call him back.

"Have a nice day at school, Alexandria," Mom said. "I'll have a snack ready for you before judo, okay?"

"Thanks, Mom. Bye, Ian."

Ian waved half-heartedly.

Alexandria darted for the bus stop, arriving just before it left.

"Almost missed it." Nikos patted the seat he'd saved for her.

She sighed. "Bad day."

"Already?"

"The parents are fighting."

"Oh." He grimaced.

"And Dad said he's too busy to take me to the planetarium." She stared out the window and blinked hard to stop the tears. Crying on the bus was too embarrassing for words. What was she, six years old? Dad hadn't broken his promise, exactly, just delayed it. Yeah, that was it. "For now," she amended. "He'll take me later."

"Ah." Nikos cleared his throat. "I've heard you mention the stars before. Big science fan?"

"Yeah, I'm going to be an astronomer. Space is so cool. Did you know NASA is sending Lucy in a couple of months to study Jupiter's Trojan asteroids up close? There's still so much to learn about our own solar system, much less the rest of the universe!"

"Oh, you'll be expert on the whole universe, hmm?"

She elbowed him. "Of course not. But I'll be an expert on something in space. Want to come with me when Dad takes me to the planetarium? It's at the Air Force Academy, but it's open to the public. And before that, I can show you my telescopes. I have two. Grandpa Ellison gave me one for the moon when I turned twelve. He was an astronomer, too."

Nikos laughed. "Sure. Yes to all of it. Now, are you ready for the trig test?"

They discussed homework until the bus arrived at school, then walked together to Trig. After class, they split ways, and Alexandria sulked through the rest of her morning classes.

At lunch, Nikos watched her friends chatter with a peculiar look on his face.

Alexandria nudged him. "What's wrong?"

"Nothing."

She raised an eyebrow.

"I don't seem to be so good at making friends as you are," he admitted

"I'm your friend," she said.

Nikos smiled. "My best friend. But—" He shrugged.

"Well, you took my advice about clothes," she said. "You ask questions about other people and take turns in conversation. You're nice. Hmm. Maybe you need to be more interesting."

"Hey," he protested. "You think I'm not interesting?"

She bumped his shoulder. "Something interesting to other teens, not just nerds. You should find something you're good at that they think is fun. Sports or music or something."

"Hmph. No good at those." He gathered both their trays, and the bell rang. "I don't see art or mythology on that list. See you later."

Alexandria daydreamed through Social Studies and suffered through Spanish, then raced into PE ready to sweat away her worries. After changing clothes, she waved across the gym at Nikos and dropped into the warmup routine. If she ran fast enough, she could stop thinking for a while, maybe.

The pounding of her feet blocked her disappointment for a while, and by the time she stopped, out of breath and pleasantly achy, she had found her equilibrium again. Dad would relax eventually, so she just had to be patient. She took her time stretching, letting the others pass her.

Across the gym, kids cheered. Alexandria couldn't see what was going on through the crowd, but she had a clear shot to the locker room and hurried to change before the space got too busy.

She emerged and was immediately grabbed by Nikos.

"Gotta go," he said.

"What—?" Alexandria started.

"On the bus," he hissed. He smiled at the students surrounding him and edged through the chaos. "Bus is coming. Excuse us, please."

Across the hall, the school's football star, Forest McConnell, glared at both of them. He followed them to their lockers, which were in the same hallway, not too far apart, then trailed them to the bus stop.

As soon as the bus wheezed to a halt, Nikos shoved Alexandria on board and dragged her to the last row. He slumped until only his black curls topped the back of the seat.

"This is all your fault," he hissed. "You ruined PE."

Kids poured onto the bus, calling Nikos's name or some mangled version of it. Forest stood in the aisle, blocking traffic and obviously searching for something or someone.

Alexandria put her backpack on her lap to block the view to the other half of the seat where Nikos cowered. "What? What did I do? I'm not even in your PE class."

"It was your idea," he insisted. "Find something you're good at that the other students care about, you said. So I stopped going easy on the weights and went for a personal best."

"I don't see how this is bad?" she asked.

"Apparently I should have looked at the record board first," he hissed. "I almost broke the school record in the dead lift. I might have, if that football thug hadn't gasped and broken my concentration."

Alexandria coughed to hide a laugh. "Just like that? How much did you lift?"

"Four hundred pounds." He shrugged as if it was nothing.

Alexandria raised her eyebrows. "Wow, Nikos, I'm impressed." His muscled arms had always made it clear he was strong, but not *that* strong.

"You and everybody else!" he protested. "And now nobody will leave me alone, and McConnell is mad I almost broke his record. You and your bad ideas!" He sank lower on the bench.

Hiding another laugh, Alexandria pulled out her phone and opened her favorite NASA news feed. She was in the middle of the latest report from Hubble when an alert sounded and a headline scrolled past.

"Cool!" She accessed the complete article and nudged Nikos. "Listen to this. Pan-STARRS spotted a new asteroid past Jupiter."

"Can I move there?" Nikos asked.

CHAPTER 5

In Which the Bad News is True

AT MIKNON'S WORDS, Gil jerked, sending himself flying across the hall. Grandsire dead?

He bounced off the wall and fought to recover his balance. No! Grandsire was too tough to die in a stupid accident. He'd been the king's chief Companion since before Mother was born, the best of the elite. Miknon must be mistaken.

Forgetting the animals, he flew up the ramp to the next deck, where all the chaos had been. Miknon was close on his heels. They wouldn't have bothered to drag the injured up several decks in an emergency, so if the pixie was right, they'd be in the closest healer's office.

But she was wrong. She had to be wrong. Grandsire had always been there, would always be there. The king counted on him as much as Gil and his family did. Life without him was inconceivable.

He might be injured, perhaps. That was barely possible. He wasn't actually invulnerable, just very skilled and powerful. An injury must be what Miknon meant. In that case, Gil would take care of him until he recovered, like Grandsire had always cared for the rest of them.

Gil flew across the hall and burst through the door. Chaos filled the room, noise and motion and mess. The king was wrapped in a hammock on the wall while several bloodworkers bent over him.

Off to one side, Grandsire lay strapped to a bunk, silent and still and gray. No one was helping him, and Gil stepped forward to yank a healer to his side. They could spare one from the king.

But Grandsire's chest wasn't moving. Blood coated his flattened torso, and slow drops broke free and floated in the weightless air.

Gil froze, staring, holding his breath as he waited for the next breath to fill the broad chest before him.

Miknon caught up and took her usual spot on his shoulder, anchoring herself with his necklace. Her small hand stroked him as her sob echoed in his ear.

Gil ran out of air and gasped for breath. And still Grandsire's chest did not move.

"We can't work like this," one of the healers snapped. "Everything is floating away." He raised his head and searched the room. "You, boy." He pointed a bloody hand at Gil. "Run to navigation and tell them to start up the acceleration."

Gil barely heard him. How could Grandsire be dead?

"Now, boy!"

"That's Gil," someone else said.

"I don't care who he is. He can carry the message before we lose the king."

"That's Dagan's grandson," the other clarified, and now Gil recognized the voice of his usual healer, Merodach. "Gil, Gil, look at me."

Gil dragged his gaze away from his dead kin. What difference did it make what anyone said? Grandsire was dead.

"I'll talk to you about Dagan later," Merodach said, "but right now we really do need weight. Please go tell them to accelerate."

The scarlet streak of blood across his forehead made him look even paler than usual. Gil blinked. Miknon yanked on his ear, then hugged his neck and flew off.

Gil took a deep breath. Grandsire was dead, but the king still lived. He packed his sorrow into his heart and stomped it down until later.

"Oh," he said. "Yes. Navigation."

He exited and closed the door, then launched himself across the hall and up the ramp as fast as he could, barely missing other travelers. At the next floor, he turned and flew up the next ramp, and the next, and more, until he reached the ninth floor.

But this ramp didn't go all the way to the top deck. He pulled himself along the wall at racing speed to the ramp on the other side of the ship, then up the tower. At least fewer people had business here, and Gil flew even faster.

Up one side of the tower, the arboretum stretched through all four decks, tended by dryads. Tree trunks faced the staff offices and the guard hall where Grandsire trained his troops. On the next level, thick branches lined the view across from the king's quarters and office. The king, who lay injured so far below.

After that was the training and storage for navigation, and hardly anyone came up this high. Gil put on even more speed in the empty hall. The view of the arboretum scattered into millions of leaves and thousands of fruits and nuts, even as he turned the corner for the last ramp.

In just a few minutes, he burst into the navigation room at the top of the ship. The room hummed and droned, as always, and Gil folded his ears down in protest at the noise.

With a planned weightless shift, only two people were in the room, and one was sleeping. He launched himself at the one who was awake.

"Healers say to accelerate right now," he shouted.

His friend Zak, who had been floating on his back, hands behind his head, flailed through the air and reached for a safety bar to control his spin.

"It's not time," he said.

As the youngest contriver, the gremlin frequently had duty on the off-shifts, though he had grown up in that room with his father and was as experienced as most of them.

"Emergency with the healers." Gil blinked away tears and shook the sleeping pilot. "Wake up."

Like many of the pilots, this one was highborn, though his plain clothing and light brown hair indicated probable low rank and no more than mediocre power. He jerked and opened his eyes, pushing at Gil.

"Alert the others," Zak said. "Accelerate now. Gil, stop shaking him." His ears turned green again.

Gil let go of the pilot. With an exasperated look at Gil, the pilot straightened the gold circlet on his head and pressed his fingers to it. He didn't bother releasing himself from the hammock restraining him to the wall.

Zak slid into his chair in front of the noisy contrivances and flipped switches. "Feet down," he reminded Gil.

Just in time, Gil rotated his feet toward the pale green, landing softly as weight returned.

Zak tipped his head at the crackle and hiss, then adjusted something in front of him. "We are now on a safe course. What happened?"

"The last jerk injured the king," Gil said. "And killed my Grandsire."

The words nearly choked him, even in a whisper. Once out of his mouth, he couldn't deny the truth anymore. His chest cramped as if it were as smashed as Dagan's. He sucked in a breath and let it go, then struggled for another.

Zak clamped his lips together briefly. "Oh, no. We detected a rock at the last moment, tried to avoid it, and didn't quite manage. I'm sorry." He adjusted his dials again but didn't give the pilot a course correction. "We thought the bump was minor enough that we could just send an explanation with the daily reports."

The pilot said nothing and lay in his hammock with his eyes closed. Only his hand on the circlet marked him as awake and working. The other pilots might be anywhere on the ship, since their magic could push the ships from wherever they were. If they hadn't needed to communicate with navigation, they wouldn't even have a pilot in the tower.

Gil sank to the floor and wrapped his arms around himself. With only the three of them here, the room was almost as empty as his heart. The hiss and crackle of the instruments echoed from the walls like mocking laughter. He pressed his hands to his ears and rocked in misery. A fifth of his family was gone in an instant, without even a chance to say farewell.

He should go tell Mother and Ram. He started to push himself up, then stopped. They'd probably gone back to bed already. Why not let them be happy for another hour? What was the point to waking them to make them cry? The bad news would still be there later. He swallowed hard and rubbed his eyes. He'd like another hour of happy ignorance, but it was too late for that.

Ah, Grandsire.

There was no point returning to the healer's room, either. Grandsire was beyond help, and the funeral would be held later. Perhaps he ought to check on the animals, but his limbs felt numb and heavy, too heavy to move. Miknon had left, probably to finish her work so she wouldn't get in trouble. He was only supposed to be sleeping. But he couldn't go back and pretend he was fine. He certainly couldn't sleep if he tried. And anywhere else in the ship would be crowded with people.

"Zak, am I in the way?"

Zak shook his head absently, checking another instrument. Gil leaned against the wall and covered his face. Memories flashed. Grandsire, carrying him and Ram on his broad shoulders. Grandsire, guarding Mother as carefully as he did the king. Grandsire, talking and teaching, rarely laughing but frequently smiling. Always caring. Always there.

Now he was gone.

Gil smothered a sob and wiped his eyes. If he didn't think about something else, he'd fall apart despite the presence of Zak and the pilot. He forced his eyes open and examined the room.

Like every hallway in the ship, the navigation deck was painted with their destination of Ki and its neighbors. Unlike the hallways, there was no mural of Kunisu and the old worlds. This room was focused entirely on their future home.

Gil stared numbly at the mural of seven worlds separated by their circles of rock. One stony band around the outside of them all, then four worlds of bright blue, pale blue, yellow with rings, and orange-striped. Then another ring of stones, followed by three more worlds, red, blue and brown, and very pale yellow. At the end was a bright yellow sun.

The blue and brown world was Ki, their destination and their last hope. But Grandsire wouldn't be there with them.

No, think about something else.

After checking to see how busy Zak looked, he pointed at the outer ring of stones. "Is this what we hit? Are we as close to our new home as the farthest rocks?"

"Not what we hit," Zak said. "We're closer."

"I don't understand." Gil concentrated on the theoretical problem to avoid the very real one that waited for him below.

Zak unfastened his safety harness and turned in his chair to face Gil. "We went over it, coming in at an angle. So we've been flying between the worlds for several conjunctions now."

"Can't have been," Gil objected. "The adults all say they could fly from Harmakis to Chandri in less than two conjunctions, all the way from the most sunward world to the most farside. The murals for the two systems look about the same. If we'd been among these worlds for that long, we'd be at Ki, but we aren't. And we haven't stopped to leave the ice, water, or fire fae on the worlds suited for them."

"None of the worlds so far have been habitable," Zak said. "And they are much farther apart than they were painted. Much, much farther."

Zak walked to the wall and tapped it by the huge, orange-striped world that had a swirling eye in its belly. "We're actually about here now. In fact, the recent weighted shifts have been from slowing, not speeding up. We'll need to make a course correction soon, and we must go much slower in order to maneuver through the last ring."

"Why don't you just go over it?" Gil asked.

"Our destination is not far beyond that ring," Zak said. "Going around would add a long detour, and we'd still have to be going slowly, so we might as well go through and save ourselves the time."

He tapped the mural again. "The distances aren't the only inaccuracies. The painting doesn't show the many — mini-worlds circling most of these worlds." He shrugged. "I don't know why they have worldlets around worlds. And the sizes are all wrong. This striped world is over ten times as large as Kunisu, even though it's painted about the same size. The yellow one before it is almost as big, though the two blue ones are only four times the size of Kunisu."

"Really?" Gil stared at the mural. "Do you think Ki will be that big?"

They could spread out so far they'd never see a highborn again. The gardens would stretch to the horizon. He tried to imagine them and failed.

Zak shrugged. "No way to tell from here. Have to wait until we get there."

Gil touched the blue and brown world. "Do you think we'll get there safely?"

"Why not? We've only hit two rocks during our whole trip. And we're almost there."

"What do you think it will be like?"

Zak stepped back to examine the mural from a distance. "Weight all the time."

"Lots of gardens," Gil added.

"An open sky."

They both glanced at the ceiling and shrugged.

"And separate territories from the highborn," Gil said.

"Finally." Zak rubbed his hands on his tunic.

Gil said merely, "Yes," though he scented Zak's fear.

The gremlin hardly ever left the two navigation rooms. Ki would be much safer for him. He might even get to reveal his secret. Ever since Gil had sniffed it out as a cub, he'd obeyed Mother's command to not even think about it, but Zak would be happier if he could be himself.

"But what about the king?" Gil asked. "If he dies, will his promises be void?"

"Shar has been trained by his father," Zak said. "He'll keep the promises. But you're worrying too early, anyway. The bloodworkers will save Arishaka."

They didn't save Grandsire, Gil thought bitterly. But that was unfair. Miknon had reported his Grandsire as dead before Gil reached the healers' office. He might have died almost immediately, considering his broken chest. Even the best of the bloodworkers couldn't bring the dead back to life.

His sorrow choked him again, and he gasped for breath.

Zak gave him a sideways glance but kindly didn't mention his distress. "The journey to Ki will still take several more conjunctions," he said.

He rambled on about his instruments and how he could guess distances, not stopping for Gil to reply.

His voice was soft and rhythmic, and Gil let it sweep over him in a meaningless tide, drowning out his own thoughts. Then he drifted off to sleep, sitting with his back against the wall.

"Gil." Zak shook him. "Gil, wake up. The shift bell will ring soon. You have the zoo this time, yes?"

Gil fumbled to his feet and rubbed his eyes. "Zoo, yes."

"Better hurry," Zak said. "It's a long way down there."

Gil clasped his friend's shoulders for a moment, then hurried out the door. Before he reported for work, he had to tell his family about Grandsire. He ran down ten ramps and arrived at the third deck just as the shift bell rang. By the time everyone rolled out of bed, he had reached Mother and Ram.

He started to blurt out the news, then stopped. How could he tell Mother her beloved Father was dead? Like a coward, he took the easy way out.

"You need to talk to the healers this morning," he said. "Before you go to the garden. I'll meet you for the meal."

And he darted off while her mouth still hung open with a question. The bloodworkers would tell her everything and offer comfort. He had no comfort to give Mother or Ram. He had no comfort for himself.

Gil ran down the next ramp and shot across the hall. Miknon wasn't there yet, but the rest of his workers arrived quickly. He unlocked the door and assigned everyone tasks, then he found the crankiest gryphon and fed it by hand while he wept into its feathers.

CHAPTER 6

ASTEROID

October 7, 2021, Colorado Springs

Nikos waved to Mrs. Moss on his way out the door, and his host mother waved back, mouth full of sewing pins. As he rounded the corner to the bus stop, Alexandria hurried up the sidewalk, followed by her father. Nikos mentally steeled himself to hear more about the new asteroid she'd been babbling about for the last week. It was just a chunk of rock in space, without an atmosphere or anything exciting. What was so great about it? All the news was old, anyway, since NASA had lost sight of it in the vastness of space.

"Hey, Nikos." Alexandria's shoulders were hunched more than the cool weather deserved, and she kept her face turned away from her father, probably to hide her sour expression.

She obviously got her height and coloring from him, but his eyes were dark brown instead of hazel, and he was much broader. Judging from his muscles, he lifted weights almost as much as Nikos did.

Alexandria's father grabbed her arm. "I'll be home in time to take you to judo, Alex. Since your mother is *too busy*."

She shrugged her arm free and scowled harder. "Okay, Dad."

Mr. Fitch frowned. "I don't know why Ian needs *another* appointment with the doctor. Why can't the kid man up and deal with a little headache."

Little headache? Ian hadn't gotten any migraines while Nikos had been around, but he believed Alexandria when she said they were common for her brother. Obviously Mr. Fitch didn't get them himself, or he wouldn't be so disdainful. Nikos hadn't had another during school, thanks to Alexandria's tips. If he was lucky, he'd soon avoid them altogether. Poor Ian apparently wasn't so lucky. And what kind of father didn't care when his child was in pain? Nikos's parents always fussed until he was well again.

Alexandria glared at the sidewalk, her eyes lightening to bright sage green. Oh, boy, danger sign. Nikos took a step away before he caught himself.

The motion caught Mr. Fitch's eye. "You the kid next door?"

"Yes, I'm Nikolaos Antonakis. Nice to meet you, sir." The polite lie made his stomach churn.

"Yeah, Alex mentioned you. You're in her math class, right?"

Alexandria winced.

"Yes," Nikos said, "and we're study partners."

Mr. Fitch laughed. "I hope you're helping my little girl understand all that math." He nudged Alexandria.

She stepped away and glared down the street where the bus would come. Her eyes blazed even brighter green, and Nikos subtly bumped her elbow with his own to distract her.

"I'm Major Troy Fitch, Air Force. I'm an engineer and pilot, but right now I'm concentrating more on the mechanical and administrative side of things until they need their best pilot back." Mr. Fitch — Major Fitch — puffed out his chest and twitched as if he had almost saluted.

Alexandria cringed, but her eyes returned to hazel. Nikos made a noncommittal grunt. Where was the school bus?

Major Fitch kept talking. "What do you want to do with your life, boy?"

"I like history and mythology, sir." It rankled him to speak politely to this particular adult, but he would mind his manners to shield his friend from her father's displeasure.

"Pfft, like my wife." Major Fitch brushed away the importance of civilization with a careless wave of his hand. "Always mucking about in languages nobody speaks anymore, and reading old stories nobody cares about. But she misses the point!"

"What point, sir?"

"She's studying the Minoans," Major Fitch said. "You know, over by Greece."

Alexandria turned away from her father and rolled her eyes at Nikos.

He bit his cheek to keep from laughing. "Yes, sir, I know where Greece is."

"And Atlantis," Major continued, "the lost island that might have been part of the Minoan civilization. Well, Helen says it hasn't been proven to be a real story." Major Fitch waved off the idea as if it was a certainty instead of a legend. "But the reason nobody can prove anything is because the aliens hid all traces of their civilization so we can't learn anything about them and won't be prepared when they come back."

Still facing Nikos, Alexandria winced.

Nikos bit his cheek again until he could speak seriously. "The aliens, sir?" How had the military let this kuzulo fly planes?

"Yes! Haven't you heard Avi Loeb?" Major Fitch barked. "He's a member of the President's Council on Science at the White House, so he knows what he's talking about. In 2018, he broke the story wide open."

Nikos checked for the school bus again, but no luck. "What story?"

"Alien spacecraft may be in our solar system already!" Major Fitch exclaimed. "Disguised as a chunk of space rock. That's why I joined the Air Force, to be ready when they come back. I mean, way back when I joined, nobody knew for sure, not until Loeb proved it, but I've always suspected."

Nikos looked at Major Fitch, who seemed entirely earnest, then at Alexandria, who covered her eyes with her hand. The bus rounded the far corner and headed for them. Nikos edged toward escape, which was taking entirely too long to arrive.

Major Fitch kept talking. "My son takes after his mom, humph, but my daughter takes after me. She likes science and math, you know, even though she's a girl. I'm waiting for her to decide how she wants the military to use her talents. Either physics or engineering would be fine."

Alexandria grabbed Nikos and pulled him toward the bus. "Okay, Dad, gotta go. See you before judo."

She stuffed Nikos onto the bus and pushed him to the back seat, where she flopped down and banged her head on the padded seat back in front of her.

He gently pushed her upright. "That's probably not good for your girly brain," he teased.

She grimaced. "Sorry about Dad."

"I bet you are," Nikos said. "Dare I ask if you are going into the military?"

Alexandria slugged him. "No! You know I'm not."

"Still deciding how to use your talents, huh?" He grinned despite the glare she aimed at him. "All that stuff you're always reading to me about the stars, doesn't he know about that?"

Alexandria sighed, and her angry look faded into sadness. "He's known for years. He even bought me a telescope once. And he promised to take me to the observatory two weeks ago, and he still hasn't. I reminded him, and he — said no."

Saying no didn't explain her wince. Nikos narrowed his eyes. "Did he yell at you?"

She shrugged. "He had a hard day. I should have waited to ask him when he wasn't so stressed."

Nikos snorted. Major Jerk *had* yelled. What kind of pitiful father treated his kids like that? But he could do nothing about it.

"That story of his about Atlantis was pretty entertaining," he said.

Alexandria laughed. "I know. That's how he and Mom met in the first place. He attended one of her graduate-student lectures on the Minoan civilization. He was hoping she had discovered something about Atlantis. I guess they decided they liked each other after that." She gave a puzzled shrug. "You'd think he'd respect her research, but he doesn't think the rest of her work is valuable. She's trying to translate Linear A, you know. That's why she learned ancient Greek, in case there's a link."

"Nobody has found really good one yet," Nikos said. "The Greek alphabet comes from Phoenician letters. Your father doesn't take her work seriously, but he does believe aliens will invade? Really? History is a real thing. Aliens are stories."

She shook her head, eyes wide. "I don't know if he really believes in aliens or if he's just looking for an excuse to blow things up. History and theoretical science are less important than technology and the military, obviously. A total waste of time, except that Atlantis shows evidence that aliens used to live here." She rolled her eyes at the quote. "Evidence my as — teroid. He's convinced we must defend ourselves, and that's all he cares about."

Nikos took pity on her and changed the subject. "So what was that about Ian? Doesn't he think migraines are a real thing?"

"Well, you didn't either, punk."

"You convinced me. See, I've got my sunglasses, and mints for nausea, and headache meds. I'm all set, just in case." He didn't mention he had remembered to grab them because the sun seemed extra-bright this morning.

"But have you made an appointment with a doctor yet?" Alexandria asked. "You might need prescription drugs."

"Eh, I'm doing well enough."

Alexandria snorted. "You say that now, but what will you say the next time you're puking on the floor?"

The bus screeched to a halt, and Nikos was spared the need to reply in the chaos of exiting. They split at their lockers, then walked to Trig together.

At the end of class, they had a few minutes for homework. Nikos slid the book in front of Alexandria and turned the page.

"Okay, it's time for me to show you how to do this math!" He tried to mimic her father's booming tones in a whisper that wouldn't catch the teacher's attention.

She stuck out the tip of her tongue too quickly for the teacher to catch her at it. "Which one are you stuck on?"

He pointed, and she explained as he wrote quickly.

The bell rang, and they went their different ways. He finished his trig in advisory, thanks to her help, and finished most of his other homework during his classes.

Only German would have to go home with him so far. He might have finished that, too, if not for the creeping signs of another migraine. In the hopes of ending the pain quickly, he used the study time in class to close his eyes behind his sunglasses. With only a dozen students in the advanced class, the teacher didn't care what they did as long as they didn't disturb anyone else.

But the lunch bell reignited his headache, and he arrived at the cafeteria hardly able to see. Fortunately, Alexandria found him leaning against the wall and escorted him to the lunch line.

"Another headache? I told you to see the doctor," she heartlessly nagged. "Close your eyes. I'll tell you when to move. Unless you want me to take you to the nurse's office?"

He tilted his head up and tsked a negative, pushing his sunglasses farther up his nose. "Food, please."

Someone bumped him from behind, rocking him into Alexandria.

"Hey," Alexandria protested.

Nikos reluctantly slitted open his eyes and peeked over his shoulder. Forest McConnell glared at him. The football star was as tall as Alexandria and as broad as Nikos. Half the school worshiped him.

"You think you're so hot with the weights," the thug hissed. "I can lift as much as you can."

"Okay." Nikos closed his eyes again.

"You're not even American," Forest complained. "Whatcha doin' in our school?"

"Learning." Nikos didn't bother turning around again.

"I'll teach you something," Forest said.

Alexandria pulled Nikos forward a little and put his hand on the milk cartons. Nikos slitted open his eyes to select a drink.

Forest bumped Nikos hard, and the milk fell onto the floor. Alexandria snatched it up and returned it to Nikos, glaring at Forest.

Forest smirked at her and grabbed Nikos's sunglasses off his face. "These are too nice for someone like you." He slid the glasses into his shirt pocket and folded his arms. "Whatcha going to do about it, shorty?"

Nikos's tall cousins always teased him about his height, too, so it didn't bother him. He'd talk to an adult later about retrieving the sunglasses. Nikos turned to face the front and found himself staring into vivid sage green eyes.

Alexandria smiled charmingly at him. "Hey, Nikos, I can't decide if I want the fish or the burger. So that I don't hold up the line, why don't you go first?"

At least he wouldn't have to try to decipher the entrée options. He watched her bright eyes as Forest shoved him again.

"I'm fine," Nikos said. "I'll wait for you. I don't want trouble." He raised his eyebrows and hoped she took the hint.

"Nonsense." And with no further discussion, she gave him her tray and squeezed between him and Forest.

Despite himself, Nikos turned to watch. By now, everyone in line had gone silent and was watching the drama. The closest tables were gradually hushing as gossip spread. Even the lunch servers had paused, ladles and spatulas frozen in midair.

Alexandria stared eye to eye at the bully. "You should set a good example for the foreigner so he knows how Americans behave. Surely a school hero like you should be worthy of admiration." Her doubtful tone didn't match the encouraging words.

Forest turned red. "Stay out of my way and let me pass." His voice sounded too loud as more students went quiet to listen.

"Oh, but you already cut in line." Alexandria shook her head. "Once is enough, don't you think? And I still need to get my food. A nice fellow like you will let a lady go first, won't you?" She smiled and plucked the sunglasses from Forest's pocket. "Oh, and those aren't yours."

"I told you to stay out of my way." Forest grabbed her collar.

In the nearly silent cafeteria, someone sucked in a breath. Nikos stepped toward them, and someone ran into the hall, but it was already too late.

Alexandria grinned, green eyes sparkling under the harsh lights. She grabbed Forest's hand on her collar and held it to her collarbone.

"Huh?" Forest said, just as she pressed her knee into his hip and rolled him away from her, extending his arm completely. She threw her other arm over his locked elbow and then sagged. Her weight carried them both to the floor, with him underneath.

Forest howled, and she whispered something in his ear, too softly for even Nikos to hear.

"What is going on?" someone bellowed. "Are you fighting?"

Alexandria gracefully bounded to her feet and patted Forest on the shoulder. "Thanks for helping me up when I tripped."

"Violence isn't allowed at school," the principal continued, fists on his hips.

While Forest struggled upright, Alexandria smiled at the principal. Her once-again hazel eyes still sparkled. "Would I fight someone twice my size?" She formed a shocked O with her mouth. "Or are you suggesting he'd bully me? Why, that would be terrible!" She shook her head solemnly. "Look, there's not a mark on either of us. No, I tripped, and he was being a gentleman. Weren't you, Forest?"

Forest glared at her and rubbed his elbow. "Course we weren't fighting."

A hum of disapproval ran through the cafeteria, and he glared at the other students until they fell silent.

"Well. I'm glad it was just a misunderstanding." The principal turned to leave.

Nikos and Alexandria picked up their lunch trays, and the servers jerked and returned to work.

Forest stepped toward Alexandria, fists clenched. "Fitch the b—"

"Mr. McConnell!" The principal grabbed him. With the uncertainty of another fight holding their attention, nobody had noticed his return. "Let's have a chat in my office."

The students gasped in shocked pleasure and giggled as the two marched toward the exit. The hum of gossip raised the noise level from hushed to resounding, and Nikos winced. Alexandria handed over his sunglasses, which he slipped back on with relief.

Nikos held out his tray to the closest server. "Fish, please."

Eyes almost entirely closed, he let Alexandria nudge him through the rest of the line and lead him to a table. Once seated, he discovered her admiring an extra fruit cup.

She winked at him as she opened it. "Nobody likes bullies."

"I can ignore pests," he said. "That wasn't necessary."

"I don't like bullies, either," she said almost philosophically, "and somehow they never expect little ol' me to be a threat."

She thumped a lemon-lime soda on his tray. Beside the drink, she dropped a couple of headache pills.

"Little old you? You're as tall as Forest." And much more skilled. But if he told her that, she'd only say she was right to defend him.

She fluttered her eyelashes. "But not as wide as that football thug. And I certainly can't deadlift four hundred pounds."

Nikos snorted. "You're not as wide as anything, Beanpole."

"Oh, yeah, Shorty? Hurry and eat so you aren't late to class."

He obeyed, since she was right, popping the headache pills in the process. With any luck, they'd work enough to get through his last two classes and home again.

They did, barely, and he dragged himself to the bus just in time.

"Hey, Shorty." Alexandria nudged his hand to the rail. "Still hurt, huh? Call a doctor when you get home."

"Hey, Beanpole. Maybe I will."

If he didn't, Mama would be upset when she found out. Better to have it all settled by the time he called again. He slumped into their usual seat and threw his jacket over his face to block out all the sun. She sat beside him and hummed softly as she scrolled through her usual newsfeeds.

Suddenly, she jerked in her seat. "Nikos, you won't believe this!"

"What?"

"You remember that asteroid by Jupiter?"

"Sure. Your favorite space rock." He left the jacket over his head.

"Pan-STARRS found it again, much farther along than it should have been able to travel, and going a different direction."

Nikos leaned against the window and took slow breaths to settle his stomach. "Like swinging in orbit?"

"No, it turned! And it's too fast!" Alexandria bounced on the seat until he put a hand on her knee.

"Stop jostling, please," he said. "I didn't think asteroids could turn."

"Well, not usually," she agreed. "'Oumuamua did, and NASA is still trying to figure out how."

Nikos pulled down the jacket and stared at her in confusion. "So what is going on? Did somebody goof the math or track the wrong asteroid?"

She shrugged and clutched her phone. "In this case, NASA thinks it probably smashed into something and ricocheted."

He replaced the jacket. "I don't see why you're so excited."

"A collision only explains the orbit change," Alexandria said. "It doesn't explain the speed!"

CHAPTER 7

IN WHICH TROUBLE IS OVERHEARD

WEEPING, Miknon left Gil behind in the healers' office. He had to run to navigation, but if she didn't finish those filters, people would get sick from bad air, and the healers already had their hands full. Her sorrow would have to wait.

She flew back through the crowded halls to the storage hold and into the maintenance tunnel in the wall, wriggling past the last of the new filters she'd left behind. From the storeroom, the noise of people moving crates of grain competed with their shocked chatter as gossip spread.

Everyone seemed to know about the king, but nobody mentioned his dead Companion. The king was important, but Dagan, despite his position at the king's side, was not. Who cared about a mere warrior when the king's life was still in doubt? There were other guards, but only one king. One of the other Companions would be promoted, and nobody cared who so long as the king survived.

Despite Miknon's attempt to hold back the tears, they crept down her cheeks as she worked. Dagan had never been as warm to her as

Maia and the boys were, but he was unfailingly courteous and protective. Never once had he protested his daughter's decision to adopt a foundling of another race. Never once had he complained about the extra care she required. Never had he allowed anyone to speak ill of her in his hearing. Though he didn't name her directly as granddaughter, she had frequently heard him number his family members as five, not four.

Miknon worked quickly, her sorrow pushing her to hurry, hurry. She slammed each filter into place with a useless wish that events had been different. Warm or not, Dagan was the third parental figure she had lost.

She didn't remember her real parents well. A quiet touch, a whisper of feathers, a musical voice, a soft light. Nothing much. Maia had been her mother for most of her life, and Dagan had almost taken the place of her father. And even if he hadn't, she still would have wept for Gil and Ram and Maia. Poor Gil. This would break her brother's heart. It was nearly breaking her own.

The emergency bell rang, and Miknon sank to her feet as weight returned. Then Gil had reached Navigation and the healers could save the king. Try to save the king.

And what if he died, too? Was the prince ready to reign, or would chaos rule? He wasn't full-grown yet. Though Gil and Ram were the youngest on the ship, there were many children only a little older, like her and Zak and the prince. The king had been training his son, of course, but they'd expected many hundred conjunctions before the crown would pass down. And they had no idea what situations would face them on Ki. How could the prince possibly be ready?

And if he weren't, what then? If war broke out among the highborn, the death toll would be terrible, especially among the commoners. Dagan sometimes told stories of the highborn wars on the old world, where floods and fire overwhelmed entire troops, and the ground moved underfoot or plants ripped apart soldiers. Even worse, some lords could take over minds and turn warriors against their friends. With no end to the highborn magic, there would be no safety.

Miknon wiped her eyes and checked the tunnel. That was the last of the filters here. She'd worked so quickly, she could rest before she must help Gil with the animals.

But resting would only give her time to think, and she wanted to forget. Another sob tore at her throat, and she leaned her head against the wall for a moment. How could she forget?

She could start on tomorrow's work if only the weight was still off. What was tomorrow's assignment, anyway? The dragon hold, which she frequently had to rush to finish in one shift. Even though the filters were only in the ceiling, since it had no interior walls, it was big enough that getting a head start would be useful. And the work would distract her. Better yet, no one went to the hold. She could be alone with her grief and cry in peace.

But the filters? She could ask someone to carry them for her. They weren't heavy for anyone Gil's size, only for her.

Miknon made her way out of the tunnel and to the parts storeroom across the hall. Streams of workers ferried crates to the lowest deck from this grain storage and the one two decks higher, above the water tanks that had leaked.

So many crates. How much grain had they lost? Even with their journey coming to an end and the gardens still growing, would they have enough food to last?

Well, it wasn't her responsibility, and there was nothing she could do about it. The king's secretary and housekeeper and the cooks would figure out something.

She flew to the ceiling and examined the crowd for someone to help her with the filters. The halls were filled, though everyone walked calmly and quickly, arms full of a box or bag in an appropriate size for their physique.

A passing dryad shifted a crate to be more comfortable and complained to the closest worker. "Just one box, they said. Then we can return to our regular duties. But they didn't say half the ship was helping and the line would stretch down two decks. I'll be late." Vines sprouted through her hair and writhed in annoyance.

"You won't be late," her companion soothed. "And if you are, your supervisor will understand. Like you said, half the ship is helping. If you're late, half your shift will be late. They can't punish everyone."

"Can," the dryad muttered, but she merely quickened her pace a little.

Miknon found a troll who carried two boxes of grain with no signs of effort. She hovered above his burly grey shoulder and spoke directly into his ear. "Can you carry air filters to the barge room for me?"

"Just throw them over my shoulder." He split from the crowd and followed her to the parts room.

She pulled a bag of filters off the shelf, directly onto his shoulder, then flew above him to the lowest deck.

Chaos reigned in the hold. Someone had woken all three dragons from hibernation, and they stumbled groggily after the orcs that tugged on their leashes. Everyone else stayed far out of their way. Though the great beasts ate only sunlight and had slept for most of the journey, everyone had a healthy respect for their size and the danger of an accidental squashing. Even the young dragon was the size of a barge, though it couldn't pull one like its parents could.

The dragons kept their wings furled, fortunately, or half the hold would be filled. With no sunlight coming through the narrow window by the ceiling, there was no point to spreading their jewel-bright wings. If they hadn't been able to hibernate for very long periods, they would have starved by now. They would need to feed before they could pull the barges to the new world, but that was a problem for the future.

Gil must still be above deck, because if he had been here, they wouldn't have needed the leashes. Somehow, all the animals listened to him, even the ones that would bite anyone else. Miknon had heard some of the greater fae dismiss his talent as merely beast speaking to beast, but none of the other shifters could do what he did. It was useless for anyone to argue with the highborn about shifters being beasts. Their opinions were set from thousands of conjunctions of life and millions of conjunctions of tradition.

The orcs fastened the dragons' leashes to the side wall and shoved their claws to the safety bars in the floor. Slowly, the dragons gripped the bars and went back to sleep.

As workers stacked crates on the newly cleared floor in front of the airlock, others checked the clamps on the barges. Once all the bad grain was here, everyone would leave and the outer hatch would be opened.

Everything not fastened down would be sucked into space, and that had better not include the landing barges. Someone, probably Gil, would come back later to unleash the dragons.

The troll dropped his crates, hooked her bag of filters next to an access grille, and trundled back to his regular duty shift. Miknon unlocked the grille and climbed in, pulling the bag behind her. This time, she had to climb up before she could go sideways. As she worked, the chaos below her continued.

Eventually, the noise died away to nothing. The shift would be over soon, and Miknon was due at the animal den with Gil. She climbed down to the grille and listened carefully for the warning bell that would precede the airlock opening. Probably they would wait for the next shift, but if they wanted to empty the hold now, she could climb up to an exit on the next level. It would just take longer to reach another access grille.

"Are you sure we won't be overheard?" someone whined.

"All the workers are gone," another replied, "and nobody wants to be here when the hold door opens."

"Neither do I."

"Where else can we be alone on this cursed ship? We're safe; I told them to wait until the next shift. Now report."

"The healers say the king might not survive." The first man sounded smug about the bad news, and Miknon froze inside the tunnel.

"Then this is our chance to return to the old ways," the second man said gleefully. "What a fortunate accident."

"What about our promise to follow our leader's will?"

Miknon peeked through the grille but could only see the tops of their heads. Two men, probably highborn by the rich sheen of their clothes and their golden or silver hair.

"If the king dies, he won't be our leader anymore." The second man spread his hands as if the argument was obvious. Miknon decided to call him Blue, for the color of his tunic.

"What about the prince?"

"He is young, not fully grown. In our perilous situation, how can we trust our entire civilization to the inexperience of a mere whelpling? He needs experienced advisors, and we can't communicate well with the rest of the fleet." Blue's voice was very smooth.

"Oh, and we're experienced! I understand." The golden top of the first man's head bobbed, and his ornate hairstyle flopped oddly. Miknon promptly labeled him Braids.

"Yes, so let's build support among the council members for a regency. There will be time to make changes slowly to avoid alarming anyone." Blue chuckled. "Then if something... happened to the prince, who would be more natural to lead than one of the regents?"

Oh, no. Miknon stuffed her fist against her mouth. What were they planning?

"Yes, I see." Braids laughed. "One of the regents." He laid a hand on his chest.

Blue sniffed. "One of the regents, yes. We can discuss the details later. First we talk to the others and gain agreement for a regency. Then we deal with the other problem."

Braids paced, waving his arms. "But the prince has all his Companions protecting him."

All of them except Dagan. Miknon squeezed her eyes shut against the sting.

"That didn't protect the king from an accident. And remember that old contriver? Things happen. And the trip and landing will be dangerous. There might be... more accidents."

"Ah." Braids sounded pleased.

That old contriver? What contriver? Miknon didn't remember any contrivers dying on the journey.

No, not *on* the journey. Before they left! Zak's grandmother, the inventor of the new navigation system and pilot link, had died on Kunisu with Gil's father and her own parents. All Miknon and the boys had been told was that an accident affected all four at departure. Maia and Dagan and Zak's father would never give them any details.

And now Miknon knew why. These two lords had murdered the inventor on purpose, possibly with their magic so it looked natural. Somehow, her parents and Gil's father must have been too close and gotten caught up in the *accident*. The highborn below her were responsible for the loss of her parents. But who were they?

She pressed herself to the grille again, but she still couldn't see the faces of the lords below her.

Her adopted mother and Grandsire and the chief navigator must have known the deaths were no accident. That would explain why they wouldn't talk about it. If they said anything, gossip might get back to the murderers, who surely wouldn't mind another *accident* to hide their guilt. And yet, Miknon would rather have the truth. Rage burned as hotly as her sorrow, and she struggled to keep it from setting off her glow.

The highborn were still talking below her.

"Too many things have changed," Braids complained. "Women should never be allowed to have power. It goes to their heads, and they can't deal with it. We should get rid of all upstarts, not just one or two. And without the proper castes, nobody knows their place in the world. Why just today, a measly lesser fae almost crashed into me in the hallway. And did he bow and beg for my forgiveness? No! He merely offered to let me go first into the room." He snorted. "As if he was ceding a right he had! I had precedence. I always have precedence."

Blue nodded. "The respect and courtesy owed us is slipping more every day. The old ways are badly needed. After we land, we must find a way to restore the old castes and rebuild our estates with the proper servitude."

Braids chuckled nastily. "We need only wait for the right opportunity to remove the obstacles."

Miknon shivered in the tunnel, though it was no colder than anywhere else on the ship. These men had killed her parents and didn't even care enough to mention them. As much as she loved her adopted family, she would have been happier to have them as friends with her own parents.

If they destroyed her parents as casually as swatting at flies, just to get rid of Zak's grandmother, then their threats against the prince were certainly real. She was too young to remember the old world, not much older than Gil, but she loved stories. The tales of Old Kunisu spoke of oppression and fear, even during times of "peace." Though the society on the ship wasn't perfect, it was better. Unless these lords succeeded in overturning everything.

But what could any of the lesser fae do about it? Their magic was small. They were powerless compared to the highborn. Only the king's promise kept them safe, and if that came to an end, so did their freedom.

"But what if the king lives?" Braids asked.

"Then we'll wait for another opportunity," Blue replied. "Or make one. We'll find a way." He patted his pocket.

The shift bell rang, and then the alarm bell for maneuvers. The two lords bolted for the ramp. Miknon dared not leave the tunnel, or they would spot her. By the time they disappeared, she was out of time. Desperately, she hooked her belt to a safety bar inside the tunnel and held on.

The ship jerked, and a wall suddenly became the floor. Only the cramped space and her belt kept Miknon from hurtling through the air. After another shudder, the ship settled again, and the floor returned to being down. She unhooked her belt and exited the tunnel. Empty sack in hand, she flew to the ramp and upward.

Gil would be with the animals now. He deserved to hear what had happened to his father. Though he could do nothing, at least he would know the truth. And maybe she could convince her fearless friend to be a little more cautious around the powerful, before he annoyed someone too much and something "accidental" happened to him.

CHAPTER 8

SCHOOL NEWS

WHEN THE BUS STOPPED, Alexandria stuck close to Nikos until he was safely away from his new fans, then bolted for home. She burst in the front door, waving her cell.

"Dad, Dad, did you see the news?"

Dad looked up from his phone. "Sports or politics?"

Alexandria rolled her eyes. As if sports counted as news. "No, NASA! The new asteroid by Jupiter changed orbit! Check it out while I get dressed."

She dashed for her room, dumped her backpack onto her bed, and changed into a t-shirt and judogi. As she tied her blue obi, she grinned. Soon she'd have a brown belt instead.

In the kitchen, she grabbed an apple and a granola bar, then hurried back to the living room. Dad was already up, keys in hand and heading for the front door, gaze fastened on his phone screen.

"I'm here, I'm here," Alexandria mumbled through a bite of apple. She wasn't late, so why couldn't he wait patiently?

"Oh, judo." Dad didn't look up from his phone. "Sorry, Alex, I can't take you. I have something I need to do."

"But Mom is gone," Alexandria said. "You're my only ride." She opened the coat closet and snagged her jacket.

"We'll talk about it later." Dad walked out and shut the door behind him.

In the middle of dropping her keys and granola bar into her jacket pocket, Alexandria froze. Had he actually left her behind? She ran for the door, but even as she opened it, Dad's black Lexus pulled out of the driveway and screeched down the road.

Numb with shock, she stared after him. Dad had abandoned her. Now what was she supposed to do? The city bus wouldn't get her to her class in time, even if she could get to a stop. She didn't have cash for a taxi or Uber. Mom was still at the doctor's office with Ian. She couldn't run there. She said a word that would have gotten her a scolding from Mom.

After a moment of thought, she ran next door and pounded on the door. Nikos answered, an open book dangling from his hand.

"Hello." He examined her from head to foot. "Charming outfit. What's up?"

She tried to smile. "Can Mr. or Mrs. Moss drive me to judo? Please?"

Nikos swung the door open wide. "You can ask."

Mrs. Moss came into the living room, wiping her hands on her apron. "Hello, dear. What's the trouble?"

Alexandria bounced on her toes. "I'm sorry to bother you, but I need a ride to judo practice. I mean, I had a ride, but... an emergency came up."

Nikos frowned at her. He must know Dad had left only a couple of minutes ago, since his bedroom window faced the street; she'd seen him studying at his desk before. But if Dad hadn't had an emergency, he wouldn't have left her, would he?

She steadfastly ignored her friend and kept her gaze fastened pleadingly on Mrs. Moss. "I'll pay for your gas and time. Um, after I get my allowance. Please?"

"Oh, no worries, dear. I'm happy to give you a ride. Let me get my keys and purse." The elderly lady vanished down the hall.

Nikos pulled Alexandria into the house and shut the door, then wandered out of the room. She hovered anxiously, not sure if she should sit or wait by the door, then remembered the half-eaten apple in her hand. Munching quickly, she finished it and snuck into the kitchen to throw away the core.

"Here we are, dear," Mrs. Moss said, waving her keys. "I'm ready to go."

Nikos reappeared, stuffing books into his backpack. "I'm ready, too."

Alexandria cast him a startled glance. "Oh, no, you don't need—"

He took her elbow and hurried her out the door. "Don't want to be late."

Mrs. Moss got into the driver's seat, and Nikos opened the rear door for Alexandria, then hurried around to take the seat across from her.

"I wouldn't miss this for anything. After today, I really want to see what you learn." He grinned.

She crossed her eyes at him. "Very funny."

"Oh, what happened at school, dear?" Mrs. Moss asked as she backed out of the driveway.

"Nothing," Alexandria blurted, reaching across to smack Nikos.

He laughed, but mimed locking his lips. "Nothing, Mrs. Moss. Somebody tripped in the cafeteria, and Alexandria helped him."

Out of the driver's sight, he raised his hand and then tipped it flat, indicating Forest's fall from her "help." Ungrateful brat. See if she helped him with the next bully.

"Take Academy Boulevard downtown," she said, then gave directions to Mrs. Moss for the next twenty minutes.

Once they arrived, she hurried inside, Nikos trailing her, while Mrs. Moss found a parking spot. Alexandria dropped her jacket onto the parent benches and kicked her shoes underneath.

"You two can sit there." She glared at Nikos. "But be quiet and don't embarrass me."

He locked his mouth again, eyes twinkling. What a punk! If he made a scene, she'd pretend she didn't know him. The sensei would throw him out, and that would be the end of it. Serve him right.

Warm-ups were just starting, and Alexandria hurried to join the class. She took a deep breath and tried to clear her mind. Concentrate.

Listen. Watch. Think only of judo. The familiar routine calmed her, and the physical exertion blocked out her mental distress.

After the stretches, they practiced falls and rolls for a bit, then the sensei demonstrated a new hold. The judoka broke into pairs to practice as the sensei walked around and gave feedback. Once everyone was doing the hold correctly, he allowed some time to try the new move integrated with whatever old techniques and feints they wanted.

After that, the sensei gave them some combinations to try, then they hauled out the crash mats and practiced throws. That was followed by groundwork practice, conditioning, and live sparring.

The sparring was what Alexandria had been waiting for. Now was her chance to demonstrate she was ready for her brown belt. She would have already gotten it if they hadn't moved around so much for Dad's career. He preferred karate's dramatic kicks and offensive style, but if she could impress him with her skills, he'd understand why she liked judo and be proud of her. She glanced over at the parent benches, already grinning at him.

But Dad wasn't there.

Nikos waved his pencil, and Mrs. Moss mouthed, "Be careful."

Alexandria's grin faded. Oh, yeah. Dad hadn't come.

Her first opponent bowed, and the sparring began. Alexandria fought half-heartedly. What had been so important that Dad couldn't come with her? He'd promised to bring her today. If she got her brown belt today, he wouldn't see her triumph. Telling him about it wouldn't be the same.

She feinted, her opponent dodged, and they swapped a few moves. When an opportunity arrived, she grabbed her opponent in an arm lock and leaned on his elbow. He wiggled free, threw her to the ground, and pinned her. Alexandria tapped out.

Sensei awarded the bout to the other judoka, narrowing his eyes at her. Okay, so she hadn't been subtle enough.

She shrugged. "Next time? I'll practice harder." She'd be ready the next time Dad brought her.

He shook his head and turned to the next pair.

Through the last few minutes of class, her attention wandered back to Dad. Why hadn't he come? Didn't he want to see her advance?

Class dismissed, and she grabbed her jacket and shoes and followed Nikos and Mrs. Moss to the car. Nikos held the doors for both of them, then climbed in and stared at her.

After buckling her seatbelt, Alexandria pulled her granola bar from her pocket and unwrapped it. Judo made her so hungry, even twenty minutes was a long time to wait for dinner.

Nikos cleared his throat. She stared out the car window and chewed. Was Dad home yet? Where had he gone? What was so important that he couldn't come watch her earn her brown belt?

Nikos tapped her elbow. "Hey, Alexandria?"

"What?"

"That last move of yours looked like what you did to McConnell."

"Did it?"

"Yes, but this time it didn't work." His voice was heavy with suspicion.

Alexandria shrugged. "It's harder against someone who knows the counter move."

Nikos didn't say anything for a minute. "Oh, is that it?"

"What else could it be?" Not locking his elbow enough, her guilty conscience prodded.

Nikos paused again. "It's too bad your Dad couldn't come tonight."

"He had something important to do." More important than her. She sighed and leaned her head against the window.

Her much too insightful friend grunted but stopped talking.

When they reached home, Alexandria thanked Mrs. Moss and dragged her feet inside. The smell of pizza filled the house.

"Dinner's ready," Mom called from the kitchen.

Alexandria hung up her jacket and dropped her judogi top and belt on the couch. In just her t-shirt and judogi pants, she shuffled to her seat at the table and flopped down. Ian passed her the pizza box. Half pineapple ham, half pepperoni. Something for everyone.

"Where's your dad?" Mom leaned back to peer toward the living room.

Alexandria grabbed several slices of pizza and dropped the almost empty box onto Dad's plate. "He had to do something this afternoon."

"Hopefully it was fixing the house papers," Mom said. "He left earlier, not right now? How did you get to judo?"

"Got a ride from next door." Alexandria rearranged her pizza and spread her napkin over her lap, not looking at Mom.

Mom sighed. "I'm sorry. I won't make any more of Ian's appointments on judo days. Ian, will you please bless the food?"

They had almost finished eating by the time Dad finally arrived. He grabbed the last of the pizza and crammed it into his mouth, not even sitting.

"Is the deed ready for me to sign?" Mom asked.

He shook his head. "Had to do something more important. Didn't you hear the news?"

Mom stacked the plates and took them to the sink. "No, I spent several hours in the doctor's office, waiting for them to deal with another emergency before they could see Ian."

Alexandria wrinkled her nose at Ian in sympathy. That explained the pizza, not that she minded. She tapped her head, and he shrugged. So the doctor didn't have any better treatment than his current one. Well, could be worse.

"Alex, tell her the news." Dad leaned back in his chair, looking serious.

And how did he know already? Did he just assume she was no good? Her chest pinched. Maybe she should have advanced anyway, to prove she could.

"I didn't get my brown belt," she said.

"No, not that," Dad scoffed.

Alexandria blinked. Didn't he even care she hadn't advanced?

"Oh, Alexandria, I'm so sorry," Mom said. "What happened?"

"No," Dad interrupted. "Tell her the other news! About the asteroid."

Alexandria raised her eyebrows. Since when did Dad care about the science news? He never listened to anything that wasn't engineering or military. Now, if someone invented a new bomb, he'd care about that.

"The new asteroid by Jupiter changed orbit today," she said. "NASA thinks maybe it smashed into something."

"Right," Dad said, "so that's why I couldn't take Alex to judo."

Alexandria, she thought wearily. But what did the asteroid have to do with anything?

Mom stopped filling the sink and turned to look at Dad, hands dripping soap suds. "That's why you disappeared today? How is the random movement of a chunk of space rock more important than settling the paperwork for the house or taking Alexandria to judo?"

Dad grinned, spreading his arms wide. "I reenlisted!"

Alexandria and Ian shared a wide-eyed gaze. Dad hated his new desk job. He'd been threatening to quit for months, despite being close to retirement.

Mom frowned. "I don't understand the connection. You reenlisted because of the asteroid?"

"Yes," he said, "I want to protect Earth from the aliens."

Alexandria put up a hand to block her face and rolled her eyes at Ian. There were no aliens on the asteroid. There never would be aliens within visiting distance of Earth. This was real life, not a dumb science fiction movie. Even light, the fastest thing in the universe, took more than four years to travel to the solar system from the closest star, which had no signs of life around it.

She couldn't even blame Dad's PTSD for shaking loose his mental stability, because aliens had always been his choice of conspiracy theory, clear back to college or earlier. That didn't mean he was right.

Mom pressed her lips together, and Ian covered a giggle.

"Okay, fine," Mom said, "it's a good idea to stay in the Air Force until retirement." She turned back to the dishes with an air of resignation.

"Oh, my news is even better." Dad kissed Mom on the cheek. "I switched to the Space Force and got a big bonus for enrolling for six years."

Mom gasped. "You did what?"

Dad frowned. "You wanted me to stay until retirement, and now I am. I did what you wanted, and you're still mad." His voice rose to a bellow. "Can't I ever make you happy? What do you want from me?"

Alexandria pulled Ian from his chair and sidled down the hall with him on her far side. Behind them, the fight continued loud enough for them to hear every word.

"I wanted you to stay until retirement. ONLY two years." Mom's voice was strained but not quite yelling.

Dad shouted back. "Well, there's a threat to Earth, and I have to protect it." He took a noisy breath. "Besides, the bonus will be useful."

Mom splashed water. "Okay, it can go toward Alexandria's college fund. We have more time to save for Ian."

"Oh, that's not necessary," Dad said. "The Air Force Academy is free. We can spend the bonus on a car for her."

Alexandria gasped. Oh, no. No way. She was a future astronomer.

She left Ian in the hallway and ran back enough to shout at Dad. "I'm not going to the Academy!"

"Of course you are," Dad said. "Your country needs you, and the military is great. Once you get used to it, you'll love it." He narrowed his eyes and scowled. "The discipline will do you some good."

"I don't want to be in the military at all. Ever!" She slashed her hands through the air in negation. "Not for a single day."

Dad stomped toward her, swearing in Russian. Ian ran for his bedroom and slammed the door.

Mom chased after Dad and grabbed his arm. "No swearing! Stop yelling at Alexandria! She doesn't have to enlist."

He slapped her off without looking at her. "You're going into the military! Both of my kids will carry on my legacy! I prefer the Air Force or Space Force, and either complements your silly star hobby. But if you really want a different branch, I'll go along with it." He rolled his eyes. "Even the Navy. Physics is a great major, and they'll be lucky to have you."

He leaned to peer around Alexandria. "I'm less confident about your brother. Languages are less useful, except to spies, but Ian can learn something else. He can't be totally useless."

Yet the sneer on his face gave his true opinion. His shoulders tightened, and he clenched his hands.

Alexandria backed up a few steps, trying to seem casual about it. When Dad was like this, it was better not to annoy him more. He couldn't make her enlist, after all. And she had little more than two years before she turned eighteen. If she kept up her grades and worked hard, he'd see reason by then.

"Honey, the kids don't have to enter the military. They'll be fine in civilian jobs." Mom kept her hands visible and didn't touch Dad again.

"Oh, yes, they do," Dad said. "And speaking of Ian, it's time for him to go to school."

"He is in school," Mom said. "I teach him every day."

"Real school." The sneer was back, and he raised his voice loud enough to be heard through Ian's closed door. "Maybe a military school. How would you like that?"

He marched toward Ian's bedroom, and Mom ran in front of him, blocking his progress.

"Okay, real school," she said. "I'll enroll him in junior high tomorrow, though they probably won't have him start until after fall break."

Poor Ian. He'd hate public school. And he wouldn't even be with Alexandria.

Dad leaned down, nose to nose with Mom. "I'll check after work tomorrow to be sure you obeyed. If he isn't enrolled, I'll start calling military boarding schools."

He stormed off and slammed the door of his den behind him.

Mom sagged against Ian's door and bit her lip. "I'm really tired of being treated like a mere soldier who has to take orders. When did I stop being his partner?"

There was no answer to that, so Alexandria just hugged her.

After a deep breath, Mom knocked on the door. "Ian? May we come in and talk to you?"

We. Alexandria squared her shoulders and took her own deep breath. Yes, they'd face this as a team.

CHAPTER 9

IN WHICH THE PRINCE MUST BE WARNED

149 CONJUNCTIONS AFTER DEPARTURE, *NEW KUNISU*, ON THE WAY TO KI

GIL WHISPERED his sorrow into the gryphon's ear and choked back more tears. Soon, he'd have to direct the workers, and he needed to be dry-eyed to avoid questions or teasing. Some of them already didn't like him supervising because of his youth; bawling wouldn't make him look more competent.

"Gil," a tiny voice piped. "Gil, Gil!"

He blinked and wiped his eyes and patted the grey-and-tan gryphon one last time. When he raised his head, he faked a mild smile. Blue wings flew toward him, dodging animals and workers and tools in use.

"Miknon?" She rarely flew so frantically. What had happened? He hurried toward his sister, holding out his hands.

She dropped into them, shivering. "I need to talk to you," she whispered. "In private."

Casually, he moved down the hall to the garden that grew feed for the animals. Though workers had already moved animals in to graze, he found a far corner that was empty, recently harvested and waiting for replanting. He sank to the stubbled ground, cross-legged, and Miknon settled onto his knee.

"What's wrong?" he asked.

She shook again, her feathers quivering. "I was changing filters in the dragon's den, and I overheard two of the lords talking about the king's accident."

"Everyone is," Gil said.

But nobody was talking about his Grandsire's death. It was as if Dagan didn't matter to anyone but his family.

"They said it was their chance to return to the old ways," Miknon continued. "If the king dies, they want a regency for the prince so they can make him restore the old castes and remove all women from power. Then they'll divide the rest of us among their estates as vassals."

"But they promised us a new society," he said.

She shrugged. "Yes, well, they think a change in leadership will release them from that promise."

"That's terrible," Gil said. "I'd be separated from most of my friends." He gasped. "They'll make me be in the army like Ram! I won't get to take care of the animals anymore." He clutched his hair. "I don't want to be a soldier. How can they do this to me?"

Miknon kicked his knee. "That's not all. Are you still listening to me?"

"What else?" Gil groaned. "Don't tell me they won't let us visit?"

Miknon yelled, "They're planning to—" She took a deep breath and lowered her voice to a mere whisper. "To kill the prince!"

"No they aren't." The denial was automatic. How would they dare rebel against the rightful heir?

Miknon stuck her fists on her hips. "You weren't there, and I was. They talked about accidents and opportunities. They said if the king died, only the prince would stand in the way of the regents taking over."

"That means nothing," Gil protested more doubtfully. Truthfully, it did sound odd. "What could they do?"

"With magic, they could do anything. They hinted they already arranged an accident for someone else in the past. An old contriver."

Gil shrugged. "No contrivers have died on this trip."

"Not since we left, no. But what about Zak's grandmother?"

"Not possible," Gil said. "If she'd been killed on purpose, that would mean my sire's death was no accident, and neither were your parents'." Of course the accident was terrible, but murder was an entirely different scenario. Why would anyone kill a bunch of harmless commoners?

Miknon raised her eyebrows. "And we've never been told the whole story of how our parents died, have we? Mother and Grandsire always get very quiet and tell us now is not the time. And why is that?" She stuck her fists on her hips. "Because if we knew they were *murdered*, we might have given away our distress around the wrong people. They were *protecting* us, you numbskull, which means there is something to protect us *from*, which means those lords probably *did* murder our parents!"

She stopped, panting for breath, and Gil found he was breathing as hard as she was. Could she possibly be right? Were there murderers on the ship?

"Did they really murder four people?" he asked, even though he knew Miknon couldn't know for sure. "And for what? Just to get rid of a female contriver? There must be more to the story than that. But Mother probably wouldn't tell the truth anymore than she had before, and Grandsire is gone." He gulped down more tears. "Maybe Zak can convince his father to tell us?"

"That's not the biggest problem," Miknon said. "We can get the truth about their deaths after we land."

"Right, right, of course. Rogue council, broken promises, ruined Ki. I'd better warn the prince to be careful and not trust the council."

"You can't just walk up to him," Miknon said. "Not only will he be mourning his father, but he's the *prince*. He doesn't talk to people like us."

Gil shrugged. "I talk to him all the time. You always leave right after you eat, but I talk to all sorts of people on the ship. Even the prince. He's only a little older than you, you know. Everyone still considers him a child, like us."

Which was why Ram's continued lectures about growing up were ridiculous.

"You still can't tell him," Miknon squeaked. "What if someone hears you? Then you'll be in trouble. I'll be in trouble. The highborn will make us disappear like we never existed!"

He touched her arm. "I'll be careful, I promise, but we can't ignore this. If we don't warn Shar and something happens to him, it will be our fault."

"We didn't do anything," she said. "It's not our fault. Can't you stay out of trouble?"

Gil set her on the ground and hopped to his feet. "I'll talk to him during my free shift today. We'd better get back to work before someone comes looking for us."

He hurried through the garden, and before long, Miknon caught up. She dropped onto his shoulder and grabbed his necklace as usual, but said nothing else. Speculation swirled through his brain. The advantages to killing the prince were obvious, but why would anyone murder Gil's father, who was nobody in particular?

As they walked into the animal room, some lounging workers jumped to their feet and tried to look busy, but others ignored Gil until he nagged them back to work. In fact, he nagged them so much that all the chores were finished a little early, and he dismissed them to grumble somewhere else.

Miknon left to get some extra sleep, so Gil went to the barge hold to check on the dragons. If something happened to them, the passengers would be stranded on the ship until they could borrow a dragon from another ship in the fleet. And the baby was too young to even be imprinted with a driver.

All three of the dragons were still asleep, as they should be. He didn't see any injuries or signs of disease, so he quietly left again and headed to the arboretum for his next work shift.

Mother greeted him, eyes rimmed with red. Obviously, she knew about her father, and Gil yet again fought the lump in his throat as he silently opened his arms.

After a tight hug, she sent him to help Ashur tighten the straps that held the trees still when the weight turned on or off. The red-haired dryad boy started talking as soon as Gil arrived, alternating instructions with ramblings about the trees and plants. Normally, Gil would have pitched in half of the conversation, resulting in a crazy mishmash of overlapping chaos that confused any eavesdroppers and amused both of them greatly. But today, Gil's grief choked him into silence, and he let Ash's talk wash over him.

Each time they finished with a tree, the hundred-handed giant who lived in the arboretum — it being the only space tall enough for him to stand up — moved his basket and plucked ripe fruit, filling baskets as fast as smaller workers could haul them away.

Once finished with the trees, Gil and Ash checked the mesh and grass that kept the dirt in place, patching any holes or replanting thin spots. And still Ash kept talking as leaves sprouted and died in his hair. He talked the whole four hours, until every word was nearly croaked through a dry throat.

Finally, the shift bell rang, and everyone automatically reached for the closest safety bar as their feet floated off the ground.

"I'm sorry about your grandfather," Ash blurted.

Before Gil could respond, his friend was gone, propelling himself through the air toward the exit. Gil stared after him. He'd known the whole time? Had he been hiding his own awkwardness or providing a distraction from sorrow? Zak, though quieter, had done similar, not making Gil speak of his grief. His friends were kind to let him forget for a few hours.

Mother called from the doorway. "It's time. Let's go meet Ram."

Gil sighed. Time to remember. He followed Mother to the healers' office, where Ram and Miknon already waited. With the help of a few of Dagan's fellow guards, they carried Grandsire's body to the dragons' hold and set it midair in front of the hold door.

Each Companion spoke a few words of honor, then they left the family alone for their last farewells.

Despite floating, Ram kept the rigid posture of the soldier he was learning to be. "I'll work hard and be as good as you. You'd be proud of me, Grandsire."

Gil touched the cold hand floating in front of him. "I'll miss you."

Miknon, yawning from her interrupted sleep, kissed Dagan's ear and straightened his collar. "You were always kind to me."

Mother opened her mouth, then closed it and cleared her throat. She tried again, then finally buried her face in her father's shoulder and wept. "Oh, Dada."

Her dark hair was the exact color of his, except for the few strands of white marking his age. Awkwardly, Ram and Gil patted her shoulders, and Miknon stroked her hair. For long moments, Mother kept weeping.

Finally, she stood erect and wiped her eyes. "Gil, go tell Zak to open the hold doors. Ram, to the healers. Miknon, hurry back to bed."

She floated out of the hold, shoulders rigid, and Ram followed her. Gil touched his Grandsire one more time, then followed them. They turned off the ramp on the third deck, but he kept going all the way to the top of the tower.

Inside Nav, Zak turned a quiet, sad gaze on him. "Is it time?"

Gil nodded, and Zak pulled a lever. Far below, gears groaned and the hold doors slid open. After a minute, Zak pushed back the lever.

"He'll travel among the stars forever," he said, "a fitting Companion for the constellations."

"As you say." Gil clasped his friend's shoulder, then headed back down.

He would rather have his Grandsire as his own companion. But now that the funeral was over, he had to move past his grief. Before he ate, he needed to report to the healers for a regular health inspection. It would also be the perfect opportunity to speak to the prince, who was almost certainly still with his father. His father, but not Grandsire. Gil pushed at the grief again, stuffing it farther into his heart until he could breathe again.

Indeed, when he drifted through the doorway, the prince was in the inner room, floating by the king's bed. Gil's family was already gone and would be waiting for him in the meal hall. He found his usual blood-worker and presented his finger for a bite from the long fangs. Merodach swallowed a drop of Gil's blood and waved him to the side.

Instead of waiting there, Gil snuck through the inner door and joined the prince. The king looked pale and still, his golden hair spread across the pillow, but he was breathing. His son kept his gaze fastened on him, though the prince's face gave away nothing. In fact, he was so quiet that his resemblance to his father was striking.

"Shar," Gil greeted his friend. The king and prince were too well known to avoid everyone knowing their first names, and too powerful for it to matter. They did keep their other names strictly private, and Gil tended to use only the polite use-names. "How is your father?"

Shar glanced at Gil and offered half a smile. "Still alive. And how did Dagan's funeral go? I regret I could not attend."

Gil managed not to flinch. "It's done. Truly, we didn't expect to see you and did not take offense."

Shar nodded. "I knew you would not, but I still wished to support you."

"And I, you," Gil said. "Can I help in any way?"

Shar touched his father's hand. "The Companions see to my needs."

Every need except restoring the king. Even though the healers were trying, Gil's heart pinched for his friend.

Gil subtly checked both rooms, then closed the door to block eavesdropping. Shar raised one eyebrow.

"There's a new problem." Gil repeated everything Miknon had told him. "Try not to oppose the council too openly, if you can. Don't give them an excuse to create an accident for you."

Shar tightened his lips. "Several of them already offered to guide me in my decisions while Father is unwell."

"Already?" Gil yelped. "They move fast."

"I declined," Shar said, "but I will expect more urgency in the future. I appreciate the warning. What do you want in reward?"

Gil snorted. Why would he need a reward for helping a friend? "Stay alive."

The prince laughed. "I hope I can accommodate you."

They sat in silence for a few moments while Gil gathered his courage. Finally, he spoke. "If your father dies — and of course I hope he doesn't — do you intend to keep his promises for a new society of equals?"

He let himself drift out of arm's reach of the prince, in case his question was too bold.

Shar sighed and faced Gil instead of his father, though he continued to hold the king's hand. "I will. Father trained me well. Besides, I have seen what equality can do, and I see the difference from Father's tales of Kunisu. Commoners saved all of us from the destruction of our world when the highborn couldn't. Though the pilots come from both high and low classes, all the navigators are 'lesser' fae. Commoners tend the gardens, prepare the meals, mend the ship, and take care of all the necessary tasks."

Gil grinned. "Even the highborn have tasks. I personally love to watch them shovel dung."

The prince stifled a chuckle. "Yes, but the commoners work without complaint. Father never spent a day without some highborn or other coming to his office to gripe about how his powers and station should exempt him from some task or other. But then there's you."

"Me? What did I do?" Gil didn't remember complaining about anything. Except boring people, maybe.

"You are common but my true friend."

Gil's ears grew hot. "Of course I am. Why wouldn't I be?"

"Perhaps you don't realize how selfish the lords tend to be. Few of the fae birthed children between the announcement of the disaster and our departure, but for very different reasons. The highborn wanted to save the resources for themselves and limit the number of passengers. Father fought them to increase the number who could be saved. In contrast, the lower classes decreased their birthrate to preserve room on the ship for as many of their neighbors as possible. And yet, they trusted each other to save everyone, and a few still had children for the future. My father followed their example." He waved a hand at himself.

"And so I grew up among 'lesser' fae," he said, "eating, sleeping, playing, and working together. All of you accepted me without question. With the highborn, I must weigh every word and guard my back at all times. I need not do that with the commoners. I know your worth, regardless of your lesser magic. And now you are here, warning me against plots against my authority and my life, all for no reward."

"I'll help however I can," Gil assured him.

"For now," Shar said, "stay out of trouble. Don't confront the lords or try to spy on them. We will see how events unfold."

Gil frowned. "I have to do something more. I know a lot of people. What if I talk to them subtly, assure them you will continue your father's policies until he recovers, and encourage their loyalty?"

"If you can manage that," Shar said, "I will be grateful, but don't feel discouraged if you can't. We both know our elders still consider us children."

Someone knocked on the door. Shar held a finger to his lips and turned back to his father. Gil opened the door to the healer.

"I have your analysis," Merodach said, a frown on his pale, narrow face. "You haven't been eating your plums, have you?"

"Yuck," Gil protested.

"I don't care if you like them or not. You need them for your bones, so eat two today, then one every day. After today's ration, shift twice to pull the nutrition into your bones."

Gil cheered. He loved shifting forms but rarely got the opportunity because of the extra food it required to fuel the change.

"Just twice, please." The healer smiled. "You know, after we land, you can shift as often as you like. In fact, you should shift as often as possible. You shifters have an advantage over the rest of us. We'll have to rehabilitate our skeletons the slow way. It will take months for most of us to even walk again, assuming we weigh as much on Ki as we did on Old Kunisu."

Gil flipped a somersault in the air. Shar laughed.

Merodach said, "Don't you think you're a little old for that?"

Gil widened his eyes in fake surprise. "I'm only one day older than the evacuation. I'm the youngest person on this ship. If I'm not young enough, who is?"

He had no intention of giving up his play, no matter what Ram said. And if it encouraged people to underestimate him, so much the better.

"I suppose you have a point. Hurry to your meal, *young* one, and make sure to eat your plums."

With another somersault and a wave to the prince, Gil left. He expected to find Mother and his siblings already in the meal room but found them standing at the back of the line, still waiting in the hall. Ram looked furious, Mother was biting her lip, and Miknon flew to Gil's shoulder as soon as he arrived, cowering against his neck.

"You didn't have to wait for me," Gil said. "I would have found you."

"Nik just announced rationing due to the grain infection," Mother said. "We're already at maximum garden production, so we can't make up for the losses."

Gil shrugged off the news from the king's secretary. "We're in the final approach. We'll survive a little rationing for a few months. It will be fine. Did you wait here just to tell me that?"

"No." Ram clenched his fists. "Now that we have no head of the family and thus no status, we are bumped to the back of the line with the other orphans and unaffiliated women."

"Wouldn't Mother be the head of the family?" Gil asked. "Or you?"

Ram glared at him, and Gil realized the problem. Women had status only through their father, husband, or adult sons. Mother no longer had a mate or father, and he and Ram were still considered children.

"Uh-oh." Gil rubbed his hungry belly and settled down for a long wait.

Chapter 10

Alien Expectations

October 8-10, 2021, Colorado Springs

As Nikos walked into the cafeteria on Friday, the students were in chaos. The noise was so loud that the words blended into an incoherent mess. He collected a tray and selected Chinese chicken and noodles. He picked through the vegetables to find the freshest, though they were still pitiful compared to home, then found a place at a table in the corner. Within minutes, Alexandria sat next to him, folded her arms for a private blessing on the food, and started eating her chicken salad. She tilted her head sideways, listening intently, and he concentrated to distinguish what had caught her attention.

The teacher on cafeteria duty seemed to have given up trying to control the noise level, and the conversations around him were all the same.

"It can't be an asteroid, then."

"I know, right? It must be aliens!"

"They'll attack Earth!"

Alexandria finished her dessert and raised her hands for attention from the other students at her table. "Look, NASA just hasn't tracked down the natural forces that moved the asteroid. They're still working on that for 'Oumuamua, too. Since this asteroid is now smaller than it used to be, it probably smashed into something. No big deal. If there's a danger to Earth, they'll say so. Be patient and wait for the scientists to figure it out. Keep in mind that it's very far away and hard to see."

"No way!" the students called. "It's aliens!"

Alexandria sighed. "Why does everybody sound like my dad?" she muttered to Nikos. "And despite his new interest in space, he still won't take me to the planetarium."

"Aliens are exciting," he said, "but this is nothing new for your dad. Or so you said."

"I know, but it can't be aliens!" She pounded on the table. "Do you know what the chances are of meeting other intelligent life in the universe?"

"Not impossible?" Nikos guessed.

"Pretty much, yeah. I mean, I believe God created other intelligent life. But not close to us! Doesn't anyone realize how big space is? Without traveling at light speed, it takes much too long to get anywhere at all. Even light takes decades or millennia. Do I really need to remind everyone we can't travel at light speed? We'll be amazingly lucky if we ever even get a radio signal from another world. And everybody should calm down, because NASA will tell us what's going on as soon as they figure it out. That's their job, and they're good at it. Chill, folks!"

The other students kept chattering at full speed.

Nikos squinted at his friend, who was stabbing her salad as if it would run away. "Is something wrong?"

Alexandria scowled. "Dad totally flipped out yesterday and transferred to the Space Force. *And* he re-enlisted for six years!"

"Youch," Nikos said. "I'm sorry. What will he do when NASA proves it's a weird orbit or something?"

"He already thinks 'Oumuamua's proof of aliens," she said flatly. "Besides, it's too late for Dad to change his mind about enlistment. I just hope they'll figure it out before Dad enrolls me in the Air Force Academy without my permission."

Nikos lowered his fork and stared at her. "Can he do that?"

It was bad enough Major Fitch wouldn't keep his promises, but forcing his daughter into the military was too much. He almost spit on the floor to fend off the possibility before remembering he was inside.

"Probably not," Alexandria said. "If nothing else, by the time I graduate, I won't be a minor anymore. But he also wants to put Ian in a military boarding academy *this year*, and I don't know if Mom can change his mind. She's enrolling him in the local junior high today, hoping that will delay matters long enough for this to all blow over."

"Ian in military school?" Nikos feigned a whistle. "Doesn't seem like a good idea to me." He liked Ian a lot, but the kid was not robust.

Alexandria groaned. "No kidding. Worst idea ever. But you know he wants us to be like him, and he and all his military friends want to take their planes to blow the aliens out of the sky."

Her voice rose at the end, and the students across the table leaned forward.

"Yeah, let's blow up the aliens!"

Nearby tables erupted into agreement.

Alexandria stood on the cafeteria bench and raised her voice loud enough to be heard several tables away. "Okay, guys, I've had enough of this. We can't blow up the aliens."

"Why not?" someone bellowed.

"So many reasons the whole idea is terrible," she said. "First, we don't have space planes to go track down the aliens that certainly aren't coming here, by the way, because space is too big and travel is too slow."

"Sure they are," a student argued.

"Second," Alexandria continued, "the asteroid is by Jupiter, which is two years away with our best technology. If the Air Force or Space Force or astronauts or anybody else spent four years in space without gravity, there and back again, their bones would break when they landed."

The students hushed, listening intently.

"Third," Alexandria said, "if it was aliens — but it's not — who had good enough technology to get all the way out here, then what makes you think they don't have the tech to swat any of our planes or spaceships like a fly?"

Now the students looked embarrassed and worried. Nikos smothered a smile. She'd already convinced him.

"Fourth," she continued, "if the military decides taking the fight to Jupiter is useless — which it is — and waits for the aliens to get here before trying to fight them in the atmosphere with our planes—"

The students interrupted her with cheers. She folded her arms and waited. By now, everyone in the lunch room was listening to the conversation.

When they finally quieted, she continued. "What makes us think we have the tech to defeat anyone who could survive a trip through space from who-knows-how-many light years away? The best we have is either a nuclear bomb — and I hope I don't have to explain why exploding one of those in our atmosphere is a bad idea — or aiming a kinetic impactor at their ship before they enter the atmosphere."

"Okay, let's do that," someone yelled, and more students cheered.

Alexandria rolled her eyes at Nikos, and he grinned. His best friend was more entertaining than any of his teachers, especially when she was excited.

Alexandria spoke slowly, as if explaining something to a child. "A kinetic impactor is intended to change the orbit of a near-Earth object by striking it at high speed. But it can only move an NEO a tiny bit, which means we have to hit it while it's far enough away that the small change in orbit will make enough of a difference to avoid Earth. And if this *were* aliens — which it isn't — then what's to stop them from readjusting their trajectory and aiming at Earth again? And then they'll be annoyed we threw a rock and hit them in the head, so to speak."

"Not fair," Forest McConnell protested. "Humans win in the movies!"

"Yeah," another student volunteered. "Independence Day."

More students pitched in. "Men in Black, Ender's Game."

"War of the Worlds."

"That doesn't count! Earth only won by accident."

Nikos hopped up onto the bench beside Alexandria. "Those are all science fiction, and not realistic. Do you really think aliens use computers that run on the same code we use? And where is our tech like the movies have?"

One of the drama students stood, arms wrapped around herself.

"And sometimes the movie aliens win. What about The Day the Earth Stood Still or Infinity War?"

That started another round of suggestions around the cafeteria. "Invasion of the Body Snatchers, Hitchhikers Guide to the Galaxy, The Host."

Now the students looked worried, and fearful murmurs circled the lunch room. Time to bring them back to reality.

Nikos touched Alexandria's elbow. "What would you do, Alexandria, if it were aliens, which it isn't?"

She took a deep breath. "Well, assuming they didn't blast Earth into smithereens right away, and we had a chance, I'd try to make peace. Can't we make friends with them?"

Of course that was her answer. Alexandria was excellent at making friends. Half the students listening to her counted her as a friend, and the other half just hadn't met her yet.

As before, students called examples from the film industry.

"Bumblebee, Guardians of the Galaxy, ET."

"Star Trek!" The science nerds gave each other high-fives.

Mr. Reynolds, Nikos's American history teacher and one of the lunch monitors, clapped slowly. "Making friends is a great idea. Not that I think it's aliens, either, but it would be a good exercise in our history classes to discuss the history of cultures meeting each other, and how we could make it go smoother than it has in the past. Every era has bad examples."

Other teachers, presumably in the history department, nodded.

One stood. "But we really do need to cover the state curriculum. We can't spend more than a little time discussing aliens." Her last word dripped with skepticism.

"Oh, like that will stop the students," Nikos muttered to Alexandria. "They won't get any teaching done with all the gossip."

"What about an after-school club?" Alexandria asked the lunch room in general. "We could get a sponsor from the history department, and one of the math or physics teachers could help with technical questions."

Mr. Reynolds nodded. "I'm willing to sponsor you. Clubs normally meet once a week, but considering the excitement, maybe we should meet two or three times a week for a while, to calm any worries."

"Judo, judo," Alexandria muttered. "What about Monday-Wednesday-Friday?" she called out.

Nikos ripped a page from his notebook and passed it to the closest student. "Sign up if you're interested."

"Hold on," Mr. Reynolds said. "I want people to take this seriously, so if you join, expect homework. If you don't want to do the work, don't sign up. We'll start in two weeks, after fall break, to give me time to find a science advisor."

Someone on the far side of the cafeteria ripped out another notebook page and started a list on that side.

Nikos and Alexandria hopped down and grabbed their empty trays. On the way to the trash can, Nikos nudged her.

"Way to go, rabble-rouser," he said.

It wouldn't do to let her know how amazed he'd been at her ability to calm the crowd and pull them toward a common goal.

Alexandria rolled her eyes. "Pretty sure an organized club is the opposite of a rabble."

The warning bell rang, and both hurried to class.

In the rest of his classes, the students were still excited and inattentive, but they stayed quiet enough to not get sent to detention. As word spread, teachers posted the days for the new club on their boards and passed around sign-up sheets. They usually ended with a useless plea to pay attention until the bell rang. Most of them gave up teaching halfway through class and let students either talk or have a study hall. Nikos got through all his homework that way, did some personal research on the internet, and rode the bus home in a very good mood.

When he walked into his host home, Mrs. Moss had a snack ready, as usual. The Mosses had four sons and a daughter, and even though they were all grown, Mrs. Moss obviously remembered teen appetites.

"How was school, dear?" she asked.

"Crazy," he said. "Lots of worry about aliens."

Mrs. Moss shook her head. "I've been watching tv, and it's amazing what some people believe."

"Yeah." He finished his snack while he double-checked the times he'd researched earlier. "Hey, Mrs. Moss?"

"Yes, dear?"

"Would you take me and some friends into town next week during the break?" he asked. "They're only open midday, so we can't do it after school."

He couldn't make up for Alexandria's dad being rotten, but maybe he could help in another way. He didn't say which friends, but his foster mother could probably guess, since he didn't see any of his other friends outside of school. Even the girls he dated seemed happy with a couple of dates before bouncing on to the next guy.

She beamed at him. "Of course, dear. We're happy to help. Would Monday be okay?"

"Monday is perfect," he said.

And she hadn't even asked who or where. He hugged her and ran next door to bang on the door.

Alexandria answered. "Hi, Nikos. Were we supposed to study today? I thought you finished all your trig in class?"

He grinned. "I did. May I speak with your mother, please?"

Alexandria raised her eyebrows but let him in. "Mom, you have a visitor."

Wiping her hands on her apron, Mrs. Fitch came to the living room. "Oh, hi, Nikos." She frowned at Alexandria. "Did I forget you were coming for dinner?"

Alexandria shook her head. "We don't even have trig tonight."

"No, Mrs. Fitch," he said. "I want your permission to take Alexandria on an activity next Monday, before lunch."

"I'm not dating until I turn sixteen," Alexandria said, "and Nikos—" She stopped and grimaced.

Quickly, Nikos rescued her. "Not date! Just somewhere I thought you'd like to go. As friends, I promise! My host parents are driving, so we'll have chaperones. Ian can come if he wants! Your mother could come, except I don't think the car is big enough."

He stopped talking, trying not to sweat. Why did it have to be this hard to treat his friend?

Now Alexandria looked intrigued. "Where?"

He smiled. "It's a surprise. Please come. Mrs. Fitch, may she go? We'll be back before dinner."

"Ian," Mrs. Fitch called. When Ian arrived, book open in his hands, she asked, "Would you like to go on a mystery activity with Nikos and Alexandria next Monday?" Ian's eyes widened, and Mrs. Fitch added, "I've been promised it isn't a date."

"Okay, sure." Ian flashed a quizzical grin at Nikos and wandered off, nose in his book.

"Then you have my permission." Mrs. Fitch returned to the kitchen.

Alexandria opened the door. "You know she'll check to see if Mr. and Mrs. Moss are in the car Monday," she whispered.

"I don't have my driver's license yet," Nikos whispered back. He winked and strolled out.

The door shut rather firmly behind him.

ON MONDAY, Nikos knocked on the Fitch's door while Mr. Moss held the car door for his wife. Both of them had been chuckling all morning, anticipating Alexandria's reaction as much as Nikos did. Apparently, they loved being in on surprises.

Ian and Alexandria ran out of the house almost immediately, shouted "Bye, Mom," and slammed the door before Nikos could say anything. The front curtains parted and Mrs. Fitch waved, smiling.

Ian climbed into the middle of the back seat and folded his arms, grinning. After Alexandria took the right seat, Nikos closed her door and sat on the left side.

"Mr. Moss," Nikos said, "we are ready."

Ian bounced a little, and Alexandria grinned at Nikos over his head.

"Ready to tell us where we're going?" she asked.

"Nope," Nikos said.

In the front seat, Mrs. Moss said, "Take I-25."

When Alexandria tried to peek over the seat at the directions, Mrs. Moss folded the paper. Mr. Moss nodded and pulled out of the driveway.

Nikos chatted with Ian while they traveled, studiously ignoring

Alexandria's piercing stare. Eventually, Mrs. Moss looked at the paper again, shielding it to prevent spying.

"Take exit 156, dear."

Alexandria sat bolt upright and looked at Nikos with wide eyes. Unable to resist, he winked at her.

She rolled down her window and leaned out, watching intently until they reached the north gate of the Air Force Academy. Mr. Moss showed his driver's license to the soldier on duty before being waved through.

Alexandria began making a low squeal, like a tea kettle coming to a boil.

"Now straight ahead for four miles," Mrs. Moss instructed.

She and her husband grinned as they watched their passengers in the rearview mirror. As they traveled down the road and a white dome came into view amid the hills and trees, Alexandria bounced in her seat, the tea-kettle squeal getting louder.

"Please be real," she whispered.

Mr. Moss turned left and parked, and Alexandria jumped out of the car almost before it stopped moving.

"Hurry up," she called. "You boys are slowpokes."

Ian leaned over to Nikos. "Where are we?"

"The planetarium." He ruffled the younger boy's hair and followed Alexandria.

"I didn't know you like the stars," Alexandria said. "Your eyes always glaze over when I talk about them."

"Eh, they're not so bad." Nikos shrugged casually, hiding a grin. "But I thought you'd enjoy this."

Because her father kept breaking his promise to bring her, the jerk.

"It's too bad they don't have a real observatory," Alexandria said, "or we could see Jupiter. Next year, Jupiter will be the closest it's been in fifty-nine years!"

She headed for the planetarium at nearly a jog, and Nikos stretched his legs to catch up. Mr. and Mrs. Moss trailed them.

Ian slipped between Nikos and Alexandria. "That's cool?"

"Yes, silly. That's very cool." Inside the planetarium, displays listed the shows for the day. Alexandria turned to the Mosses. "Do we have time to watch both movies?"

"Of course, dear."

Alexandria hauled the boys into the large, domed movie room and grabbed front row seats. With the Mosses behind them, she sat silently through two films, one about telescopes and one about astronauts. They weren't bad, but Nikos spent most of his time watching Alexandria's enjoyment instead of the movie screen.

When the movies ended, she blinked and looked around. Her smile faded, and she dragged her feet out of the building and got into the car without a word. Nikos and Ian exchanged a confused look, and the other four joined her. Mr. Moss started for home, speaking quietly to his wife.

"Didn't you like the movies?" Ian asked. "For star stuff, it was pretty good."

She shook herself and reached over her brother to touch Nikos's shoulder. "I'm sorry for being a brat, Nikos. Thank you very much for bringing me here. I loved it. I really did. I was just thinking..." She sighed.

"I know." Nikos smiled wryly. "It's okay."

He wasn't the person she wanted on this trip, but he couldn't fix that.

Alexandria sat up straight. "So, did you know professional and amateur astronomers report possible NEO's to the Minor Planet Center in Massachusetts? The Center calculates orbits of new discoveries so other observatories can confirm its existence. If it's in an impact orbit, they'll keep scanning it. Amateurs usually either confirm the asteroids that professionals find, or they try to answer questions about them, like what they look like or how fast they spin."

Ian groaned. "Oh, no, Nikos. She activated lecture mode."

Alexandria poked her brother in the ribs. "In 2009, Hubble found a tiny object in the Kuiper Belt. At thirty-two hundred feet across and 4.2 billion miles away, that's like seeing a flea eleven thousand miles away. Amazing, even if they can't see any details."

Ian put his hands over his face, and Nikos started to laugh.

"I already told you NASA watches for potential problems," Alexandria continued, "but I didn't tell you there are two kinds they watch for: a very close encounter, or a potential impact. They tell the public about the close encounters just for fun. They might not be the first to announce it, because they'll wait until they know for sure. Stop laughing, Nikos."

Nikos asked Ian, "How do you turn off the lecture?"

Alexandria glared at him and kept talking. "If NASA detects something bigger than thirty feet across with more than a one percent chance of hitting Earth, they'll warn the White House, Congress, and other agencies. Then the White House takes over for the U.S. If the asteroid will hit somewhere else, then the European Space Agency might take the lead."

Ian leaned away from Alexandria. "I usually drown her out with ancient Greek. I don't know if modern Greek will work, but you can try it."

"Oh, I know some ancient Greek," Nikos said. "It's standard curriculum."

Eyes lighting with joy, Ian started chattering in ancient Greek.

"Slow down," Nikos said. "I read it better than I speak it."

Ian nodded and complied. Nikos answered all his questions in detail, sometimes in Greek and sometimes in English, until Alexandria threw up her hands and stopped talking halfway home.

"Can you teach me modern Greek?" Ian asked.

"Sure." It would be great to speak his native language to someone, even someone barely learning it. "German, too? I'm not fluent, but I'm learning it in school."

"Yeah!" Ian beamed at Nikos like he was a superhero.

Alexandria leaned forward to chat quietly with the Mosses while the boys discussed the basics of verbs until they pulled into the driveway. As soon as they opened the car doors, they heard the major yelling inside the house, with periodic silences that probably marked Mrs. Fitch's too-quiet replies.

Alexandria's face fell, but she spoke politely to the Mosses. "Thanks for the trip."

"Yeah." Ian hunched his shoulders and followed his sister through their front door.

"What a shame," Mrs. Moss said. "The kids are lovely, and Mrs. Fitch is so kind."

"Can't we call the police or something?" Nikos asked.

Mr. Moss shook his head. "I tried that while you were at school. Mrs. Fitch wouldn't press charges. But if you ever see suspicious bruises, let me know." He took his wife's arm and went inside the house.

For long minutes, Nikos stared next door. Even though the aliens didn't exist, they were ruining Alexandria's life.

No, her father was ruining her life. And he could do nothing to help his friend.

CHAPTER 11

IN WHICH TREACHERY ARRIVES AT LAST

MIKNON FLEW above Gil and Zak, keeping watch. A full conjunction had passed since the accident, and the king was still alive, though his recovery was uncertain. Most of the passengers wanted him to get well so their future would be secure.

Miknon wanted to ask him if he knew who had murdered her parents. Ever since she'd overheard the unknown lords in the dragon's hold, anger had etched every vein. She examined each highborn she ever passed, but there was no way to identify the plotters. Fancy hair and clothes were common among the lords, and their voices hadn't been distinct enough for her to recognize. But the king knew his lords better than she did.

Sadly, the king's internal injuries didn't seem to be healing. The mages didn't know healing, and the healers didn't know other magic, so they couldn't tell if the problematic healing was natural or some subtle magic poisoning his flesh. Many of the highborn had talents that could be turned to mischief, and some were masterful enough to avoid detection if they wished.

With the king almost too weak to talk, it had taken the prince a while to discover that whenever the lords brought his meals, they sent away all witnesses and ate the food themselves, which explained at least some of the king's lingering ill health. Nobody had the rank to disobey the lords except the prince, and he didn't have the age.

So Gil had arranged a sneakier solution himself. Despite being on short rations themselves, his friends had been taking turns sharing their meals. While the prince guarded his father, Gil escorted the food to the king and made sure he ate it, or delegated the task to a trusted friend if he couldn't get away.

Miknon zipped faster and ducked into the air filter tunnel to spy if the king was alone.

Alone enough. Only his son sat with him, with a troll guard in the outer room.

She exited the tunnel and waved Gil and Zak into the room, then followed them.

The prince looked up, relief obvious on his face. "I thought you'd never get here."

From his cot, the king smiled and waved. His face was pale but less grey than before, and someone had braided his hair. He almost looked well, if she ignored the obvious effort his wave had taken.

"Had to detour around some lords," Miknon said.

She opened a maintenance grille and sat at the edge, watching down the long tunnel for shadows that might indicate unwanted visitors approaching in the hall.

Zak pulled fruit from his tunic pockets while Gil emptied mush-rooms from a kelpie's feed bag. Gil helped the prince settle the king higher on pillows, then flung himself into a hammock. Zak stood awkwardly against the wall, hunching in his father's too-large tunic.

"Tell me the news," the king whispered.

Gil raised an eyebrow. "You are feeling well today, Sire." He rubbed his chin. "The lord with water magic—"

"Zaidu," the king whispered.

"Zaidu wasn't able to retrieve the water lost inside the walls," Gil said, "so the gardeners have been prioritizing crops. Trees first, then water-wise plants. Mother and Ash say we should have enough food to make it to Ki." He rocked his hand back and forth to signal uncertainty. "Probably, though we might have to cut rations again."

"We're slowing even more for maneuvering," Zak said. "Plus, we need to be slow enough for landing."

"So more rationing, since the dragons will have to take many trips to unload." Gil sighed. "It's too bad the dragons can't fly fast enough to make transfers between ships while we're moving."

The king nodded and opened his mouth for another bite from his son.

Miknon rubbed her own aching belly. She was always hungry now, like everyone else. Nobody was starving yet, but nobody was comfortable.

Zak wound his fingers together. "There's more. I haven't told the council yet."

Miknon leaned forward. She wasn't as gossip-hungry as Gil, but Zak looked worried.

"Good or bad?" the king asked.

Zak shrugged. "You know the navigation system detects power from stars and worlds. Ki glows with much power."

The prince frowned. "It must be the magic of the rebel colony. Surely that is a sign the world is doing well."

"But something is odd about the signals." Zak shrugged again. "I can't tell what with our equipment."

"Can you alter the equipment?" the king asked.

"Perhaps with Father's help," Zak said. "He worked the closest with Grandmother."

At the reminder, Miknon glowered. Zak's grandmother had died with her parents, and someone on this ship was responsible. One day she would find out who, and then... And then what? She could do nothing against a powerful highborn.

"Keep me informed," the king said.

Zak bowed and left.

"Now that you're feeling better," Gil cheekily asked, "what are your plans, Sire?"

"I must finish training my son and write my will before I die," the king said.

In the tunnel, Miknon froze as still as Gil did. Head bowed, the prince lifted another mushroom to his father's lips. His hand shook, but he said nothing.

"But—" Gil protested.

The king lifted one hand for a moment. "I will try to live. But if I die, I must leave my kingdom and heir prepared. Shar told me about the proposed regency. None of my council has mentioned it to me yet, which is worrisome. If they were truly concerned with the good of our people, they would discuss the issue with me. That they have not implies they hope I will leave my son vulnerable to their manipulations." He patted the prince's arm. "I shall not. And I know I can count on his friends to help him."

Gil bowed his head. "Yes, Sire."

Miknon murmured agreement, though she didn't know what she could do, small and powerless as she was. No way to find or punish her parent's murderers, no way to protect the prince.

At the king's prompting, Gil recited the gossip of the ship, both large and small, that he heard from his many friends. She listened absently, still missing her parents. Eventually, he finished the serious gossip and moved on to merely entertaining tales. He was in the middle of the latest disaster in the kitchen when a shadow briefly darkened the maintenance tunnel.

"Hush," Miknon said.

"—spilled all over—" Gil stopped mid-sentence and froze.

The outer door opened and closed, and a highborn voice murmured.

"He's sleeping," the guard said loudly, "with the prince watching him."

Footsteps marched to the inner door and stopped, as if the troll had moved to block the bedchamber. The voice murmured again, a little louder but not quite audible.

"Yes, I will tell you when he wakes."

Silence, and Miknon held her breath. Finally, the outer door opened and closed again.

The guard opened the inner door. "Lord Kishar insists he must talk to you, Sire."

The king pressed his lips tightly. "Yes, I suppose he must. Shar, I will be designating Kishar as your heir, until you bear your own children."

The prince winced, and Miknon shuddered. If Kishar was the heir, how eager would he be to inherit? Would he conspire to bring down the prince? She didn't know what kind of magic Kishar had, but for him to be the backup heir, he must be powerful. And the prince was still young, still learning his own magic.

"Is that a good idea?" the prince asked. "You know what he's like."

"If there is no heir," the king explained, "the lords will fight among themselves and drag us into chaos. You will be an adult soon, and when you marry and have your own heirs, Kishar will no longer be a consideration."

"Please, Father, stay with me." The prince rested his head on his father's shoulder.

The king stroked his hair. "I love you, and you'll be a good king when your time comes."

Miknon wiped tears from her cheeks. She couldn't remember her parents, and her heart still ached. How much worse must it hurt for the prince who knew and loved his father? And he had no loving foster mother like she did, no brothers to keep him company.

The troll Companion cleared his throat. "Before Kishar returns, you young ones should clear out."

Gil hopped to his feet and held out his hands for Miknon. She closed the grille and flew to him, and after bowing to the king and prince, they hurried out.

Through the next conjunction, Miknon, Gil, and their friends continued their secret mission to feed the king and keep him informed. Despite his temporary recovery and the continued meals, the king gradually faded. The prince spent every day with him, learning as fast as he could with the help of the sirin housekeeper's songs. From time to time while the king slept, Gil dragged the prince out for a rest with his friends. It rarely improved his mood.

Not that Miknon could blame him. Watching a parent slowly die had to be the worst kind of torture, even without the other problems.

"The council has finally broached the regency issue," the prince said glumly when Gil and Miknon showed up again. "Every day, they pressure me to choose someone to *guide my steps*. I'd hide when they come, but I don't dare leave Father alone with them." He looked back over his shoulder.

"Ash will take care of him while he sleeps," Gil assured him. "Come on, we've set up food under the trees so you can relax."

And then he didn't listen to any more complaints until they were all settled among the trees with their meager food. Miknon, sitting on a branch too thin for the rest of them, listened to them chatter. Eventually, the prince even laughed at one of Gil's frequent jokes.

From her high perch, she was the first to see the Companion enter the arboretum. His face was solemn, even for a troll, and his shoulders were tight. Miknon flew to the prince and tugged on his ear. When he turned to face her, still laughing, he saw the guard coming. The laughter died, and his skin drained of color as he shot to his feet. The others followed his gaze and also jumped up.

"Prince," the grey troll started. "Your father—"

The prince raced from the arboretum without waiting for the rest of the sentence.

"Is he dead?" Gil whispered.

The Companion shook his head, lips tight. "Not yet. Shar should make it in time."

Zak brushed off his tunic. "We should go."

"Don't say anything to anyone," Gil cautioned.

Zak nodded and headed up the ramp to Navigation. The others disappeared almost as quickly. Miknon and Gil climbed the closest tree, two decks high until they could watch the king's offices.

Healers streamed in the door as highborn left. The king's secretary and housekeeper went in with the new chief Companion, and Gil stiffened. Only two conjunctions ago, that would have been Dagan instead of the naga whose snake scales gleamed even in his two-legged form.

Gil's dryad friend Ash slipped out amid the crowd. He stepped from the hall directly to a branch and disappeared among the leaves.

When the chaos ended, silence fell. The guards outside the door watched the hall but listened inward.

Miknon snuggled closer to Gil's warm neck. The key to the animal hold clinked against his family emblem as she shifted the chain. And then they waited.

"Maybe it was a false alarm," Gil breathed. His knuckles paled as he tightened his grip on the tree trunk.

"It isn't," someone whispered.

Gil jerked so hard he almost knocked Miknon off his shoulder. They both looked up. The dryad's red hair dangled above them as he hung upside-down, knees hooked over a branch.

"Oh," Gil mouthed silently, and they returned to waiting.

Soon, much too soon, the bloodworkers filed out, heads bowed. As they passed each light sconce, they whispered to the pixie sitting there, and the light faded halfway. The dimness spread through the ship along with the news.

The king was dead.

The dryad vanished among the leaves again. Gil slipped down the tree with Miknon and headed for Mother, who waited with Ram, arms ready for a comforting embrace. Miknon huddled in the middle and shivered.

With the king dead, would the prince be forced into a regency, or would he be able to fulfill his father's promises? And if he could not resist the council, would their civilization return to the oppression of Old Kunisu? Would the lords find it as easy to murder their opponents as they had her parents?

When the shift bell rang, so did the meeting bell, summoning the entire ship for an announcement. Everyone squeezed into the ninth-deck meeting hall and waited breathlessly until the prince arrived in the midst of his guards. His face was pale and set, with lines of pain etched around his mouth and eyes. Without waiting, he raised a tablet and read aloud the king's will. Murmurs of surprise almost drowned out the first few sentences.

Miknon didn't understand most of the legal language, but the last terms gave the crown to the prince without a regent. The lords of the council watched the prince with smooth, smiling faces.

She didn't trust a single one of them.

Somewhere in that smiling lot were two lords who had plotted against the prince. And either they had killed her parents themselves, or they knew who had. By now, the entire council might be on their side.

She spent the rest of the meeting in a worried daze, constantly watching the highborn for any sign of immediate treachery. At bedtime, she crawled even farther into the wall than normal so no one could find her without knowing she was there.

The next morning, Gil hunted down Miknon in her tunnel sanctuary.

"We'll eat with the prince," he said cheerfully. "Before the king's funeral, so hurry."

She yawned. "We?"

"Zak and Ash and Mother and me and you," he said. "Ram had to work. Get up, lazy. Zak is drawing water while we get cereal and Ash picks fruit."

Miknon tumbled out of the wall into his hands. "Don't you have to take care of the animals right now?"

"I traded my free shift," he said. "With the weight on, the kitchen will make hot cereal. Ready?"

And he took off in his bounding gait. In his usual charming way, he wiggled his way through the crowded kitchen and collected a big enough pot of mush to feed everyone, guards and servants included. Miknon held on, desperate to stay on his shoulder in the crowd. If she was knocked to the ground, any of the larger fae could crush her without even noticing.

Once back in the less crowded hallway, Gil whistled as he swung the pot. Ahead of them, someone tripped and brought down three other people in a noisy crash. Gil put down the pot to help untangle the mess. As he straightened the smallest victim and checked for injuries, Miknon thought someone in an embroidered tunic stopped briefly in the hall to gawk at the accident. Gil turned to help the next person, spinning Miknon with him, and when she could reorient for a good view, the tunic was gone. They could have helped, but a highborn wouldn't care if commoners were hurt.

"May this be the most impact you have this day," Gil joked to the clumsy fae, grabbing the pot and hurrying on their way.

When they arrived at the king's offices, everyone else was already there, with the door closed to keep out the noise of the ship. Gil dropped the cereal on the desk, hugged the dryad casually, then rumpled Zak's hair and kissed Mother.

The housekeeper got out bowls, and the secretary passed around spoons and fruit and cups of water. Miknon leaned over the pot, squinting. Was that a dash of color on top? Where had that come from?

"What's that?" she asked.

"Porridge."

"No, I mean—"

"Hey, Miknon," Gil asked, "do you want an apple or a plum?"

She pointed to the plum in his left hand, then turned back to the cereal. Too late. A guard was already stirring it, his long claws clicking against the ladle's wooden handle as he dished out the first serving.

"Wait," she said.

"Don't worry," the baubau said. "There's enough for everyone."

He slid the bowl along the desk into someone's hands and filled another bowl. Miknon flew to Gil and tugged on his ear.

"Make them stop," she yelled over the happy chatter. "Something's wrong."

Gil raised an eyebrow but hurried to the guard shoveling cereal between his fangs. "Hey, now, don't start eating before the prince."

The baubau swallowed his large mouthful and bowed his head until his horns touched the floor. "Sorry, Sire. I didn't think."

The prince looked quizzically at Gil. "I don't mind."

Gil threw his hands in the air. "Protocol, Sire?" He frowned at Miknon.

The king's secretary raised his hand, but the hungry Companion clutched his stomach and vomited.

"I told you something was wrong," Miknon squeaked.

She flew for the door, which the young navigator barely opened in time, and zipped down one deck to the closest healer's office.

But she was still too slow. By the time she got back with Gil's favorite bloodworker hot on her wings, the baubau was dead and Gil was held in the strong fists of the other Companions. The healer closed the door behind himself and rushed to the dead guard.

"Now we know why you were so concerned that the prince eat first," an ogre bellowed in her brother's face. "You poisoned the cereal on the way here."

He laid the point of his sword against Gil's chest. Gil gaped at him, then at the prince, whose look of surprise was almost as strong as Mother's fear.

"I didn't," he swore.

If he'd been capable of sweating, Miknon was sure he would have been dripping. She flew to her brother, inserting herself between him and the ogre's angry face. Her wings pressed against Gil's nose.

"I think I saw the poisoner," she gasped. "In the hallway."

"Everyone *sit down*," the prince bellowed. "I can't think with all this noise."

The guards shoved Gil into a chair and stood over him.

The prince flung himself into another chair and pointed at Miknon. "Tell me what happened, because I can't imagine my friend trying to kill me."

So Miknon explained about the tripping in the hallway and how everyone had stopped to stare at the accident.

"But I thought one of the highborn…" She gulped. "Maybe paused by the cereal, though he wasn't that close to it, really. And then in here, I thought I saw something in the food. But nobody would stop long enough for me to be sure." She finished in a wail.

The dryad grabbed the pot of cereal and cautiously poked a finger into it. Even more cautiously, the dryad touched his tongue despite the healer's yelp.

"It's that grain fungus," he said. "Someone dried and powdered it to concentrate the toxin."

The healer yanked the pot away. "So don't put it in your mouth! Idiot!"

"How did anyone know we were bringing food for the prince?" Gil asked.

"My poor taste in friends is becoming better known," the prince teased. "Did you see which highborn? If he wasn't actually close, perhaps he used telekinesis to drop in the powder, rather than by hand."

He looked at his secretary, who nodded and moved to collect tablets that would presumably list highborn talents.

"I don't know who," Miknon said. "I just saw a flash of embroidery and jewels."

Mother choked. "Zaidu."

"Many highborn wear embroidery and jewels," the housekeeper murmured cautiously.

"And his power is with water," the secretary said, "not telekinesis."

"Oh, I've seen him use it," Mother said. "It's weak, but he knows how to make the best use at the right time."

She clenched her teeth, angrier than Miknon had ever seen her.

"When?" Gil asked.

Mother looked away. "I'll tell you after we land."

Miknon settled on Gil's shoulder and folded her arms. "We want to know now. Does this have anything to do with him murdering four people?"

Most of the people in the room gasped, but Miknon continued relentlessly. "My parents, your mate, and Zak's grandmother? Did anyone else help him?"

Zak sat abruptly on the floor, and the guards stopped threatening Gil.

Mother sighed. "Five people died; there was another female navigator." She flickered a glance at Zak before shaking her finger at Miknon. "And I don't know if anyone worked with him, so don't you dare ask questions. If you ask the wrong questions of the wrong person, you'll be dead."

"Then he *was* one of the lords in the dragon's den," Miknon choked out to the prince. "The ones Gil warned you about. They said they knew how to keep you safe, in a voice that definitely didn't mean safe for you. Safe for them to continue their scheming, perhaps, since you rejected their regency."

Hatred burned in her throat. Now she knew the identity of one of her parents' killers, but would she ever get justice? And when would their perfidy stop? Only the risk of getting caught kept her from searching everyone right now. That lord's water magic was strong enough to pull water from the tanks from anywhere on the ship, as he had proved cleaning up the leaking tank. With even a little telekinesis, he could form a ball of water around her until she drowned, and then send the water back to its source, leaving her dead with no trace of the weapon. She shivered. Was that what happened to her parents?

The prince rose to his feet. "Companions, arrest Lord Zaidu."

The secretary raised his hands. "Shar, you can't do that. If you accuse him with no proof, you'll antagonize his allies. They are too powerful to fight until we land and can get support from the other ships."

"We can't wait until they succeed, either," Gil said.

"Then what can we do?" the prince asked.

Miknon glanced at the door to the bedchamber, where the king's body waited. "Let them think they won. Tell everyone a poisoner attacked the prince, and send the guard's body between the stars with the king. Let them assume he's the prince. Then hide the prince until we land."

"Won't that give the council exactly what they want?" the prince asked.

"They're determined to get it anyway," Gil said, "but at least this way you'll be alive to take back your power after we land."

The secretary rubbed his chin. "Not bad. But how can we hide him for so long?"

Miknon shrugged. "He won't fit into the maintenance tunnels."

A lopsided grin tugged at Gil's mouth. "Disguise him as a girl and put him with the navigators. Hardly anyone goes to the top of the tower, and if they do, they'll only think Zak is sneaking in a sweetheart."

His eyes crinkled with mirth, and he winked at the navigator, who frowned back at him.

"Not as a girl," the prince protested.

"I can manage that disguise," the housekeeper said, and the prince's shoulders slumped.

"Won't anyone miss the dead baubau?" Miknon asked. Worried relatives or friends would ruin the whole plan.

The secretary rummaged for another slate in a cupboard. "He didn't have any family. I can change his assignment to another floor and rearrange his schedule so if he were alive, he would never see anyone he knew before. If I also put him 'on duty' in the most out of the way rooms, nobody will be surprised they don't see him."

"Do it," the prince said.

"Only those here in this room can know," the chief guard said. "Don't tell your families, your fellow guards, your best friends. Nobody." He barked orders for the funeral, clothes, and other arrangements, and everyone scattered.

Gil and Mother carried Miknon off with the dryad, while the navigator hurried upward to prepare a hammock for his new "sweetheart."

But would it work? Could they keep the prince hidden long enough to get to Ki?

CHAPTER 12

HAPPY BIRTHDAY

NOVEMBER 17, 2021, COLORADO SPRINGS

ALEXANDRIA CHECKED HER NOTES. "Okay, can anyone think of anything else to add?"

Despite most of the benches being full, the cafeteria was silent. Some students checked their own notes, and some merely sat. Alexandria waited while they thought. They'd already run through this cycle every day last week, thinking they had everything and then adding something else at the last minute.

Diplomacy Club, so named because the school absolutely refused to call it Alien Club, had been running for a month. For the first week, it had been so popular that it met in the auditorium. Once the initial thrill faded and students realized it would be as much work as Mr. Reynolds had promised with a lot less discussion of aliens than they hoped, half of them dropped out. After weeks of discussion, the remaining students had finally worked out their version of first contact protocol.

While checking for any last-minute raised hands, Alexandria read aloud the summary. "Then our chosen protocol includes choosing a formal ambassador and a linguist, assuming the aliens haven't already learned an Earth language from the radio and don't have an interpreter; asking about greeting customs and forms of address; offering a tour of non-secret places; and asking about interests and goals. When we need to make an agreement, we state our position and then try to find common ground while being open-minded. Did I get that all correct?"

"We'll fine-tune it through the year," Mr. Reynolds said, "but I think that's a good start."

"Okay," she said, "I'll type up this summary, along with all the details so far, and email everyone a copy."

"Why do we need a copy?" a cheerleader asked. "We're just kids. We'll never meet aliens. That will be the President or the U.N. or somebody important."

Seated across the lunch table from Alexandria, Nikos rolled his eyes. "No aliens," he mouthed.

"If you don't like it, drop out," Forest grouched.

Alexandria wasn't sure if he stayed in the after-school club because he was still hoping for aliens or in order to bother Nikos. It certainly wasn't because he was interested in actual diplomacy.

"Most of these strategies can be adapted to welcome new kids to the school," Alexandria said. "Only in that case, you're automatically the ambassador."

At least with her attending the club every time, someone besides the teachers was there to keep the other students in the Land of Sane instead of detouring to Alien Sightseeing every chance they got.

Mr. Reynolds nodded. "They're also good ideas for job interviews or settling in to a new job or new neighborhood, among other life skills. Diplomacy always has a use." He clapped his hands once. "Okay, time's up. I'll see you on Friday, when we will discuss the science and math behind alien encounters."

Alexandria and Nikos shrugged on their coats.

"The science, meaning the impossibility," Alexandria whispered. "That asteroid hasn't done anything odd in months, which means we'll eventually figure out what made it change orbits. When will they believe there are no aliens?"

Nikos laughed. "When will your dad?"

She stuck out her tongue but didn't reply. They gathered their books and notes and ran outside to meet Mom.

Alexandria hopped in while Nikos held her door. "Good timing, Mom."

Yesterday had been pleasant and warm for autumn, but today was literally freezing, and she didn't want to stand around until she turned into an icicle.

Nikos took the back seat, as gentlemanly as always. "Thanks, ma'am."

"No problem," Mom said. "How was school? Lots of homework?"

"Just a bit of German," Nikos said.

"I'm almost done," Alexandria said. "I'll have plenty of time for ice cream and games."

"Nikos, you could come over for birthday cake, if you like." Mom winked at Alexandria. "Sixteen is a big year, you know."

"Sixteen is an excellent year," Nikos agreed solemnly.

"Driving," Mom continued, "dating."

"Mom," Alexandria groaned. "I can hang out with my friends on Saturday, right?"

She emphasized "friends" as strongly as she dared and smiled over her shoulder at Nikos. He'd been so adamant about the planetarium trip only being between friends that she knew he felt the same way. If Mom embarrassed her best friend, Alexandria would die.

"Dad promised to be home today," she said. "I mean, you're always welcome, Nikos, but I wanted to spend time with just the family, since Dad's been so busy lately. We've barely even had time to talk. You're okay with later, aren't you?"

"I wouldn't dream of intruding," Nikos said. "Happy birthday, Bean-pole. I hope your birthday is everything you wish for."

He looked worried, but he didn't say why. She turned a little and watched him as they chatted about school and Diplomacy Club, but he still didn't volunteer anything that would explain the creases on his forehead.

When Mom parked in their driveway, he thanked her again and headed next door. Well, if he still looked upset tomorrow, she'd talk to him then. Right now, she had a birthday to celebrate. Alexandria darted ahead and had the door unlocked by the time Mom caught up. As soon as she opened it, she heard yelling in the kitchen.

Oh, no. What now?

Mom headed for the noise, with Alexandria close on her heels. Ian cowered at the table while Dad stood over him, yelling and stabbing a book with his finger. Alexandria quickly checked the room for a forgotten mess, but she couldn't see the problem.

"Honey?" Mom asked. "What's wrong?"

Dad turned around, face red. "Where were you?" he bellowed. "I got home, and you weren't here, and Ian was all alone."

"Twelve is old enough to stay home alone or to babysit younger children," Mom said calmly. "He has his own cell phone, and I have mine with me. I was gone less than an hour, and he was perfectly safe."

Dad grabbed the book off the table. "And he was reading one of his stupid language books, not doing his homework. He's in a real school now, and he can't afford to waste his opportunity to learn. If he falls behind, he'll have to settle for a grunt job in the military instead of being an officer."

Ian gulped and scrubbed at his wet cheeks. "My homework is all finished except for one math problem. I was waiting for Alexandria to help me with it. And—"

Alexandria shot him a warning look, and he stopped before mentioning his career plans again. Now was not the time to start another fight about the military.

"You could ask me," Dad yelled. "I know math."

Ian grabbed his book from Dad and ran to his room.

Alexandria started to follow, then thought better of it. She'd talk to him later, when Dad wasn't so worked up. Ian would understand Dad needed a chance to cool down from work before he dealt with problems at home. Why hadn't he been reading in his room, where Dad wouldn't see him?

"Rude," Dad shouted after him.

"Honey," Mom said. "Calm down. Everything is fine. Ian's doing well in school, and his teachers are very pleased with him. And dinner is ready, and it's Alexandria's birthday. You're home just in time."

Alexandria ran to the counter and waved her hands over the cake, grinning at Dad.

"I know," he said. "That's why I came home early. Happy birthday, Alex." He turned to Mom and loudly whispered, "Did we get her something?"

Mom tipped her head toward the wrapped present on top of the microwave. Dad gave her a thumbs up.

Alexandria bit her lip and collected the plates. She set the table by herself to give Ian time to compose himself, setting out the nice glasses and the fancy napkins. This was a celebration, and her birthday should look good. If she'd been born in spring, like Ian, she could have had flowers, too. But November was a terrible time for flowers, as Dad always pointed out when Mom admired the florist's booth in the grocery store.

Mom continued to soothe Dad while she pulled the roast and potatoes from the oven and finished the last details. Alexandria's favorite meal was actually lasagna, but she wanted to please Dad on his rare night home. She'd even picked his favorite flavor of ice cream to go with the cake.

Once everything was perfect and Dad's face had returned to its normal color, Alexandria went for Ian. She had to coax him out with a reminder of dessert and her birthday wish for a family dinner. Everyone sat for the blessing on the food, then Mom sliced the roast and served the potatoes and carrots. Dad, as usual, skipped the carrots.

Dad asked Alexandria about school, then cross-examined Ian, dissecting every class he was taking, even the eighth-grade English and history the school had put him in because he was so advanced. All the questions didn't slow his eating, and he chomped through two servings while everyone else picked through just one.

Every time Dad paused to breathe or chew, Ian eyed the cake, the present, and Alexandria, then inhaled and took another bite. Under the table, Alexandria nudged him encouragingly with her toe. He could make it. Just a little longer.

Eventually, Mom distracted Dad with questions about work long enough for Ian to finish eating in peace. Finally, it was time for dessert and presents. Mom sliced the cake while Dad dished up the ice cream.

He didn't even notice it was cookies and cream. Maybe she should have gone for rocky road, if it didn't matter to him.

Ian brought her the large box wrapped in solar system paper and tied with a sunny yellow bow. It was heavier than she expected, and she had to put it on the table instead of her lap.

Her family sang happy birthday, then Ian pushed the box closer.

Slowly, she untied the ribbon and sliced the tape. Even more slowly, she folded down the paper, watching Ian to see how long she could prolong his torture before he exploded with excitement. She almost forgot to look at the contents of the package until he pointed, eyebrows raised.

The weight and bulk came from a globe of Mars. "So cool," she squealed, turning the box to read the details.

A small package taped on top opened to a wrap-around bracelet of beads, including large beads representing each planet.

"I love them both," she said.

Ian squeezed her in a hug. "Happy birthday."

"Happy birthday, sweetheart," Mom said.

"That's not even Earth," Dad said. "How will that help her in the Air Force?"

With a great deal of effort, Alexandria ignored him, as did Mom.

Ian said, "She's not going into the Air Force."

"Yes, she is," Dad insisted.

Ian shut his mouth again, but it was too late.

Dad frowned at Ian, then turned to Mom. "Why don't you take better care of our son? Why is he always wearing the same shirt? Didn't you do the laundry?" He looked around the kitchen and glared at the mail on the counter and the dirty dishes by the sink. "Why isn't the house clean?"

Alexandria glanced at her school backpack abandoned in the hallway and winced. Ian hunched in his chair and stuffed cake into his mouth.

"He wears a school uniform," Mom said mildly. "They're only allowed certain colors and styles, and Ian only likes the navy. He wears different shirts that all look the same. And it takes longer to get the housework done when I'm running the kids to school and all of their activities. If you want to drive them, I'm happy to spend the time cleaning instead."

Dad grunted. "I work hard to provide a good life for all of you. I'm defending you and all of Earth against the aliens coming to attack us. You're not working or bringing in any money. The least you could do is take care of the house and kids like you're supposed to. Have it all cleaned up by tomorrow."

Mom put down her fork and tightened her lips. "I'm not one of your soldiers. Don't order me around."

Dad sneered at her. "You're not worthy to be one of my airmen, but you'd better follow my orders."

Alexandria blinked back tears. Did they have to fight at her birthday party? At least Nikos wasn't here to see this.

"I'm not worthy?" Mom blurted. "I do everything around the house and take care of the kids all by myself. I do all the shopping, the cooking, the cleaning, the organizing, the bills, everything. And I don't deserve you yelling at me." She took a deep breath. "I've had enough. I want a divorce."

Dad slammed his hands on the table, and Ian bolted for his room.

Alexandria sucked in a breath and froze. She felt like running, too, but she'd have to pass Dad. Why couldn't Mom just wait out his bad mood? He'd be fine again tomorrow.

"If that's what you want, you can have it!" Dad shouted. "But I earned all the money, so I'm keeping it all! You'll get nothing!" He inhaled and smiled. Very calmly, he added, "And the kids are mine, so you can't take them. If you want to move out, go by yourself."

"They're mine, too," Mom said.

"Well, the military will be on my side. You can't win against the entire Air Force." Dad sat back and folded his arms. "Go ahead and divorce me. I'll sell the house and take the kids to a foreign base. You'll never see them again."

Mom burst into tears.

"You know I hate tears. Stupid cow." Dad stormed out of the house, slamming the door behind him.

After a minute, Ian crept back into the kitchen and threw himself onto Mom's lap. Both of them shook with tears.

"Nice, Mom," Alexandria said. "You know he'll sulk until you apologize and tell him you didn't mean it."

Why couldn't the two of them talk about their problems like adults? For that matter, why wouldn't Dad just go to therapy and fix his PTSD and his stupid belief in aliens?

Mom grabbed a tissue and blew her nose. "I'm totally serious. I'm tired of living like this. He isn't changing his attitudes or behavior. He doesn't even seem to *want* to get better. I've had enough. I want a divorce." She faced Alexandria steadily, but more tears crept down her cheeks, and her lip trembled. "I don't know how I'll fight him, but I'll talk to a lawyer. There's no way I'll leave you kids at his mercy." She clutched Ian tighter and kissed his hair.

Mom couldn't be serious. Alexandria jammed her fists on her hips. "What about eternal families?"

Mom's lip quivered again. "He doesn't seem to want one. At least not with us."

"He wants me," Alexandria argued.

He had even come home early for her birthday. She burst into tears and ran to her bedroom. Happy birthday! What day could be more perfect for losing her family? Dad had been getting better, sort of, and with a little more time, he'd be back to normal. But now it wouldn't matter. Mom didn't want him anymore. No matter which adult won in the divorce, Alexandria had already lost.

Without her whole family together, what difference did it make if they were invaded by imaginary aliens? At least if aliens killed her, she wouldn't have to live with the Dad-shaped ache in her chest.

She'd almost rather be invaded by aliens.

CHAPTER 13

IN WHICH THEIR NEW HOME IS OCCUPIED

153 CONJUNCTIONS AFTER DEPARTURE, *NEW KUNISU*, STONE RING around Ki

A SCUTTLING whisper caught Gil's ear, and he immediately froze. The whisper died, but still he waited. After a moment, it started again. In stops and starts, it grew closer. Without moving his head, Gil looked sideways. Yes, there it was. A dark line waved from a crack in the wall, retreating and testing. Breathing quietly, Gil held perfectly still and waited. Fortunately, nobody else was wandering the hall right now, so if he was quiet enough, his prey might emerge.

After another few moments, a small black body emerged onto the wall. Gil whipped down his arm and grabbed the cockroach before it could hide again. Popping it into his mouth, he chewed quickly, crunching through the shell to get at the greasy, bland meat inside.

His stomach still growled, as it always did now. In the two conjunctions since the king had died, rations decreased twice more, and the fleet still wasn't safely through the ring of stones. Between the infected grain and the lost water that shrank their gardens, only the pilots and others with essential magic still ate well. Gil had suspicions about which of the highborn were cheating the rationing, but with Shar feigning death and in hiding, nobody could control the lords. The commoners tried to stay out of their way, and when they couldn't do that, they obeyed quickly and disappeared.

At least, they obeyed when they could. Several of the lords had tried to commandeer Gil's key to the zoo with flimsy excuses. Gil, smiling like an idiot, always told them he'd have to get approval from Nik, the king's secretary. The lords invariably told him he needn't bother, which was proof, if he had needed it, that they were up to no good.

He'd already discussed the matter with Nik and Shalla and Shar. All of them agreed that if they ate the animals, they'd have nothing to breed later. Since nobody was actually starving yet, the animals were worth saving.

Besides, the lords didn't normally take care of animals or prepare their own food, and Gil had no faith in their abilities to distinguish mere animals from the fae with animal bodies but intelligent minds. Confinement in the zoo equally prevented an attempt at escape or defense. What if someone ate a kelpie or a hydra or a gryphon? The prospect gave him nightmares, so he never removed his key except when he unlocked the door.

Gil listened but heard no more insect feet, so he continued on his way up the tower. On the next-to-last deck, he checked for observers, then slipped inside the navigation storeroom. The nav auxiliary room held the specialized repair parts for the navigation system, and a backup system that also served for practice and training, and the room allowed off-duty contrivers to rest in a quieter place than the general dormitories. Nobody came here but the few contrivers, so it was one of the most private rooms on the ship. They had even dismissed the light pixies now that it held the hidden prince, and Shar lit the room with his own magic.

Now Zak and his father were trying to get the backup system to better read the odd signals they'd detected from Ki. Using the new adjustments as an excuse, Zak's father had declared it off limits except in an emergency, decreasing the possibility of the prince being discovered.

Gil closed the door and turned around. The room was chaos. One of Shar's ball-lights illuminated parts scattered everywhere on the floor, next to open crates waiting to contain everything before the next time the weight turned off. The backup navigation system was half-disassembled, and Zak's feet stuck out among mysterious boxes.

Shar lay in a hammock, and whether he'd been watching or sleeping before, the sound of the door had made him alert.

"Greetings, Gil." Shar turned red as he smoothed his flounced skirt over his knees and pushed curls out of his face.

Gil didn't bother hiding his smile at the prince's disguise, so different from his usual tunic and simple hairstyle. "Greetings, Sharra. How goes the courtship with Zak?"

A tool spun from under the nav system and cracked into Gil's foot.

"Ow," Gil howled.

"I don't think my suitor cares for you," Shar said dryly. "Perhaps you should stop teasing him about it. He hears enough jokes when he has to tell other visitors I'm here to keep him company."

Gil sniffed and rubbed his bruised toe. "Perhaps so, but you do make a pretty girl."

Shar hopped out of the hammock, adjusting his bodice with an angry jerk. "If you only came here to make fun of us, you should leave."

"Does that mean you aren't hungry?" Gil held out a bucket with a quarter of his own meal and bits and pieces from others who knew the secret.

The prince growled, then sank into a graceful curtsy, skirt spread wide. "I apologize for my rancor and humbly beg for sustenance."

Gil dropped the bucket at his friend's feet. "Shut up and eat, Shar. Nice curtsy, though."

"Shalla taught me," Shar mumbled through his first bite.

Watching the prince eat only made Gil hungrier, so he settled cross-legged by Zak and asked questions about the changes the gremlin was attempting. Sadly, he couldn't understand more than one word in ten of the answers, but he let Zak talk anyway. When he returned to the main decks, he had to give an update to excuse his time up here. As usual, he'd wait until Zak ran out of words, then ask for a simpler summary "for the passengers."

As much as he could understand so far, Zak's father had been here carlier and made another suggestion, which Zak was now trying to apply.

"So we think it might improve the sound output," Zak finished. His bare feet twitched as he stretched farther under the equipment.

Better sound. That was simple enough to report to the others.

"Any idea how long it will take?" Gil asked.

Zak slithered out and glared at him. Dust coated his hair and tunic, and grease was smeared across one cheek. "Until it works."

"Right, right. Sorry." Gil held up both hands in surrender. "I didn't mean to argue with the expert."

The gremlin pulled himself back under the equipment and banged on something. "I'm not—" Bang. "The expert." Bang. "Father is." Bang.

And yet Zak was the one making the actual changes. Was that because his father had to be in Navigation, or was Zak underestimating his skills?

"Will you turn the red dial, please?" Zak asked.

Gil popped to his feet and examined the confusing array of buttons and levers and dials. "Red, red, red," he chanted. "Here it is. Right or left? How much?"

"Just play with it a little," Zak said. "Slowly, so I can make adjustments."

Obediently, Gil slowly turned the dial right. The constant hum in the room crackled and popped. When he couldn't turn the dial any more, he reversed it slowly.

He couldn't hear any difference, but Zak suddenly said, "Stop."

Gil snatched his fingers off the dial and waited. More banging echoed, then Zak crawled out.

"I think that's all I can do for now." The gremlin gently touched the dial, rotating it no more than a hair.

To the shock of all three of them, the hum and crackle in the room suddenly changed to music.

Zak yelped and spun the dial until the noise returned to a meaningless hum. He stared wide-eyed at Gil and the prince. "Did you hear that?"

"Magic," Shar whispered.

Gil swallowed hard. "This is good news, isn't it? The colony must be thriving to send so much magic toward the stars."

"But what is the purpose of the magic?" Shar asked. "Is it merely running something on Ki, or is it meant to strike invaders? They are rebels. What makes us think they would welcome us?"

"We could find out," Zak said slowly.

Gil raised his eyebrows. "How?"

"By listening to them. Shar, do you know enough about magic to detect which spells they're using? I could wear earplugs and turn off the signal at your command or if you look peculiar."

Shar rubbed his chin. "That might work. Perhaps. What if the magic works too quickly for you to stop it?"

"We could tell the council now," Gil said.

The prince grimaced. "Before we know how dangerous it is? No, I think we will have to go with Zak's plan."

"What if we asked the secretary and housekeeper to join us?" Gil asked.

Shalla and Nik used the office one deck down, and though neither had much magic, Shalla's was at least in the realm of music, and Nik would know who they dared ask for help without endangering the prince's secret.

"Good idea," Shar said.

"I'm getting Father." Zak whirled and ran.

"I'll tell Nik," Gil said. "You stay here."

As he ran out, Shar dropped him an ironic curtsy.

When he banged through the door into the king's office, Nik and Shalla were discussing schedules and rationing with the new chief Companion, a tall naga with scaled skin.

All of them knew about Shar-in-hiding, so Gil gasped for breath and jumped to the point. "Come hear the magic Zak found."

"He found what?" the naga asked, but all three followed him up to the auxiliary room.

When they arrived, Zak was already back with his father, Izdu. Shar explained the plan, and after discussing what hand signs they'd use, everyone but Shar stuffed their ears and spread out across the room. Zak took control of the dial, Shar strapped himself into the hammock closest to the door, and Gil stood between the prince and the exit. If something went wrong, Zak would turn off the magic beacon immediately, while the guard tried to deal with the prince. If that didn't work, Gil would run for help, hoping that untangling the hammock restraints would slow Shar for long enough.

With Gil's ears full, the crackle in the room faded to almost nothing. It was a relief from the usual noise, but he kept his gaze fastened on the prince, watching for any odd behavior.

Shar pointed at Zak to start. Gil could barely hear anything, but the prince frowned in concentration. Long moments passed, and Gil wondered if the prince was enchanted after all, until Shar waved his hand in the agreed "all is well" signal. Yet the lines on his forehead deepened, and his eyes narrowed.

Still he listened, and still Gil kept watch. The prince didn't try to leave the hammock, and his hands rested easily on his skirt. He didn't look in physical distress, and he periodically waved "all is well."

And then his eyes widened, and the frown disappeared as his jaw dropped in shock. Gil stepped forward, ready to do — something — but Shar sucked in a breath and motioned for Zak to stop the sound.

Once Zak appeared in his peripheral vision, removing the stuffing from his ears, Gil unstopped his own hearing.

"What happened?" he asked, at the same time Zak asked, "What did you hear?"

"At first, the music," Shar said. "And it was only music. I couldn't detect any magic at all. That doesn't mean there wasn't any, just that I couldn't find it. They might be more powerful than I am, or more subtle, or their magic might have changed from ours since they left Kunisu."

He inhaled and winced. "Then the music changed to speech."

"What did they say?" Nik asked.

"I don't know. I didn't recognize the language."

"Were they speaking the ocean dialect?" Shalla asked. "Or the fire tongue? Something from the beasts?"

"I know all those," Shar said, "at least enough to recognize them. This was entirely different. I don't think the speakers were fae at all."

Gil scratched his head. "I don't understand what you mean. We know the Starry Lovers took their retainers to this world. Or intended to, at any rate. They were fae."

They hadn't taken many of the ice, water, or fire beings with them, which simplified their escape. The current fleet was still looking for appropriate worlds to leave those beings who had other living requirements.

"Listen, and see what you think." Shar motioned to Zak, who played the new signal for them all.

As the music echoed softly, the adults looked as stunned as Gil felt. He'd expected a singer, like Shalla, but whatever made the very complex music didn't sound like any singer he'd ever heard. In fact, he was almost positive he heard more than one thing, making different sounds. Many things, perhaps. If he wasn't still worried about being enchanted, he might have enjoyed it.

This time, Izdu touched the red dial, and the sound changed. This time, there was a singer as well as the other music-makers, but Gil couldn't understand a single word.

Izdu changed the signal again, and now it was only words. Multiple voices talked in an obvious conversation that was completely incomprehensible.

Again, Zak turned the dial, and more speech rolled forth, sounding different from the first but still nothing like the fae.

"Turn it off," Nik said numbly. In the silence that followed, he rubbed his forehead. "I see what you mean. Without more information, the colony — or the natives — must be considered foreign and hostile. And I would give almost anything to know if that *is* the rebel colony or if we're dealing with unknown beings with undiscovered powers."

"The colony might have met resistance and failed," the guard said. "But from whom?"

"We might never know," Shar said. "But that doesn't matter. Our problem is what we should do now."

"We have to tell the council," Izdu said.

"No," Gil protested. "You know what they're like."

"He's right," Nik said. "I do not have the authority to deal with this situation. Unless Shar were to come out of hiding, which I do not recommend, the lords must make decisions about what we do next. At the least, they need to know we might face greater challenges than we anticipated." He sighed and rubbed his head again. "The prince must hide. Can we sneak him to the upper deck or down to the king's office?"

Gil bounced to the back wall and yanked open a cupboard door. "There's room for both of us to hide here."

"Both of you?" Nik repeated. "No, Gil, you should leave before the lords arrive."

Gil folded his arms and planted his feet firmly. "And leave Shar without defense if they send the rest of you away? No."

"And what will you tell the council if they discover both of you?" Shalla asked. "How will it help to have both of you punished?"

Gil winked at her. "He's a girl, right? I'll pretend we snuck in here for a little kissing and didn't notice when you all came into the room. If we tell them we were too... busy to notice what they said, they might believe us."

Shar groaned. "I won't actually kiss you, you know."

"I appreciate that. You're a pretty 'girl,' but I prefer the real thing." He danced away from the swat Shar aimed at him.

Nik grunted. "I suppose it's the best plan, under the circumstances. Zak, please make sure they are well hidden before you leave. I'll go find the council members."

The king's servants left, closing the door behind them, and Zak showed his father how to tune the signal while Gil and Shar made themselves as comfortable as possible in the small cupboard. Sitting on overturned buckets helped a little, but they could barely move by the time they wedged themselves into the space.

Zak held his finger to his lips and closed the door on them, and then all was dark. Shar's breath was warm on Gil's neck, and the stupid skirt tickled his feet. He shoved at the flounces until the prince gathered them up and tucked them somewhere.

The outer door opened, and Zak's father murmured to his son. The door closed again. Now Izdu muttered as he worked, random phrases that could have been reminders to himself but kept Gil and Shar informed of his progress.

The room's door opened abruptly, and Gil jerked into Shar, then froze.

"Welcome, lords," Izdu said loudly.

Clothing rustled and makeshift seats thumped as the lords found places in hammocks or on crates or buckets. Muttered complaints revealed their dissatisfaction with the accommodations. Gil rolled his eyes in the dark cupboard. They'd like it in here even less.

Nik took charge of the meeting, explaining the bad news. As expected, the lords didn't believe him, so Izdu turned on the navigation system. The strange music was accompanied by bangs and shouts and the door slamming as the council apparently bolted for safety.

Gil and Shar held still, covering their mouths to stifle chuckles. True, they had been as alarmed the first time they'd heard the signals, but they were youngsters, not supposedly seasoned and mature lords with magical defenses.

The music stopped, and Nik persuaded the councilors to return.

"We told you Ki glowed with power," he said, "but now we know it's more complicated. The navigation system is intended to detect the natural frequencies of stars and worlds so we can maneuver around them, but these signals aren't natural."

"It's magic!" one of the lords gasped. "Evil magic!"

"No," someone else said. "It's proof the rebel colony survived. Their magic shifted over the long time we've been separated, but they will surely remember us. We can move in with friends."

Shar leaned forward and whispered directly into Gil's ear. "Friends? They ran away from us."

Gil nodded. If the rebels were still around and did remember Kunisu, they wouldn't remember their old world and old neighbors kindly.

"There's more," Nik said. "Please keep your seats this time."

Someone's protest was cut off when the signal played again, shifting to words instead of music. Then again, to different words, and again. They were clearly words, not nonsense, but in a completely unknown language.

The signal stopped playing, and the lords all shouted at the same time.

"That's not fae." "Who is that?" "That can't be from Ki!"

Nik let them babble until they faded to silence. "That isn't the colony, but neither is it an empty world. We must consider Ki foreign and hostile. What do we do now, Commanders?"

"What happened to the colony?" someone asked. "Did they go somewhere else? Integrate with the natives?"

"Die," someone else suggested.

"Does that matter right now?" Nik asked. "What do we do?"

"We should go home," a lord whined.

Gil wanted to jump out and smack the stupid highborn for wasting time on impossibilities.

"We don't have enough food to make it back," Nik said, "and Kunisu is still on the way to destruction. Even if we made it back without starving, which we wouldn't, we would only live until the world died."

"What about the other worlds here?"

"Good question," Nik said. "We can check, but so far they haven't been livable. In fact, they are so far from habitable that we can't even change them with magic, even if we had enough food to take the time. Which we don't."

"Can we find another world near another star?"

Nik shrugged. "Perhaps. If there's one close enough for us to arrive while the food lasts. But tell me — do you know which way to go?"

The room was silent. Gil already knew the answer. The only reason they had found Ki was because of the Starry Lover's vision, and she'd only left one goal for them. They had no other map.

One of the lords spoke in an eager voice. "If we can't go home and can't stay in the ships and can't go anywhere else, there's only one choice left. We must conquer Ki and take it for ourselves."

"Yes," another said. "Let's leave the rest of the fleet hidden among these stones. We can move faster alone, and hide better, too. We can go spy, and when we have a plan, we'll come back for the other ships."

"We'd have to cut rations again in order to have time to spy on Ki," Shalla said.

"Sacrifices must be made," the lord said pompously.

The council discussed details a little longer, then left. Izdu let Gil and Shar out of the cupboard. Nik and Shalla and the chief Companion were still there.

"Speaking of spying," Shar said, "we need to keep informed of the council's plans. I don't trust them to tell Nik everything."

"And how are we supposed to do that?" Shalla asked. "They have enough magic to detect anything we might use."

"Magically," Gil said. "What about physically? I can talk Miknon into listening to them. She knows all the maintenance tunnels, and she's small enough to fit anywhere."

"Are you sure you want her to do that?" Nik's forehead creased with concern. "It might be dangerous."

"Do you have a better idea?"

Nik grimaced but didn't reply.

Gil turned to Shar. "Will you really let the lords conquer the new world? That's not very nice. What if they're friendly?"

"What if they aren't?" Shar asked. "Should we die quietly?"

Gil threw out his hands in frustration. "There has to be some way to find out!"

Shar sighed. "I'll think about it."

And that was as far as the conversation got. Gil left to find Miknon and talk to her about spying.

He didn't envy the weight on the prince's shoulders. At least it wasn't Gil's job to figure out what to do about Ki.

CHAPTER 14

SPRAINED

December 15, 2021, Colorado Springs

BEFORE HE HEADED for the bus stop, Nikos double-checked that he had all his homework and books. Tomorrow was the last day of the semester, and half of his classes were giving finals today. The other half were turning in the last assignments and reviewing for tests tomorrow. Either way, he must not leave anything home. As he exited the house, he spit to fend off bad luck.

He still reached the stop early and tipped up his head to enjoy the pale sunshine. Most of the past week had been near freezing, but this morning was warm enough not to zip his coat. Too bad it hadn't been that warm on the sixth when Alexandria and Ian had come to dinner for his name day. When he'd called his parents after the party, they'd reported over sixty degrees at home. Well, seventeen degrees in Celsius, which still made more sense even though he was getting used to Fahrenheit. He missed the warmth of Greece, though.

Pounding footsteps rounded the corner. Ian ran down the sidewalk like Cerberus was chasing him, head down and backpack clutched in his arms instead of on his back. He screeched to a halt by Nikos and jumped behind him.

"What's wrong?" Nikos asked.

Trembling, Ian shook his head but said nothing. Around the corner came a procession of the Fitch family. Alexandria walked in front, weaving from side to side across the entire sidewalk. Major Fitch tried to duck around one side of her, then the other, but she kept in front of him. At the back, Mrs. Fitch tugged on her husband's arm, talking fast but too low to be heard.

Uh oh. Nikos turned a little to shield Ian better. "The bus will be here soon," he murmured.

"Not soon enough," Ian squeaked.

"Ian," the major bellowed, "get over here. I'm not finished talking to you!"

"Troy, let it go," Mrs. Fitch said. "We can talk after school. As a family."

"What family?" he roared. "You're taking my family from me!"

He turned to his wife, leaning over her and glaring, nose to nose. Alexandria reached the stop and stood shoulder to shoulder with Nikos, hiding Ian entirely.

"Dad, you're embarrassing me in public," she said.

Nikos felt her shoulders tense, and he leaned a little harder against her in encouragement.

"Embarrassing *you?*" Major Fitch yelled. "What about your mother? She embarrassed *me.* She served me divorce papers *at work.* With all my airmen watching!"

"I didn't tell the lawyer to do that," Mrs. Fitch said. "They must not have been able to find you anywhere else. You haven't been spending much time at home."

"No, because I'm giving you *space* to change your mind!" His voice grew louder.

Nikos winced. Could the entire neighborhood hear him? Speaking of embarrassment, the major would become the favorite topic of local gossip if he didn't settle down. His parents would never behave like this in public.

Mrs. Fitch let go of her husband's sleeve and stepped backward. "I won't change my mind."

"Fine." Now the major's voice dropped to a lethal whisper. "If this is really what you want, I'll ruin you!"

He pushed past his wife and marched toward their home. Mrs. Fitch pressed a trembling hand to her face, and Alexandria and Ian both ran to hug her. Nikos awkwardly sidled closer and patted her shoulder.

"Is there any way I can help?" he asked.

She shook her head. "I'm sorry you got stuck in that. I have to go to work. Alexandria, I'll pick you and Nikos up after club, okay?" She hurried around the corner, shoulders shaking.

"I didn't know she had a job," Nikos said.

Alexandria sighed. "It's new, to pay for the divorce lawyer."

Ian scrubbed at his cheeks. "Dad says at least she's finally off her lazy duff and working." His lip quivered until he clamped his mouth shut.

Alexandria took his hand. "This won't last forever. Either they'll come to their senses, or the divorce will go through. Either way, the fighting will stop."

Nikos grimaced. He knew plenty of divorced families that still fought, but saying so wouldn't help. When the Fitches weren't looking, he spit on the ground again.

The bus turned the corner, and Ian pulled his hand free. The three of them took their customary back seat and hunched down, speaking quietly to avoid being overheard.

"I don't want to live with Dad anymore," Ian said.

"He can't take us from Mom," Alexandria said. "The judge will require joint custody, and with Dad in the military, I bet he only gets weekends and summers."

Ian flopped his head onto the backpack on his lap. "I don't want to live with Dad *at all*. He doesn't like me. He's mean."

Nikos had to agree. Whether natural temperament or the PTSD Alexandria had told him about, the major was terrible.

"He didn't use to be like that," Alexandria muttered. "I thought he'd be better by now."

"He was always like that to me," Ian whispered. "He's just worse now."

And Nikos could do nothing about it. He clenched a fist and wished the major's nose was available.

Alexandria silently stroked her brother's hair until the bus pulled up at the high school. She waved to Ian until he left, then walked inside with Nikos.

"Dad loves me, you know," she said wistfully. "We used to be best friends."

Nikos grunted. And now her dad broke his promises to her on a regular basis and abandoned his responsibilities. But if she couldn't see his worthlessness herself, it wouldn't do any good to point it out.

They went to their lockers, then walked together to Trig. She took her seat and pulled out her math book without further comment. Her brow stayed furrowed all during the test review, and Nikos didn't think trigonometry was the problem.

At the end of class, he touched her elbow to get her attention. "See you in club? And can we study after school?"

"You can come for dinner." She waved as she disappeared into the crowded hallway.

Did he want to eat with the major? No, but he would suffer if it made Alexandria feel better.

Nikos gave his last speech, took the health test, and spent an hour studying for his German final. At lunch, he stole half of Alexandria's broccoli before she jolted to attention and passed him the rest of it. By the end of lunch, she still hadn't said more than a few words to him.

American History was another test prep, but he had a final in his world lit class, followed by a final assessment in his weights class. Conscious of Forest's gaze on him, Nikos carefully broke his own record by a couple of pounds, avoiding the school record. When Forest groaned his way to a new school record, Nikos politely applauded with the rest of the class.

The teacher dismissed them a few minutes early, and Nikos had already changed into his regular clothes when a commotion in the gym caught his ears.

"Call the nurse," someone screeched.

"Go away," someone else yelled.

Nikos recognized that voice. What had she done now?

He wiggled through the crowd until he reached the center of the excitement. Alexandria lay on the polished floor, holding her ankle and groaning.

Every time someone reached for her, she swatted at them. "Don't touch me! Leave me alone! I can get up myself." But she didn't even sit up.

Nikos edged next to the teacher. "If you get rid of the crowd, I'll help her. She's my friend."

The teacher looked dubious, but she blew her whistle. "Everyone go change. Anyone still here in thirty seconds gets to run laps."

Complaining, the students vanished into the locker rooms.

Nikos sat on the floor by Alexandria and leaned back on his arms. "What did you do?"

"It's just a sprain. I'm fine." She flopped on her back and stared at the ceiling. "I'll get up in a minute."

"I don't want to interfere with your independence," he said, "but I could carry you."

Her voice was ragged with pain. "You can't lift me. Give me a minute."

Nikos nodded solemnly. "You have a good point. I can only dead-lift four hundred pounds." He took a slow breath to control his laughter before he continued. "If you weigh more than four hundred, tell me now so I don't embarrass myself."

"That's not funny!" She glared at him, eyes green. "As soon as I can stand, I'll kill you."

"Oh, I'm properly terrified," Nikos said, "but if you weigh less than that, where's the problem?"

"I. Can. Do it. Myself." Alexandria sat up and wiggled into a half-kneeling position, then pushed herself upright. "See? I'm standing." She hopped once and groaned.

Nikos stood out of arm's reach. "Need any help?"

She hopped again and bit back a scream.

Nikos took a step closer. "You do weigh less than four hundred, right?"

With a ferocious glare, she held up her arms. "I'll kill you later."

He swept her into his arms and waited until her head was tucked under his chin before he grinned. Her weight was no trouble; despite her height and fit muscles, she was so skinny he didn't have to strain at all.

At the entrance to the locker room, he paused. Yeah, that was a problem. From just inside, the gym teacher raised an eyebrow at him.

Ah ha. "May I borrow your chair, ma'am?"

The teacher grabbed her wheeled office chair, and Nikos deposited Alexandria on it, then shoved her into the locker room.

"I'll meet you back here when you're dressed," he called after her.

He ran to get the books and coats from both their lockers, using the combination she'd given him a month ago when she had to talk to a teacher after school and was afraid she'd miss the bus. By the time he got back, she was on the chair outside the locker room, arms folded around her gym bag and one sneaker untied.

"I'm excused from PE tomorrow," she grumbled.

"I'm sure that's just so you won't kill anyone," he teased. "It's certainly not because anyone thinks you can't run laps with a sprained ankle."

He dropped the coats onto her lap and stuffed her gym bag inside her backpack. His backpack went on his back, hers over one elbow, and then he picked up her and their coats in one load.

She looped one arm around his neck and tugged on his hair. "I hate being broken. Why can't I magically fix everything?"

Her voice was much sadder than a sprained ankle deserved, and he thought of her father. Family meant everything to his Beanpole. It was one of the qualities he most admired in his friend.

"Because life doesn't work that way," he said softly.

He hugged her a little tighter and headed for the cafeteria where Diplomacy Club had already started. All her friends exclaimed over her injury and set her in a comfortable seat with her foot reclining on another chair padded by coats. With this being the last meeting before Christmas break, everyone listened intently to the science teacher giving updates on the mysterious asteroid that definitely wasn't aliens.

"So NASA lost track of it when it entered the asteroid belt. It's simply not big enough to track with accuracy among all the other rocks.

They've calculated where it ought to emerge if it stays in a regular orbit, so we'll check back in a few months."

"A few months," a student protested. "Why so long?"

"Math," Alexandria said, sounding much more like her normal scientific self. "Even though things move very quickly through space compared to on Earth, space is huge. Huuuuge. Our best travel speed to Jupiter is about two years, remember."

"Yes," the science teacher continued. "And this asteroid might smash up in the asteroid field, so we never see it again."

"But," Mr. Reynolds added, "we won't have wasted our time here, because all of you will be so much better prepared to be diplomatic and kind through the rest of your life. You'll change history for the better, right?"

The students sighed. "Right."

"But that isn't as exciting as aliens," Forest grumbled as everyone collected their coats and backpacks.

Nikos helped Alexandria with her coat and donned his own and his backpack, then picked her up again.

"Are you still coming over for dinner and studying?" she asked as he carried her through the school halls.

"Will you poison the meal?"

She flicked his ear. "No, I might accidentally kill someone else. I'll wait until my ankle is better, and then I'll kick your rear myself. You know I can do it."

"Fair enough." He leaned backward against the door to open it and maneuvered her through.

Mrs. Fitch was already waiting, and she sprang from the driver's seat to open the front passenger door. "What happened?"

"Just a sprained ankle," Alexandria said.

"But she needs a doctor to look at it," Nikos added. "She likes having professionals make sure everything's okay."

He pretended to ward off the glare she cast at him as he climbed into the back seat. Fair was fair, and she made him see a doctor for his migraines.

"I invited Nikos for dinner, Mom," Alexandria said, "so we can study for the trig final. Is that okay?"

"Fine with me, but I think we'll have to pick up pizza after Urgent Care."

After he texted his host parents about his plans, Nikos and Alexandria squabbled pleasantly over pizza toppings while they waited for the doctor to rewrap her ankle and find crutches. They agreed in time for Mrs. Fitch to call in the order and pick it up on their way home.

Since Alexandria wouldn't let him carry her now that she had crutches, he stole her backpack instead and followed the ladies to their front step. As soon as Mrs. Fitch unlocked the door, they heard the major yelling. Mrs. Fitch marched in, and Nikos dropped Alexandria's backpack inside and tried to sneak off.

"Oh, no," she whispered fiercely at him. "We're studying trig, and I promised you pizza. Please don't leave me."

Her eyes shone green again, but this time he suspected fear instead of anger. He'd never seen the major as angry as that morning, even when yelling. Did she suspect her father would hurt someone if he didn't have an audience to restrain him?

Nikos held his breath and stepped inside the house behind Alexandria. Once she closed and locked the door, he felt like a prisoner.

"He'll have to get used to not being pampered anymore," the major bellowed at his wife. "And so will Alex. She'll go to the Air Force Academy like I said."

Alexandria thumped her way into the kitchen on her crutches, and Nikos followed reluctantly.

"I'm going to Boulder U and living at home," Alexandria stated calmly, though her knuckles turned white around the crutch handles.

The major looked over her shoulder and glared at Nikos. In a softer bark, he said, "Air Force for you. As for Ian, some branch of the military will take him when they're desperate to defend Earth from the aliens."

"Ian isn't going into the military," Mrs. Fitch said.

Her husband ignored her.

"There are no aliens," Alexandria said. "NASA has been giving regular updates, and none of them have included the threat of invasion or collision. They are still monitoring, but there are no aliens." She pushed forward and flopped into a chair.

"Yeah, they want you to think they aren't invading, until it's too late!"

Shoulders tight, Alexandria patted the chair next to her and raised her eyebrows at Nikos. "Can we just eat dinner, Dad? We need to study for finals tomorrow. You and Mom can talk later, can't you?"

Reluctantly, Nikos sat beside her, still wearing his coat. Ian bolted to collect glasses and napkins.

"Once I have full custody," the major said with a sneer, "Ian will go to military school and shape up. Alex will go to the Air Force Academy, and neither will ever see you again." He turned to Nikos. "And you get out of my house. My daughter didn't have permission to invite you tonight."

Alexandria grabbed Nikos's arm, but he patted her hand and slid free.

"My apologies, sir." Nikos rose and grabbed his backpack from against the wall.

He nodded at Alexandria and walked out. What else could he do? It wasn't his house or his family. At least the major wasn't yelling anymore, and his face was back to its normal color. The family was probably safe now. He walked next door and repeated the whole story to the Mosses while he ate leftover meatloaf. Even though he was late and supposedly eating with the Fitches, Mrs. Moss had saved him half the pan.

"Can I call the police again?" he asked at the end. "He's so mean to them."

"I don't think Mrs. Fitch will file charges," Mr. Moss said. "He didn't hit them, and until the kids are eighteen, he has the right to decide where they go to school. If he gets full custody, he can keep them from their mother, but the court will decide. We have to trust the system to get it right in the end."

"It's not fair," Nikos said.

"No, not fair at all." Mrs. Moss handed Nikos a dish of ice cream and patted his hand. "I'm sorry, dear."

Nikos smashed the ice cream flat, wishing it was Major Fitch under his spoon. An alien invasion might be a blessing, if the major ran off to fight it and got killed. At least his family would be free of him then.

CHAPTER 15

IN WHICH SPYING UNCOVERS TREACHERY

155 CONJUNCTIONS AFTER DEPARTURE, *NEW KUNISU*, BY THE RED WORLD before Ki

MIKNON CREPT through the maintenance tunnel, listening hard through the periodic grilles for which way the voices were going. Why had she ever let Gil talk her into this? If the council lords caught her spying on them, she'd be dead or enchanted before she could take two breaths.

"You're the only one who can help, Miknon," Gil had said.

Ha! Every light in the hall was a pixie glow, though alternate sconces were now left empty to reduce energy demands during the food rationing. And besides the pixies, there were plenty of other fae small enough to sneak through the tunnels.

The prince needs you, Miknon.

No, he needed *someone*. Anyone. It didn't have to be her getting into trouble, and she'd said so. Not that it helped.

I don't trust anyone else, Miknon.

She sighed. What a fool she was. When would she stop letting her brother talk her into helping with every bad idea he had?

The lords' voices faded, and she tiptoed forward until she heard them again. So far, they only talked about unimportant things. They were hungry. They had chores to do. They were anxious to arrive at their new home. They wondered where the ice, water, and fire beings would live. They were worried about what enemy might be inhabiting Ki. The same things everyone on the ship talked about, except the potential enemy was still a secret.

A conjunction ago, the king's ship had abandoned the rest of the fleet in the last ring of stones before Ki, where they were stranded without access to the navigation contrivance. Ever since, *New Kunisu* had flown alone, trying to reach a place from which they could see the new world and develop a plan of attack. Miknon had spent the entire time sneaking around, spying on the council lords.

And for what? So far, they had done nothing out of the ordinary. They didn't discuss treachery. They thought the prince was dead and their position was secure. They did talk about how to conquer Ki, but that was only to be expected. Miknon faithfully carried every word back to the prince, even though there had been no hint of treachery so far.

"I got the news on the red world from the seers," one of the lords said.

Miknon hurried closer to catch every word, neck tingling with fear, ready to dart away if they looked behind. So far, none of the worlds they had passed had been livable, even with magic. If they could find one that was, they could end the conflict before it ever started. The prospect was worth a little risk, and yet her wings still quivered, shaking her flight path.

"It's about half the size of Ki," the lord continued. "Oddly, it has two miniature worlds rotating around it."

"How can that be?" another asked. "Wouldn't they collide with its neighbor?"

"I suppose they don't because the worlds are farther apart here. Anyway, there are tracks of old mining all over it, but no air and no free water, and no recent traces of work. It's not habitable, not even for the other beings."

Disappointment made her wings heavy. She wrapped her arms around herself and bit her lip. The prince would have been happy for an alternative to war, and Gil would have been even happier. Her brother thought the whole universe should be his friend. One of these days, he'd discover the universe didn't work that way.

"Why would the rebels abandon an established mine?"

"I can think of several reasons," a third replied, "and none of them are good. Can the seers tell how long it has been abandoned?"

"A long time. Thousands of conjunctions, if not tens of thousands."

Someone grunted. "Much too long for temporary troubles. I find myself wondering if the rebel colony still exists at all."

"If the natives destroyed the rebels, they might have enough magic to prove a challenge to us, too."

"There are more of us than the rebels, and more highborn. Our magic is more powerful than theirs."

Too powerful for the commoners to fight them, certainly, but Miknon wouldn't mourn if the highborn died fighting the Ki natives. But if Ki was powerful enough to defeat the lords, why would they spare the commoners? If that even mattered, since the commoners were sure to die in a magical battle, one way or another. They always did.

"You don't know if the colony was destroyed quickly," a lord said, "while it was still weak, or later, when it had grown strong."

"Or even later, when it had withered," someone countered.

"Or if the rebels joined the natives and we must face both of them."

As if they didn't already have enough troubles, Miknon thought. They were approaching starvation and a questionable landing, and now this. Maybe they could win against one enemy with known capabilities, but against two, and one completely unknown? Did they even have a chance?

"Enough arguing," the first one commanded. "It is time to tell everyone what we have discovered — the unknown signal, the mining world that can't support us, the potential enemy. We must start preparations."

"And while everyone is busy..." The lord didn't finish his sentence.

Miknon held her breath. That sounded suspicious.

"Yes, it's time. We've waited long enough."

It was time. She had to tell the prince. But who were the lords?

The voices grew louder, as if the councilors had reversed direction and were suddenly coming toward her. This was her chance to identify them, if she could without being caught. Miknon froze inside the tunnel. She carefully leaned toward the grille and tried to see who was in the hall, but she was too far away and they were moving too quickly. Her stomach clenched, and nausea burned the back of her throat.

Once they passed, she hurried to the prince and repeated everything, including their vague mention of something it was now time to do. Soon after she finished, a guard arrived with the news that a meeting had been called for everyone on the ship. This time, they would meet on the seventh deck instead of the ninth, supposedly to be more central.

The prince, of course, could not attend. Even disguised as a girl, he dared not risk the attention of the council. If they discovered he still lived, they'd want to fix their mistake. A navigator and a pilot must remain on duty, and a few of the pixies on light duty, but everyone else would go.

Sour suspicion flooded Miknon's tongue. Everyone would be together, would they? Except, apparently, some of the lords who had something to do that they didn't want anyone to notice. And since they had arranged to clear the ninth deck, that was the first place she would check.

The prince beckoned Miknon closer. "Can you follow them?"

She shrugged and nodded. "Maybe."

"Be careful," he said.

Then he returned to staring at the mural on the wall that showed Ki and its neighbors. Slowly, he grabbed a paintbrush and a can of grey paint and dabbed two small globes circling the red world.

Miknon returned to the ninth deck, the last place she had overheard the lords. More highborn slept on the ninth deck than lower in the ship, so that hall was near their dormitory as well as to the tower with the king's chambers that had been taken over by the council. And if everyone else was on the side with the meeting hall, then the opposite side by the garden was more likely for a secret mission.

As fellow passengers crowded into the halls, Miknon slipped inside the wall again. It would have been faster to fly through the hallway, but then people would see her going the opposite direction. At least the noise of the crowd covered any whisper of sound from her movements. She reached her chosen position across from the garden without being detected, and sat far enough from the grille that nobody could see her as they passed.

And then she waited. The chaos of ten thousand beings making their way through the ship lasted a long time. Miknon tried to keep her breathing quiet, even as her headache grew. She tugged on a loose feather, then sat on her hands. If she left a feather behind, it might betray her. As important as it was to find out what was going on, she didn't want to be caught by murderers.

When silence fell, she still waited, long enough that she thought she was in the wrong place after all. With a whole ship available, there was no real reason for the lords to come here. She would have to tell the prince — and her brother — she had failed. And while she'd been wasting time here, the lords were probably carrying out their plan somewhere else. Maybe the prince would discover their mischief in time to stop it, or maybe it was already too late.

As she climbed to her feet to return, she heard a sound. A door opened and closed, and then many feet whispered down the hall. Sandaled feet, rather than bare.

Heart beating fast, Miknon flattened herself against the inner wall and peeked out of the grille. A row of lords and ladies tiptoed past, easily carrying wooden crates from one of the storerooms.

"Remember," a lord whispered, "move fast. Leave your empty in exchange for a full, and then get back here. Don't worry about what kind of grain; just take the first heavy box you find."

Miknon shuddered, and her wings cramped. If they took all the grain from the lower levels, thousands of commoners would starve. The prince had to know. There had to be some way to stop them before half the passengers died. Miknon slipped backward silently, then turned and fled. As soon as she reached a vertical tunnel, she flew to the third tower deck and emerged in the navigation auxiliary room.

As she closed the grille behind her, the prince sat up in his hammock. The wall glistened with wet paint around the gleaming red world, but the supplies were already put away.

"They're stealing grain from the lower levels," she blurted.

"That would be noticed at the next inventory," the prince protested.

"They're exchanging empty crates for full. The cooks will think they mis-remembered how much there was."

Because the highborn protected knowledge of their spells, few of the fae could read or write, though some of them knew numbers. Mostly, they left the written records to the king's secretary.

"I see." He pressed a hand to his forehead, concentrating. Though his thought magic was less than his father's, he did have enough for a simple call.

Within minutes, several guards appeared.

"Go check all the storerooms on the lower levels," the prince said, "starting with those for grain. Also check the gardens. Stop anyone who is carrying boxes, and inspect the contents."

"You suspect theft, Sire?"

The prince nodded briskly, and the guards trotted from the room.

Miknon grabbed the collar of the last one and let him tow her along, hidden behind his broad shoulders. Smallness was sometimes useful outside the tunnels, too.

Nobody was on the seventh deck, or the fifth, but when they reached the third, they could already see a thin stream of highborn transporting crates.

Miknon let go of the collar and swung up into an empty sconce. A bit of concentration turned on her glow, and then she looked like every other pixie shedding light in the hall, disguised by her sheer ordinariness. Except she paid attention to the events below her, and the others all daydreamed, as usual. Light-duty was extremely boring, which was why she hated it.

"What is this?" a troll guard asked the closest lord.

"No — nothing," he stammered.

The guard took the crate and opened it, revealing grain. "What are you doing with this?"

The other guards spread out to block the hall and keep any of the highborn from returning to their deck with their contraband.

A lord in an embroidered tunic and elaborate braids swept through the crowd. "Our deck is short on food."

The troll folded his massive arms across his equally massive chest. "Everyone is."

"But we deserve it more," the lord argued. "We need more energy to use our magic."

"Nobody is using much magic now," the guard said. "Only the pilots and the pixies, and even the lights are dimmer now."

"But we want our magic back," the lord complained.

That whine — Miknon's light wavered, and she took a deep breath to calm herself. Was that the lord with the floppy golden hair that she had overheard in the dragon's den? The one involved in her parents' murder? What had Mother called him? Zaidu? She squinted hard, trying to remember. He looked similar, but was he the same?

The troll somehow kept his patience with the thieving lord. "Everyone needs to be patient until we reach Ki. We only have a few conjunctions left, and rations aren't so short anyone will starve in that time. The king promised equality, and sadly, that includes equal hunger."

"Actually," Zaidu said smugly, "we promised to obey our leader, which is now the council."

The guard lowered his hands to his belt, not quite touching his weapons. "And would the lower decks agree with your rearrangement of the deal? What would they say if I told them you're taking extra food?"

"Our magic is stronger," Zaidu threatened.

"And how much energy do you have for your magic when you're on short rations?"

Other guards stepped up to flank the first, hands also close to their weapons.

"We wouldn't be on short rations if you would let us take the food!" Zaidu almost stomped his feet.

He raised his hands, and water droplets appeared on the walls. As they grew larger, they merged into thin streams down the walls. The guards inhaled sharply, but they stood their ground. Water dripped into Miknon's sconce, and she slid to the edge, trying to move slowly enough to not be noticed.

Another lord approached, blue silk chiton gleaming in the dim light. "We apologize for the misunderstanding," he said smoothly, putting a hand on Zaidu's shoulder. "We didn't realize the other decks were also short on food, rather than a simple clerical error of distribution."

Miknon squinted at him, too. The blue chiton looked familiar, but she couldn't be sure he was the other plotting lord. His hair was the right silver, but it was too common to mean anything. Nonetheless, she peered at him, trying to see his face. The shadow of the troll hid the lord's features, no matter how she leaned to one side or the other.

"Everyone," the blue-garbed lord said, "take the crates back into the hold. We've made a terrible mistake." He bowed his head to the guards, who bowed low in return.

The water drops vanished back into the wall, but the guards didn't leave until all the crates had been put back, the door locked, and the crowd dispersed.

Petrified in feigned boredom, impatience crawling under her skin like gnats, Miknon waited until the hall was completely empty, then turned off her glow. She shook the water from her feet and wrung out her skirt.

As she swung out of the sconce, footsteps approached. Someone was coming. She froze. Maybe it was a random passenger, but she couldn't take the chance. And she didn't have time to climb back up and pretend to be a good little light pixie.

It was a good thing she'd been overcautious, because Zaidu immediately rounded the curve of the hall.

"Why did you do that?" Zaidu complained, tugging on the locked door uselessly. "We could have ordered him to let us take the grain."

With her light off, they didn't seem to notice her hanging from the sconce, and she held her wings motionless. Her arms ached from the weight of her body, but if she flew, they would see her. If she twitched a muscle, they would see her. If she tried to see the blue lord's face, they would see her.

They might see her anyway. Which part of the mural was she by, the colorful planets or the black between worlds? Which would hide her blue wings better?

She spared a desperate glance to the side. The blue and brown of Ki swirled next to her, the closest match possible to her blue wings and dirty skirt. Maybe she had a chance without her glow. She closed her eyes and pretended she was part of the mural. *Nothing to see here. Don't look at me.*

Don't kill me.

"We can't afford a riot," the blue lord said. "Wait patiently. Our time will come after we land. Once we have enough energy to restore our magic, we can do whatever we want. Then those upstarts will be sorry they opposed us."

The two kept walking. Her arms trembled, but she hung motionless, holding her breath until they were out of sight. Then she waited a moment longer to be sure they wouldn't return.

When she could hold on no longer, she let go and flew swiftly back to the tower to update the prince.

The guards had beaten her there, and so had the king's secretary, apparently also summoned from the meeting. They and the prince were already deep in a discussion about a new inventory of supplies.

"Inventory everything," the prince said. "Don't make it obvious we're targeting food. Tell everyone we want to see what might run short before we land."

"That's true enough," the secretary said.

He made a note across the tablet he held, reversing when he reached the end of the line and again for the next line.

The prince frowned. "I want to confront the lords, but I don't suppose that would help."

Miknon landed on his shoulder. "No, Sire, dying in a useless conflict would not help."

And would waste all her brother's efforts to keep his friend alive. And then who would protect the rest of the fae?

The secretary raised an eyebrow. "We'll take care of it."

He made a few more notes, then left to organize the inventory. As he closed the door, the noise of everyone returning to their duty shifts filled the hall.

For the next day, Miknon stayed with the prince. In case the lords had noticed her, she wanted to stay far away to avoid triggering recognition in their memories.

While in hiding, she listened to all the reports of the commotion. Apparently this wasn't the first time the highborn had stolen grain, though prior thefts had been in smaller quantities. Even after all the supplies were counted, the guards were kept busy redistributing the food in equal amounts among all four decks.

The highborn were furious but not commenting.

For now. What would they do once the fleet landed?

After all, some of them had already proved they were willing to murder to get what they wanted.

CHAPTER 16

FUNDING PROBLEMS

WHERE WAS IAN? Alexandria straddled the cafeteria bench sideways so she could watch both the door and Mr. Reynolds lecturing. Ever since school started last week, Ian had walked over from the junior high to catch a ride with her after Diplomacy Club instead of riding the bus. After the last time Dad's yelling left him in tears, she'd much rather not risk him being alone if Dad came home early. At least, not until Dad started making progress in his PTSD counseling.

She checked her watch. It was only a fifteen-minute walk most of the time, but today it was snowing and freezing, and Ian was late. He'd texted her as he walked out the school door, as usual and on time, but his halfway text had been late, and he still hadn't arrived.

Yet again, she peeked inside her backpack to check her new secret phone. Mom had gotten one for each of them without Dad knowing, so they could keep in touch without his interference. No new texts.

Just in case, she also checked her regular cell. Nothing. Maybe she should go after him. She tapped her fingers and pulled her coat closer. The zipper grated on the table top, and Nikos looked over.

"He'll be here," Nikos murmured. "Don't risk your ankle."

As of this morning, she wasn't even using the crutches anymore, but she still had to wrap her wobbly ankle and walk gently. But what if Ian had slipped on ice and hurt himself? Or been run over by an out-of-control car? She tugged her coat another inch across the table until Nikos leaned an elbow on it.

"I'll go look in a few minutes," he said.

And what if that was too late? What if her brother was already hurt? She glared at Nikos and reached for her coat again.

The back door of the cafeteria opened, and Ian crept in. He knocked snow off his hair and draped his wet coat over a table. Waving subtly at Alexandria, he took a seat and pulled out his homework. Most days, he finished half of it even before they got home.

Nikos took his elbow off her coat and winked at her. She sniffed. One of the high school students scooted by Ian, and Alexandria made sure no bullying was involved before she turned her attention back to Mr. Reynolds, who was still talking about bad first encounters in human history. Between two groups of humans, obviously, not aliens.

Fewer students had enrolled in Diplomacy Club this semester. Between the required homework and the lack of news while the asteroid was crossing the asteroid belt, the appeal of aliens had finally faded. Those who stayed were taking the diplomacy aspect more seriously.

Once the club ended, Alexandria and Nikos put on their coats. He grabbed her backpack as well as his own and followed her at her careful pace to Ian's table.

The high school student with Ian saw them coming and hopped up. "See you next week, U.N. Thanks for the help."

Ian stuffed his books into his backpack and gingerly put on his still-damp coat. "It's slippery out there, sis. Are you taking my arm or Nikos's?"

Nikos held out an elbow. "Both."

Alexandria sighed, hooked one hand through his elbow, and threw the other arm over Ian's shoulder. "My ankle's fine, guys."

"And we'd like to keep it that way," Ian said. "So you can kick some butt."

Nikos gave him a high five, and Alexandria groaned. Some days Nikos was as bad as her brother.

"Did that kid mispronounce your name?" she asked. "Why didn't you correct him?"

"Um, no." Ian blushed. "Some of the kids have started calling me U.N., like the United Nations. They saw all my language books and asked for help with homework."

Nikos laughed. "Sure, because you know, what, six languages now?"

Ian blushed harder. "Not really. I'm still a bare beginner at German and modern Greek. And I only know as much French as I've picked up from helping here."

Alexandria rolled her eyes. "So, only four fluently, plus bits of another three? I see the problem."

As they exited the building into the snow, her foot skidded on the slush and ice, and she tightened her grip on the boys so she wouldn't fall. Okay, maybe it was really slippery, and maybe her ankle wasn't ready to compensate. Whatever. The three of them slowed to a crawl, though neither boy commented.

From the curb, Mrs. Moss tapped her horn and waved, and Ian waved back. By the time they got into the car a few minutes later, all of them were sprinkled with snow. Alexandria arranged her ankle to be straight and supported, and listened to the boys chatter in the back seat. Greek, probably. Or German. She quirked her mouth. It was all Greek to her, anyway.

Despite living next door, Mrs. Moss parked in the Fitches' driveway instead of her own. While Nikos helped Ian get Alexandria to the front door, his host mother backed up and parked at her own house.

"I could have made it a few extra feet," Alexandria grouched at Nikos, though she didn't let go of his elbow.

"No need," he said breezily, "unless you want me to carry you again."

Ian snickered as she dug in her pocket for her key.

She unlocked the front door and stuck out her tongue at both of them. "I'm home now; that won't be necessary."

With a grin, Nikos reached around her to drop her backpack onto the floor. "See you tomorrow." And then he was gone, black curls highlighted with snowflakes.

Alexandria walked in and closed the door behind Ian. Scrumptious food odors filled the house, and she let Ian hang up her coat while she hobbled into the kitchen and transferred the contents of the slow cooker to another pan. She popped that into the oven and turned it on, then ran hot water into the slow cooker.

With Mom working more hours than Dad knew, they'd had to be creative to keep him from finding out how late she got home. So far, Dad hadn't discovered their secret, but if he ever did come home early, it was better to find dinner in the slow cooker than catch Ian alone. If necessary, Mom could claim to be covering a coworker's shift "just this once."

Mom wasn't putting her paycheck into her joint account with Dad. All the money she earned went into a new account under Alexandria's name. To pay for the divorce. Alexandria grimaced as she started scrubbing. Why couldn't the adults just act like adults and stop fighting? They still loved each other, so why couldn't they get along? She wanted her whole family happy together, the way they used to be.

Instead, her parents argued every time they were together. Mom couldn't get equity from the house because it was Dad's inheritance from his parents, and not having her name on the deed didn't help her case. Alimony, custody, and child support had joined the fight roster of housework, budget, and Ian.

Poor Ian. Dad seemed determined to take out all his frustration on him, no matter how hard he tried to stay out of the way, especially since Mom had started sleeping on the bottom bunk in Ian's room.

But if Alexandria could make Dad see how unhappy Ian was, she could talk him out of his insane idea to forbid visitation rights to Mom.

By the time she got the slow cooker washed and put away, Ian had finished his homework and the door was opening right on time. Mom shook snow from her hair and hurried to her bedroom to change out of her work clothes.

Alexandria and Ian set the table, finishing just as Dad came home. Silently, the kids sat as Mom pulled dinner from the oven. Despite their efforts to be obedient and quiet, Dad was in another bad mood.

This time, the nightly fight concerned college expenses, and Alexandria's stomach clenched. Ian had years before he was going to college, but it was almost around the corner for her.

"I don't care," Dad said. "I'll only pay for college if the kids live with me and take majors I approve. And go to military schools."

"The military schools don't even charge tuition," Mom said.

"So? If they did, I'd pay it." Dad smirked as if he'd scored a point.

Alexandria and Ian exchanged glances. Astronomy wasn't on Dad's approved list, but she could major in physics in a pinch and add astronomy later. But languages weren't even close to anything Dad liked. One language, sure, for a couple of years to add versatility to a resumé, but not *majoring* in a language. Or languages. That was for sissies. They'd heard the rant so many times they could almost recite it. The last time Dad had caught Ian reading one of his foreign language books, he'd ripped it in half and thrown it away.

Ian shrank into his chair again, eating so carefully that his fork didn't scrape his plate.

Even if they lived with Mom part-time, Alexandria couldn't afford college by herself. Monday was a holiday, but on Tuesday, she'd go talk to the school counselor. If she had to finance college herself, she needed to find some scholarships.

But one way or another, she would be an astronomer. She hadn't talked herself into the high school astronomy class for nothing.

"You're wise to plan ahead," the school counselor said. "Even as a sophomore, you should be thinking about college applications and financing." He pulled Alexandria's school record closer. "You have fairly good grades in advanced classes, so that's a start. You still have room to raise your GPA, though. Other things you can do include being involved in service or the community, doing sports, or developing a hobby. Keep in mind, a lot of little scholarships pay as well as one or two big ones but might be a lot easier to get."

He slid a bunch of pamphlets across his desk. "See if any of these spark ideas."

She thanked him and limped out, already reading the information.

Were there any scholarships for astronomy? She'd gotten in the junior/senior class based on her good trig grades and an essay she submitted to the teacher on the sly about how badly she wanted to be an astronomer.

Did service projects with her church youth group count? Was Diplomacy Club enough involvement in the school? Did it at least count as a hobby?

As for sports, she wasn't a bad runner, but she wasn't interested in track, and she was no good at all in any other sport. Would she even be good enough to get a track scholarship? And what if her ankle wasn't completely healed by track season? There was always next year, but was suffering through track worth it for scholarship money?

Bah. She stuffed the pamphlets into her locker and hurried to Trig. Her morning classes were all the same as last semester, as was Spanish, but instead of social studies and PE, she had geography and astronomy. She hated waiting all day for her favorite class, but at least it gave a nice finish to the school day.

All through her classes, she tried to pay more attention and forget about Dad. Better grades seemed more achievable than anything else right now, so that's where she'd start.

After switching books at her locker, she rode the bus home with Nikos and Ian, and walked in to find Dad already there.

"Where is your mother?" Dad yelled.

"She had errands to run," Alexandria automatically lied as Ian ran for his room. "She'll be home in time to take me to judo."

"Judo." Dad sneered. "Judo is for defensive babies. You need something better to prepare for the military. Karate or krav maga. Something that can hurt people."

"I've got to change, Dad."

She sidled past him to her bedroom and changed into her judogi, tying her belt with shaking hands. Why didn't anything she did make him happy? He used to love watching her in judo, throwing bigger opponents over her shoulder. "That's my girl," he'd said. Now he didn't ever come to class.

Mom beeped the horn from the driveway, and Alexandria grabbed her coat and a granola bar. Ian's door was firmly closed, and Dad had disappeared into his den. As long as the two of them stayed apart, they'd be fine.

She slammed the house door and barely managed not to stomp her way through the snow. Stupid ankle.

"Dad's home," she said as she climbed into the car, "but Ian's in his room."

Mom tightened her grip on the steering wheel and backed out of the driveway. "We'll have to hurry home, then."

Alexandria folded her arms and sulked all the way to class. Mom re-wrapped her ankle firmly and warned her to be careful. But warm-ups failed to calm Alexandria, and when it came time for sparring, she beat three opponents in less than five minutes, imagining each of them as Dad.

"Congratulations," her sensei said, though he gave her a concerned look. "And how is your ankle?"

Alexandria shrugged, not willing to admit how much it hurt at the moment.

"School?"

"It's fine."

"Hmm. And how is your family?"

Alexandria looked at Mom and then at the floor. How could she explain what she didn't understand? Everything was falling apart, and she didn't know who to blame.

"Ah." Her sensei frowned slightly. "Well, I think your ankle has had enough for the day. You may watch until the end of class or leave early."

They bowed to each other, and Alexandria hobbled to the benches to put on her boots and coat.

"We can go," she said. "He says I'm done."

"Oh, good." Mom paused. "I mean, I'm sorry, but I'm sure Ian will be happy to have us back."

"Yeah." Alexandria limped to the car and rubbed her ankle as Mom drove home.

"I'm proud of you," Mom said. "You were very impressive in there."

"Thanks."

"You're a great athlete."

"Sure." And then she straightened. Athlete? Like in a sport? She was so used to thinking of judo as self defense or even just exercise. But if it counted as a sport, did it have any scholarship opportunities?

The thought occupied her all through dinner and homework. While she soaked her ankle in Epsom salts, she researched possible scholarships on her phone. Judo was included in the Olympics, which she knew, and a nonprofit associated with the Olympics offered a college scholarship to student athletes — there was the word again — who had the potential to become elite competitors. The grants could be as high as two thousand dollars each semester, and could be used for miscellaneous expenses if she managed to cover her tuition with other scholarships.

As she read through the requirements, she realized why nobody had ever mentioned the scholarship to her before. Besides the athletic potential, the scholarship was based on financial need, with an income limit far below what her father made in the Air Force. She would never qualify under Dad.

But living with Mom... Well, that was completely different. Mom's income would be low enough to qualify; that was the whole reason Alexandria needed the scholarship in the first place.

She read the requirements again and emailed herself the link. In order to qualify, she'd have to advance through the ranks during the next two years, faster than she had been. And somehow she had to do that while protecting Ian and helping Mom.

But if she could get enough scholarships to pay for her own college, she could ignore Dad's ultimatums and go where she liked. She could still be an astronomer. Relief buzzed through her veins like an overindulgence of soda.

And maybe none of this would be necessary. Dad could still calm down and be reasonable, especially if he'd start going to the therapist to talk about his PTSD. Maybe Mom would change her mind about the divorce. Or if not, maybe Dad would agree to joint custody and child support and reasonable college plans.

But whatever happened, Alexandria's future career would no longer rely on anyone's whims.

One way or another, she'd take care of herself. Nothing could stop her now.

CHAPTER 17

IN WHICH THEY SPY ON KI

156 CONJUNCTIONS AFTER DEPARTURE, *NEW KUNISU*, BY KI

GIL PEERED into the hole in the floor. "She's almost got it."

Shar nodded and held his ball of light a little closer. In the space between decks, Miknon tugged aside the air filter and replaced it with one that looked the same but was much thinner and more loosely woven. She flew out, breathing hard, and let Gil and Shar replace the normal air filter in the floor and lock down the barred cover that was now removable instead of fixed in place.

"You're a genius," Gil told his sister. "Nobody will examine the air filter to see if it's any different, especially since everyone knows the covers don't come off."

"Didn't come off before we got to it." Shar chuckled and strapped a crate over the new spyhole, just in case.

While the rest of the fleet hid in the ring of stones beyond the red world, *New Kunisu* had traveled for another conjunction until they landed on the big rock spinning around Ki. Now that they were parked instead of traveling, they never had much weight and everything had to be locked or strapped down at all times. That wasn't actually very different, since even during weighted times, nobody wanted a sudden maneuver to fling something at their head — Gil sighed at the pang of memory — but the change in weight was odd, as was the constancy rather than the on-and-off Gil had experienced his entire life.

Based on the bounciness of his steps, Gil figured he had a third or fourth of the weight he normally had when the ship was accelerating, which was about half of Old Kunisu normal. But the lower-but-constant weight wasn't the point of their current perch. The advantage was being close enough for their scrying magics to see the land below them. And since nobody on Ki knew they were here, they'd have no reason to use their own scrying against the ship. Ki wasn't even using this rock for anything — there were no signs of mining or habitation — so the fae could sit here and spy in perfect secrecy.

And they desperately needed information. The more they learned, the greater their chances of safely winning the new world.

The others were still talking, and Gil shook himself back to attention.

Miknon nodded. "Now you can do your own spying when the council meets below."

She glared at Gil and folded her arms. Ever since she'd almost gotten caught in the hallway, it had been much harder to persuade her to do any eavesdropping, no matter how much he assured her the highborn wouldn't see her in the maintenance tunnels.

Gil shrugged. "We'll hear when we open the top, but we still can't see anything."

"They'll have to describe what they see in the scrying for the others anyway," Miknon said. "You can listen to that. Just remember to be absolutely silent when you have the tunnel open."

"Yes, Mother," Gil said.

Miknon pinched him and flew off. She had sacrificed some of her sleep time for this project, and dark circles already marked her eyes.

Gil and Shar buckled themselves into hammocks and chatted while they waited for either a secret council meeting or for Zak to get off duty and join them.

"The council announced the results of the scry on the first planet from the sun," Gil said.

"I heard," Shar said. "About three-quarters the size, rotates backwards, and much too hot under the reflective clouds, even for the fire beings."

"Not as hot as a volcano," Gil said. "Harmakis used to be inhabited."

"But it was only that hot *in* the volcanoes," Shar said. "Besides, do *you* want to live there?"

Gil rolled in the hammock to hang upside-down and grin at the prince. "Nope. What about here?" He waved his hand vaguely to indicate the rock the ship sat on. "It's not too hot."

"They checked this out first," Shar reminded him. "No water, no air, and even less weight than the red world we passed. And we don't have enough food to live long enough to fix it with magic. If we had enough magic, which we probably don't." He ran his fingers over his girlish hair and winced. "And it's not big enough to be a real world, like the tiny worldlet they found even closer to the sun than the hot one. Here makes a good place to spy on Ki, but that's all. You know all this. Why do you keep fighting against settling on the colony world?"

"Because the council wants to conquer it," Gil said. "Like an enemy. Destroy the rebels, if they're still there, or the natives. I don't think that's nice."

"They are enemies," Shar said wearily. "Or at least, they certainly aren't friends. If they were the rebels, we could offer them the same class-equality deal Father made with our commoners, and offer to move into their choice of territory, but they aren't the rebels. We don't even know *what* they are. I must take care of my people, and we have nowhere else to go. What do you want us to do? Stay here until we starve?"

"They could be friends." Gil wiggled his eyebrows. "What if we sent an envoy to discuss peace?"

The door opened, and both of them stopped talking to see who was entering. But it was only Zak and three of the guards who knew about the hidden prince. With a sigh, Shar smoothed the flounces of his skirt and sat up in the hammock instead of lounging like Gil.

The naga chief Companion opened his mouth to speak, and the prince raised his hand to silence him.

"Who can I trust that has enough power to treat with Ki?" Shar asked. "I certainly can't trust the lords on the council. And my trustworthy, loyal friends have no power. Even if that would work, I have no one to send."

"Maybe you should go yourself," Gil said.

"Absolutely not," the naga blurted despite the prince's request to wait. "We can't risk the prince's life until safety is established."

"And I can't leave my people here," Shar said. "If the council gets bad enough, I might have to reveal myself to protect everyone else."

Gil rolled his eyes. "I don't see how that's any safer."

Zak floated to his instruments and gently touched a dial. The constant hum and crackle in the room faded to a sigh. "At least he has allies and guards here, Gil. He'd have no one on Ki."

"He could take allies and guards with him," Gil grumbled.

"And we do plan to eventually tell everyone I'm alive," Shar continued as if Gil hadn't spoken. "Preferably after we recover the fleet we left behind, so we can call on them for help. But Ki is too unknown."

"Which is why we came up," the naga said. "The council is heading in for a scrying session. Is the spyhole ready?"

Gil rolled out of the hammock. "All ready. Let's learn more about Ki."

He held his finger to his lips and waited for Shar to extinguish his light. When everyone was silent in the dark, he moved the crate and bars.

Quietly, ever so quietly, he eased himself to the floor and gripped one of the bars used to anchor straps. Shar was a warmth at one shoulder and Zak at his other. A Companion or two filled the remaining space around the hole. After everyone stilled, he removed the top air filter.

From the council chamber below, voices drifted up.

"And this time, don't bump my elbow," someone whined. "If you knock off the glass cover again, it will take forever to clean up the spilled water. It floats everywhere."

"I'll sit over here, Zaidu, but remember to tell us *everything* you see. You never know what might be important."

"Yes, yes, I know. But be quiet and let me concentrate."

Shuffling and bumping echoed through the spyhole, and Gil held still, trying to breathe silently.

"I'm focusing on the sunlit side, of course," Zaidu muttered. "No point looking where I can't see and nothing can live."

"Yes, yes. Get on with it."

"Hmm. The magic from Ki is making the sunlight seem a hundred times brighter than it really is. Just a moment while I reduce the light on my scrying before I go blind."

After a moment, he continued. "There's a mix of palaces and small houses. Many of both kinds. Some of the palaces are as big as a village. And so tall! They must use magic to support them."

"So we were right." The other lord sounded smug. "The king's notion of equal classes would have put us at a disadvantage. The old ways are better."

Gil stirred in protest, and Shar bumped his shoulder. Gil inhaled softly and exhaled even more so. Now was not the time to worry about the king's promise, and if he alerted the lords to their spying, all would be lost.

"I see few beasts," Zaidu said. "They ride in magic wagons or walk."

"Does that give us an advantage or not? The wagons won't tire, presumably, but how much do they tire themselves casting the magic? We will have to watch more. What else do you see?"

Gil wrinkled his nose. He'd rather have the beasts, but he had no magic anyway, beyond that born in him for shifting.

"So many lights," Zaidu continued. "I see lights shining from the windows of houses and palaces alike. Every building is lit. They even have colored lights outdoors. Why would they need lights outdoors in the sunshine?" He didn't wait for an answer. "They must have a hundred thousand pixies."

"Or ten thousand light mages," the other lord mused.

"I see magic everywhere," Zaidu said, his voice as shocked as Gil felt. "Everywhere!"

If Ki could afford to devote ten thousand mages just to light, how many mages did they have altogether? Shar flinched a trifle against Gil's shoulder. Zak had already demonstrated the constant music that streamed from Ki, sending their magic into the air without ceasing. How much magic did that take? Or if their magic didn't work when the music was sent over the navigation system, why didn't they mind revealing their spells? Weren't they afraid of others learning them and turning them against them? Did they always have more magic, more spells?

And even after the constant music, they still had enough magic left for a hundred thousand lights. *New Kunisu* would definitely have to retrieve the rest of the fleet before they could attack. One ship alone could never fight so much magic, even though they were the biggest ship. No, they needed everyone for this battle.

Unless Shar changed his mind and sought a treaty.

Zaidu was still describing all the magic he saw, and the other lord finally cut him off. "There is much magic, but is it strong, or is it all lights and flash, with no substance?"

Zaidu paused, then said, "You're right. It's plentiful, but it's not strong. It doesn't seem to *do* much besides make lights."

"Then let's not worry about it. What about the people? Are they fae or something else?"

Zaidu groaned. "I will narrow my focus." He muttered to himself for a few minutes. "They seem about the same size as most highborn, but they wear peasant clothes. No jewels, no silk, no fine gowns or tunics. Their masters must be inside the palaces."

"And their faces and forms?"

Zaidu muttered again. "Not quite the same as the highborn, but close enough for a little magic to disguise the differences."

And what if someone went to talk to them that didn't have magic, Gil wondered. Would they be so obvious that an ambassador would be caught at once, or was there a chance?

"How many are there?" the second lord asked.

"Well, I can't look everywhere at once, but here I see perhaps a few thousand."

The other lord hummed. "A few thousand in each city, one or two cities per mountaintop to avoid the valley tides, on a world the same size as Kunisu. Mmm. It's possible they have as many inhabitants as Kunisu did, outnumbering us ten to one."

Ten to one! And with so much magic! Zak twitched, and Gil shifted enough to pat his shoulder. Everything he heard only made him think peace was a better idea. If only he could persuade Shar.

"But they are peasants," Zaidu sneered. "We can conquer them all." He groaned. "That's enough for today. I need a nap."

"You've done well. I will update the others on what you have seen. Tomorrow, we will look again."

The door below opened and closed. Gil and his friends waited breathlessly until they were sure the highborn were gone, then replaced the air filter and the bars. They let go of their handholds and drifted upright, and Shar rekindled his light globe.

After strapping the crate over the hole again, they looked solemnly at each other.

"Gil," Shar said, "stop asking me to make friends with Ki. We can't afford to show weakness in the face of that much magic. And I certainly won't send anyone alone."

"Nor will the king expose himself to danger," his naga Companion declared.

Shar winced at the title of king. Though he was his father's heir, he couldn't claim his crown while he was presumed dead. And whenever he was ready to be "alive" again, he was likely to have a fight on his hands. Even more, Gil presumed, Shar missed his father as much as Gil missed his Grandsire, and the title would only remind him of his loss.

Gil sighed and bowed. "As you command. May I be excused to feed the dragons?"

Shar nodded. "I'll see you tomorrow."

After checking that the hall was clear, Gil hurried all the way to the bottom deck. He checked the dragons for illness or injury, then made sure all three were well tethered. Once he was sure they were secure, he made his way back up the tower to the navigation room at the top and told the contriver on duty to open the hold door.

The light from Ki's sun would flood the dragon's den, feeding them through their broad wings. In another few days, they might even have enough nourishment to come out of hibernation when the doors were closed. Then Gil could really spend time with them. In the meantime, he planned to spend as much time with the other animals as he could.

He'd rather be with animals than people right now. Shar was doing what he thought was right, but Gil remained unconvinced. How could friendship be the wrong choice?

But it didn't matter, because he couldn't do anything about it. He was nothing but a lowly zookeeper.

Chapter 18

Church

Nikos grabbed the mail and stood in the frosty air long enough to check the recipients. From the house next door, indistinct shouting echoed. Poor Alexandria. Hardly a day was quiet in her home anymore. And since today was Friday, she had a whole weekend of this to endure.

He walked inside and dropped the mail onto the table. "All for you two."

Mrs. Moss handed him a hot cinnamon roll. "It's a bit early for college decisions, isn't it?"

Nikos shrugged. "You never know." He was also watching for his exemption from Greek military training, which needed to go through before his eighteenth birthday. He ate the roll and licked his fingers. "The major is yelling again. Can we call the police yet?"

She bent and checked the pan in the oven. "Listen; he's stopped already. Nowadays, he never yells long enough for the police to get here."

"Well, I invited Alexandria over to study after dinner. Is that okay?"

"Any time, Nikos. Does she like chicken cacciatore? She could come earlier, if she wants."

He tilted his head up and tsked. "Better not. She doesn't want to leave Ian or her mother until the major retreats to his den for the evening."

"Poor girl." Mrs. Moss sighed. "If you want to work on the rest of your homework, I'll call you when dinner is ready, okay?"

With his backpack, Nikos retreated to his room and organized his books and laptop on the desk under the window. Half his classes had changed this semester, and thanks to his new study period, most of his homework was already done. If he finished his paper for English Composition before dinner, all he'd have left was trigonometry with Alexandria and a few sketches for art.

Sadly, the paper wasn't absorbing enough to keep him from thinking about Alexandria's troubles, especially not when his side window faced her house. He stared at the white siding next door before shaking himself and refocusing on his assignment. If he could do nothing, he could do nothing.

But he wanted to help, to do the right thing.

What was the right thing to do?

His head throbbed, and he stopped long enough to take a pill for his migraine before it got worse. Battling the sparkles in his vision made the paper take longer to finish, but he managed just in time for dinner.

After another cinnamon roll for dessert, he cleared the table and started washing the dishes.

When the doorbell rang, Mr. Moss rolled up his sleeves and bumped him out of the way. "My turn now, if that's your study partner."

Drying his hands, Nikos hurried to the front door. As soon he opened it, Alexandria came in, head bowed. She rubbed at her eyes and tried to hurry past him to the kitchen where they always studied.

Nikos grabbed her arm. "Are you — crying?" He clenched his fists. "Did your dad hit you?" His voice rose at the end, and he tilted her chin to make her look at him.

Mr. and Mrs. Moss appeared in the kitchen doorway. Mrs. Moss already had the phone in her hand, ready to dial.

"No," Alexandria said. Her eyes glistened with tears, but he didn't see any bruises.

Nikos let go of her chin and took her coat, then escorted her into the kitchen. "Then what happened this time?"

As he held her chair, she smothered a sob. "He says we can't go to church anymore. He blames it for Mom wanting a divorce."

"Does your church encourage divorce?" he asked. Greek Orthodoxy allowed divorces, and Catholicism didn't, and he didn't know much about other religions.

"No, actually. It discourages it pretty highly, if it's possible to save the marriage." She slammed her trig book on the table. "He's not a member, but he'd know that if he ever actually listened to the talks or lessons or anything. Or if he had ever let the missionaries tell him about eternal families."

Standing at the sink, Mr. Moss stiffened a little. He rinsed the last of the dishes and turned to examine Alexandria. When he said nothing, Nikos opened his math book, mind furiously working at both math and the problem next door.

Once both of them had finished their homework, Nikos walked Alexandria home. The major was gone again, and a puffy-eyed Mrs. Fitch thanked him solemnly for letting her daughter study at his house.

Deep in thought, Nikos went home and cornered his host parents. "Why would the major forbid his family from church?"

"Just to hurt them," Mrs. Moss grumbled.

"Probably to reduce their support base and knock them off-balance," Mr. Moss said.

Nikos growled. "And how is that fair? Can we make him change his mind?"

"We have no right to interfere," Mr. Moss said. "And while free practice of religion is a right, you wouldn't get far convincing the police that it mattered on a familial basis. There's nothing you can do." He patted Nikos's shoulder and picked up his newspaper.

Nikos read a book for a while before climbing into bed and staring at the ceiling for hours. There had to be something he could do.

Not too early the next morning, Nikos put on his coat and headed next door. After a precautionary spit on the frozen grass, he knocked firmly. For once, he was glad when Major Fitch answered.

"Alex," the major bellowed, turning to leave.

Nikos cleared his throat. "Actually, sir, it's you I've come to see."

The major stared at him in surprise, as did Alexandria, coming from the hallway.

Before losing his courage, Nikos hurtled into his prepared speech. "After living next door for six months and going to school with your daughter, I'm very impressed by her. She's smart, athletic, kind, and always helpful. I appreciate you letting her be my friend. She's a great example to me, and I'm a better person for knowing her."

The major crossed his arms and glared, and Alexandria raised both eyebrows to her hairline.

Nikos kept going, a little faster. "I'm sure she's wonderful mostly because of good parenting and her inborn characteristics, but I also know she's a God-fearing young lady."

Mrs. Fitch was a good parent, so he wasn't lying about anything.

"What's the point, boy?" the major asked. "If you're asking for permission to date her—"

Nikos hurried to cut off that idea. "No, sir. I think your wife and son are just as kind and neighborly. I wondered if I could go to church with your family tomorrow. To learn more about your family's beliefs, you see."

The major sneered. "Well, my family isn't going to church tomorrow, so that won't work."

With his best disappointed look, Nikos nodded. "I understand, sir. It was just a thought." But instead of leaving, he kept a pleading gaze fastened on the major. "Perhaps some other time."

Still by the inner doorway, Alexandria squinted at him as if she was examining a strange bug. Nikos ignored her so he wouldn't give away the game. He waited, still watching her father, for as long as he dared.

Finally, he gave up. "Well, sir, thank you for hearing me out, and thank you again for raising such a wonderful daughter."

The major held up a hand. "Hold on. If it means that much to you, I suppose you can come with us tomorrow."

"Thank you, sir." Nikos shook hands with him, and the major vanished down the hall.

Alexandria put her hands on her hips. "What do you think you're doing?" she whispered fiercely. "As soon as Dad doesn't see you ready tomorrow, he'll change his mind about us going. And I'll be in trouble."

"I'll be ready," Nikos said. "What time?"

She quirked an eyebrow. "You're really going?"

"If you tell me what time, yes."

"Nine a.m."

"Okay."

"For two hours."

He flashed a grin. "Okay."

She cocked her head to one side and examined him for a minute. "Thanks, Nikos."

"Okay."

She laughed and shooed him out the door. He returned home and told the Mosses he'd be going to church with the Fitches in the morning.

Mr. Moss grimaced. "I'm pretty sure they're Mormons. You sure you want to go to a non-Christian church?"

"Oh, honey," Mrs. Moss said, "once won't send him to hell. He's trying to help that sweet girl."

"I'll be fine," Nikos promised, though he was surprised by the comment. Alexandria seemed Christian to him. "Now, what chores can I help with today?"

EARLY SUNDAY MORNING, Nikos showered and gelled his hair. He pressed his shirt and pulled out the suit he had brought from home but hadn't yet had a reason to wear. Every Sunday, the Fitches left in nice clothes, and although Alexandria hadn't given him any guidelines, he didn't want to make their family look bad. If he messed up, the major would probably take revenge on his own family. If nothing else, he would surely forbid Alexandria from hanging out with Nikos anymore.

Mrs. Moss had breakfast ready by the time he was dressed to his satisfaction, and he gobbled pancakes, careful not to drop syrup on himself.

"You look nice, dear," his host mother said when he finally shrugged on his suit jacket and coat. Though the weather promised to warm up later in the day, it was still freezing now.

"Think I'll pass inspection?" he asked.

Mrs. Moss waved her hand in front of her face like a fan. "Oh, honey, no worries about that."

Nikos laughed and hurried outside.

When Alexandria opened her door, her eyebrows shot up again. "Where'd you get that suit?"

Nikos grinned. "Good enough?"

"You clean up nice, Shorty." She grabbed her coat as Ian ran up behind her.

"You're not too bad yourself, Beanpole."

In fact, she looked very nice in a blue-flowered dress that swirled around her knees. The boys at school must be blind not to notice. Or maybe they remembered what had happened to McConnell and were all scared of her.

Once the major unlocked the car, Nikos held Alexandria's door for her, then let Ian scramble into the middle seat before taking the other side. The major climbed in and started the engine while Mrs. Fitch was still letting herself in. Nikos made a mental note to catch her door on the way home, if Major Rude wouldn't do it.

"I'm glad you're coming," Ian whispered, "since Dad's coming."

Nikos nodded. He was a little surprised about that, too. Usually the major stayed home and watched sports while his family was in church.

After that, nobody talked until they parked. The sign on the brick building said The Church of Jesus Christ of Latter-day Saints. Ha, Mr. Moss was wrong. Not Mormons, and definitely Christian. It said so right on the building. Not that it surprised him, since Alexandria prayed silently in the school cafeteria every day and read the Bible. With a lighter heart, Nikos followed the family inside.

"Welcome, Sister Fitch," the man at the door said. "Alexandria, Ian. And Major Fitch, so good to see you." He shook Nikos's hand next. "And are you new?"

"Just visiting," Alexandria said.

"I'm not a member of your church," Nikos said.

"Nik wants to see what makes my family so great," the major boomed, squaring his shoulders.

The man chuckled nervously, and the family walked through a foyer into a large room with a pulpit at the front. Alexandria pulled Nikos into a pew, and Ian took a seat in what looked like choir seats. All around him, people greeted each other with "Brother So-and-So" and "Sister Whosit."

Nikos whispered at Alexandria, "Is everyone here related?"

She grinned and shrugged. "Not like you think. We believe we're all literal children of God, so that makes us all spiritual siblings, right?"

Oh, like a priest sometimes called his congregation "children." Having everyone use the titles for each other was still amusing. Nikos hid a smile and kept watching the crowd until a man stood to start the meeting.

After a few announcements, they sang a hymn in a more modern style than he normally heard at church. Someone prayed, then there were more announcements, to his confusion. They sang another hymn while several young men tore apart bread at a table built into the front. After the song, one knelt and prayed about remembering Christ and obeying his commandments. Obviously, this was some version of communion, even without a priest in vestments. To Nikos's surprise, a bunch of young men, including Ian, lined up to carry the communion to the congregation. Nikos skipped it, and so did Major Fitch.

Nikos raised a questioning eyebrow at Alexandria and tipped his head toward her father.

She mouthed, "Dad doesn't believe in God."

Oh. She'd said he wasn't a member of their church, but Nikos didn't realize he didn't believe at all. Maybe that explained a lot.

Then the young men prayed again over water instead of wine, and the boys passed that around, too.

Once communion was finished, the young men at the front joined their families. Ian slid next to Alexandria, and she put her arm around him. A lay speaker talked about having faith in Christ. After that, everybody sang a hymn, and a lady stood to speak. Nikos checked his watch and realized they'd not quite reached one hour of the two Alexandria had promised, and he subtly shifted on the bench to ease his bones. But then the congregation sang another hymn and somebody else prayed, and everybody stood and either left the room or chatted with other people. Just in case, Nikos stayed seated until Ian and Alexandria rose.

"See you after class, Mom." Alexandria grabbed Nikos and almost ran, Ian hot on their heels.

Down the hall, they piled into a large classroom filled with teenagers and took seats at the back with Nikos between the siblings.

"Can I ask questions?" Nikos asked.

"Absolutely," Alexandria said.

"Why did Ian pass communion? He's just a kid. Sorry, Ian."

"I'm a deacon," Ian said.

Nikos blinked. "I have to assume that means something different than it does in the Greek Orthodox Church."

"It's the lowest, um, order of the priesthood," Alexandria said. "It has very limited authority, but we have a lay priesthood that starts with young men so they get plenty of practice. I can give you more details, if you want."

Nikos tsked. "Nope, I'm good. I just wondered. The lowest order of the Orthodox priesthood is also the deacon, but they have to go to seminary first."

"Totally understandable." Alexandria flashed him a grin. "By the way, we also go to seminary for four years, but as teens, boys and girls, and it's not related to the priesthood. My classes are over Zoom this year, though, before school."

He raised his eyebrows and let it go, sure that asking for an extended explanation would only confuse him more.

After another prayer, an adult teacher started the class, and all the students pulled out either print scriptures or their phones. Since Nikos hadn't brought any, the teacher passed him a King James Bible.

For the next forty-five minutes, they discussed Abraham, Sarah, and Lot, talking about how to apply the lessons to their own lives. Nikos was used to studying the theology of the scriptures, not the daily practicality, so he just listened. As the class shared stories about how they'd had to escape wickedness, Alexandria and Ian stared blindly at their phones.

From his seat between them, Nikos could see both screens without them noticing. Ian was supposedly reading the scriptures under discussion, but he never scrolled down. Alexandria was looking at a picture of her family, thumb covering and uncovering her dad's face.

The teacher checked her watch. "Okay, we're out of time. This week, I want you to remember nothing is too hard for the Lord, but He will fulfill His promises in His own way and time. If you have any experiences about that, you can share them with us next week."

She called on a student for prayer, and then the class hurried out, chattering and laughing.

Alexandria sighed and blanked her phone screen. "When is His time? What is the way?"

Ian shrugged helplessly. "I guess we should find our parents."

They wove through the crowded hallways until they found Mrs. Fitch, then waited in the foyer until the major appeared, grinning and chest puffed out.

"I can't tell you how many people congratulated me for bringing Nik today and asked if he wanted to hear the missionaries." The major looked at Nikos expectantly.

"No thank you, sir." Nikos held his opinions firmly behind closed lips as he opened the door for the ladies. Even though the Mosses were wrong about the Christianity thing, he was quite happy in his own church.

His decline didn't bother Major Fitch, who kept reciting the praise he'd gotten, all the way to the car. As Nikos held the car door for Mrs. Fitch, Ian winked at him and opened the door for his sister. By the time both boys climbed into the car, the major was drumming his fingers on the steering wheel.

Halfway home, the major broke off his self-congratulations. "I guess your church is a good influence on you most of the time. You have my permission to attend, as long as you don't expect me to go."

"Thank you, dear," Mrs. Fitch said meekly.

Ian winced slightly. Alexandria mouthed "Thank you" to Nikos over Ian's head.

"No problem," he mouthed back.

Once parked, Nikos shook hands with the major and thanked him for his hospitality. True or not, he didn't want to give the man any excuse to rescind his family's permission.

"I'll see you at school tomorrow," he told Alexandria, then ruffled Ian's hair and went home next door.

Mr. Moss lowered his newspaper. "How did it go?"

"The major says they can keep going again. And I guess you'll be happy to know they aren't Mormons. The sign said The Church of Jesus Christ of Latter-day Saints."

Mr. Moss gave him an odd look. "That is the Mormons. Because they believe in the Book of Mormon instead of the Bible."

Nikos shrugged. "Then you'll be happy to know Mormons are Christians. All the songs, the prayers, the talks, the lesson — everything talked about Christ. And the lesson was from Genesis, so obviously they believe in the Bible."

Mr. Moss gave him an even odder look. "Are you going to join their church?"

"No." Nikos hung up his coat.

His host father grunted and went back to reading his newspaper.

LIFE RETURNED to its old pattern of school, Diplomacy Club, and homework, plus Alexandria's judo and listening to parental fights. Nikos and Alexandria continued to study at his house to avoid the major, and while she was never actually happy, she didn't arrive in tears again. The divorce dragged on with no end in sight.

When her worries distracted her, Nikos nagged her into studying. "You have to keep up your grades. You can't do anything about your parents, anyway, so try to focus."

Alexandria snorted, but she picked up her pencil and looked at the next trig problem.

Well, he'd remind her again, and again, and again. Just because her father was being a jerk was no reason to let him ruin her entire life.

His eighteenth birthday passed, and after he called his parents, Mr.

Moss took him to get his driver's license. Not that he had a car yet, but it wouldn't hurt him to practice driving first. His exemption for Greek military training also arrived, relieving him of that worry.

In mid-March, Mrs. Moss picked up him and both Fitch kids from Diplomacy Club, which was still studying actual diplomacy and problem-solving since the asteroid still hadn't reappeared.

His host mother waved an envelope at Nikos. "You got mail! Open it, open it, open it!"

He held the front door for Alexandria, then hopped into the back seat and took his mail. The return address was from his top-pick college, and he held his breath as he ripped open the envelope.

Congratulations, he silently read at the top. It was time to apply to extend his visa.

"Well?" Alexandria turned around in the front seat to stare at him.

"I got in."

She tilted her head to the side. "So why don't you seem excited?"

He forced a smile. "I am excited. Give me a minute to get over the pleasant shock, would you?"

He was excited, truly. But he'd be all the way in Pennsylvania, and Alexandria would still be here. If the divorce went through, her dad would still be close enough to make her life miserable. If the divorce didn't go through, she'd still be miserable.

How could he just leave his friend in trouble?

CHAPTER 19

IN WHICH THEY ARE DISCOVERED

157 CONJUNCTIONS AFTER DEPARTURE, *NEW KUNISU*, BY KI

MIKNON SPRAWLED on Gil's back as he lay on the floor, head by the hole leading to the council room below. With the prince, the king's secretary, and a couple of guards surrounding the hole to listen, there was simply nowhere else to sit and still hear. And she certainly wasn't heavy enough to hurt her brother.

"Yes, one city at a time," one of the lords below them said. "With their weak magic, they won't defeat us. Pretty lights will make no difference. We'll hit them so hard and fast, they won't have time to use their magic. And we'll destroy them completely, leaving no one to spread the word to other cities."

"Landing all the barges will take time, and once we land, our warriors will be too weak to attack at once. And won't they see us land?" another asked.

"We'll set up our base on the dark side of the world and stay there until our troops are ready. Yes, yes, I know it will be difficult, but magic will keep us warm, and we'll send the dragons high enough to feed in the sunlight. While we train, we'll keep spying to choose our first target and find more weaknesses in the Ki natives."

Miknon leaned over Gil's shoulder to hear better. What if the fae couldn't take advantage of the Ki weaknesses? What if their magic was stronger than they realized and they could do more than make pretty lights?

"We can train everyone big enough to hold a weapon," a lord said, "thus multiplying the size of our army."

"Or," a third lord said, "the useless non-warriors can take the ship back to retrieve the rest of the fleet. Once they arrive, we can conquer cities in multiple waves."

"We can't grow a garden on the dark side."

"We will take most of the ship's supplies with us."

"What about those left behind? The little folk and the weak and the slow?"

"Other than the pilots, they are less important than the warriors. If a few of them starve, what does it matter? We will honor their sacrifices to allow us to colonize our new home."

Under Miknon, Gil stirred. Why was he shocked? Of course the lords felt that way. They never had valued the commoners, especially those smaller or weaker or with less magic. They considered the pixies nothing but a source of light.

She leaned forward and whispered in his ear, a mere breath. "They always underestimate us. We are small enough to be hard to see, but we can cut bowstrings or tendons and stab eyes and throats. And we eat less than the hulks."

He patted her hand and tilted his ear toward the spyhole. She took the hint and held her tongue.

"We should start training now," a lord said.

"What good does it do with so little weight?"

"First, it will accustom the warriors, particularly the new ones, to working together and obeying their leaders. Second, they can learn the commands and tactics they will need to follow when we attack Ki. Third, if they have too little weight, we can simply add more."

"We don't have enough weapons to train everyone."

"Then we must make more. We can take apart the empty shelves to make both weapons and training weights. If that is not enough, use the bedframes and let people sleep on the floor. Now that half the storerooms and a quarter of the gardens are empty, they can be extra dormitories."

"No one will like that."

The lord almost hissed. "I don't care what they like. They. Will. Obey."

Miknon shuddered. Always the lords cared only about obedience. Not wisdom, not choice, only obedience to their wills. And though the king had promised freedom and equality, the lords would not allow either. How could the prince fight all of them to keep his father's promise? How could any of them fight against their overwhelming magic?

The conversation below deteriorated into the boring details of which room and how many men and what training routines, and Miknon flew to the corner for a nap. The others could take notes if they liked, but none of that had anything to do with her. She hadn't even been able to recognize any voices to help her find her parents' murderers. Gil had better ears, but he hadn't heard the lords in the dragon's den. The prince knew the lords better, but he hadn't heard the conspirators, either.

She woke to voices and a light in the room. The spying must be over if the others dared to speak. She yawned and sat up.

The guards and secretary had left, and only her brother and the prince remained, sitting against a wall and apparently in the middle of an argument.

"You'll just let them do this?" Gil argued, with a remarkable lack of respect.

Miknon rolled her eyes. Her brother rarely acknowledged power, and one of these days, it would get him in trouble. Or dead.

Patiently but wearily, the prince said, "What else can I do?"

"Make a treaty!"

"I told you, I have nobody both faithful and powerful to send."

Miknon shook her head. Gil didn't recognize the impossible, either. Where he got his irrepressible hope, she didn't know.

"Well, you have to do something!" Gil said.

"Do you want me to reveal myself and forbid the council from invading?"

Gil snorted. "Like that would do anything except make you dead. No, Shar, I don't want you to be stupid."

Miknon winced, but the prince only laughed.

"Then let me know when you have a better idea."

Gil leaned forward. "What would you bargain if you could make a treaty?"

The prince closed his eyes, head against the wall. "It's a little hard to say without knowing the other side, isn't it? But I'd ask for territory somewhere, either shared or private, at least for most of us, since areas for the fire, ice, and water beings don't seem likely." He sighed heavily. Losing the other beings would cost a noticeable fraction of their total population. "A way to support ourselves, of course. Trade agreements. The right to pass property and wealth to our descendants. The right to *have* descendants. Peace. If we couldn't have sovereignty, then acceptable local laws."

"You'd surrender the crown?" Gil sounded as shocked as Miknon felt. What other highborn would ever be willing to lose one handspan of their power?

The prince opened his eyes and met Gil's gaze soberly. "If it saves my people, yes. There are more important things to worry about than my rank or reign. Besides, Father promised equality among the classes, didn't he? Does that still leave room for a king?"

He closed his eyes again. "As for what I would offer for a treaty, I suppose almost anything but our death or slavery. Surely our magic must be worth something. Or Ki could salvage our ship — the whole fleet, once we land. Our labor, as long as it is fairly compensated and under fair conditions. Any of our supplies, though we don't have much left."

Ki had so much magic, would they want to trade for more, Miknon wondered. Or perhaps the fae had better or different magic that would still be of interest. But not the pixies. They already knew Ki had plenty of light.

Gil looked over, and she waved. He motioned to Miknon and waited for her to come closer before he spoke. "After you fell asleep, the council said they'll use 'their' room for dormitories from now on, after they take apart the beds. They have their plans, so they'll concentrate on the training. Can you keep an eye on them to make sure they don't tell the troops anything else?"

"As if what they already have planned isn't bad enough," the prince muttered, eyes still closed.

Miknon folded her arms. "No. I've done enough spying. Don't you remember how close they came to spotting me last time?"

"Please?" Gil put on his lost-puppy face. "You're the only one who has a chance."

"No, I'm not," she said. "Ram will be in the training. Why don't you ask him?"

Gil smacked his forehead. "Because I'm stupid. Excuse me." He ran from the room.

The prince's lip twisted. "I envy your brother, you know. He goes everywhere, knows everyone, and never lets anything stop him."

"Someday something will stop him," Miknon said sadly. "And I'm afraid he won't survive the experience."

"Will any of us?"

The two of them sat without talking until Gil returned, rather less bouncy than before. He flopped onto the floor and pouted.

"Ram doesn't mind being in the army," Gil said. "It's responsible and adult. And I think he actually finds it fun." He shrugged.

"We already knew he wanted to be like Dagan," Miknon said.

Gil frowned. "He doesn't mind fighting Ki, either. If that's what the leaders want, then that's what he'll do."

"You didn't tell him about the prince, did you?" Miknon asked.

"Not yet," Gil said, "and probably never at this rate. My own brother, and I can't even trust him! How can he be happy about conquering Ki? Doesn't he care he might slaughter perfectly innocent people?"

The prince patted his shoulder. "I keep telling you that you have a nearly unique point of view, Gil. Most people are suspicious of strangers."

Gil smiled. "Strangers are just friends you haven't met yet."

Miknon rolled her eyes and exchanged glances with the prince that were half amused and half horrified.

"So." Gil sat up and stared at Miknon. "We really do need you to spy on the lords. Ram won't do it. I can't even ask him, because he'd probably report me for being insubordinate."

"No."

Gil wrinkled his forehead in thought. "Oh, I know. Since the lords will oversee the training personally, it will give you a chance to see if you can discover who helped Lord Zaidu murder our parents." He smiled triumphantly.

Miknon scowled at him. "No. I'll get Mother to help me after we land on Ki and have space to run away."

"But when we land, we'll spread out. You might never see the right lords again." Gil raised his eyebrows and spread his hands. "You'll never find the culprits."

Miknon turned her back to him, but she couldn't ignore his words. That was the problem with siblings — they knew what strings to pull to make you dance like their puppet. Well, not this time! She'd done enough spying, and she wasn't taking any more risks.

Gil said nothing. The prince said nothing. Miknon didn't look at them. The answer was no.

But how would she identify the right lords? She was the only one who had heard them in the dragon's hold. Mother already said she didn't know who else was involved. Nobody but Miknon had any chance of finding the murderers.

And if she didn't try, her parents would go unavenged.

Miknon whirled and glared at her brother. "Fine, I'll do it."

He almost smiled. "I knew you would."

She kicked his knee. Stupid brother. Stupid puppet strings.

By the end of the day, one dormitory and two storerooms had already been disassembled. Wood from shelves and beds was made into practice weapons while the smiths worked on converting metal to either weapons or heavy splints, depending on the quality. Already, some warriors wore the metal strapped to their legs to weigh them down and exercise their muscles. Those not yet outfitted got their exercise by taking apart beds and shelves and moving crates and supplies.

And Miknon watched it all from her perch in a light sconce. Stupid, stupid, stupid.

The displaced sleepers rolled up in the abandoned garden sections, the dining halls, and anywhere else they could find space. Even the king's secretary threw up his hands in dismay and stopped trying to keep track of where everyone was staying.

By the next day, the lords started training the warriors in the newly empty rooms while more space was prepared. Miknon moved herself to a sconce in the biggest training room and watched and listened.

The seasoned warriors were intimidating, but the new ones were merely amusing. Half of them couldn't keep right straight from left, and mid-maneuver collisions flung them into the air unless they were already wearing the weighted splints strapped to their legs like footless boots.

Even with the weights, they'd still have to strengthen themselves once they landed on Ki. Everyone would. Shifters like Gil would have an advantage, but that was only a bit of a shortcut.

The trainees below her shuffled out, and a new class entered. And there was Gil, next to his twin. Both of them wore the weights, and Gil's bounces had turned into stutters. Served him right.

One of the king's guards called everyone to order and taught them a new combat move. Ram was one of the best in the class. Gil wasn't, though he was enthusiastic. Once the group mastered the move enough for the day — which meant no longer smacking into their neighbor — the guard started telling them how to use the technique to subdue an enemy.

"No, no, no," someone interrupted from right below Miknon.

Subtly, she rearranged herself to look down.

One of the highborn stepped forward, waving his arms. "No, don't waste your energy subduing the enemy. *Kill* them. It's much simpler. We don't need them, you know."

Gil took half a step, and Ram gripped his elbow. Miknon glared at the boys, even though they wouldn't see her. If Gil didn't behave himself, he'd ruin everything.

The highborn kept lecturing, marching back and forth in front of the troops while he encouraged them to kill all the Ki natives. Ram kept his hold on his twin. Eventually, the lord stopped talking, though he lurked by the door until class ended, then criticized the trainer again about the proper way to teach everyone.

When they finally left, Miknon flew to the prince and reported what she'd heard. He promptly called in his chief Companion and gave commands for all the guards in training positions.

Over the next few days, the highborn tried sending the guards away and training the army themselves, but the guards refused to leave. The troops, understandably, grew a little confused about whether they should kill the natives when they invaded or just try to capture them.

And every time the lords tried a new sneaky tactic, Miknon reported it, and the prince passed down new commands. The guards followed those no matter what the lords said, claiming greater training experience. She watched the highborn grow crankier and crankier, but she still didn't spot anyone with Zaidu who looked like the other lord she'd seen in the dragon's hold.

Depressed, she let her glow fade but stayed in the training hall after the last class. This was all useless. The lords had no intention of pacifying Ki, only of conquering it. And whoever had plotted with Zaidu was staying out of sight altogether. She couldn't help the prince, and she couldn't help herself. And Gil, who wanted peace for their new world and had equal reason to catch the murderers, wouldn't get either.

"Hush," someone said. "We need to hurry before the next shift arrives for training. What did you need to tell me?"

Something about the voice stirred a memory, and Miknon leaned to take a look. That was definitely Zaidu below her, talking to someone in blue silk.

Blue silk! This was her chance to identify the other person responsible for the death of her parents! Even if the prince couldn't do anything about it now, he would know for later. Once they landed and he revealed he was still alive, he could bring the murderers to justice.

She leaned farther, trying to see his face, and slipped. Desperately, she grabbed the sconce. Her feet pattered against the wall, and two faces turned toward her. She lunged upward, beating her wings, and grabbed the maintenance grille. Within a second, she was inside, frantically crawling far into the tunnel.

Behind her, someone roared. "Blue wings! Find everyone with blue wings. Call a thought mage! We will question everyone and find the truth!"

Oh, no. Miknon crawled faster, heart beating almost hard enough to drown out the pounding of feet as people ran to the lords.

They would catch her.

And they would kill her.

Chapter 20

Divorce

Yet again, Dad had left for work before anyone else woke. Alexandria stabbed her pancakes with more force than necessary. Didn't he even want to try to keep his family together?

"I don't know what to do," Mom said. "Your dad won't sign any divorce agreement. He won't compromise on any topic at all. Even when I offer a halfway deal, he won't budge. He doesn't want to pay alimony, so I agreed to waive it, but he says he won't pay child support, either." She rubbed her forehead. "I'll go back to work full time, but my resumé is pretty bare. Even if I can afford housing and regular expenses, I don't know how we'll pay for college."

"I'm working on scholarships," Alexandria muttered.

"The court will make him pay child support." Ian sounded much too mature for his years.

Mom shook her head. "Not until we agree on other terms and finalize the divorce. He's pushing for sole custody with no visitation rights for me."

Ian shuddered. "You're still trying for sole custody, too, aren't you?" He looked at Mom with a pleading expression.

"Yes, honey, though I expect the judge will still give your father visitation unless he transfers to another base. I can't see us having to follow the major around the world." She sighed. "I hate to admit it, but I'm tempted to report some of his behavior as unbecoming an officer and a gentleman, to give us a little leverage. But if the judge doesn't think he's bad enough for criminal charges, it won't do anything but antagonize him. And if he is charged, it might ruin his career. Why can't he just cooperate a little?"

Alexandria stabbed her breakfast again. This would all be so much easier if everyone would just apologize and make up.

Mom winced. "Alexandria, please don't scrape the glaze off the plates."

Okay, no apologies, no making up. Her family was ruined. That's all there was to it. But couldn't they save something from the mess? Dad needed to remember he was more likely to get a favorable decision if he compromised, and Mom needed to ease up on sole custody. If only she could make both of them see reason. She sighed. Mom was trying to be fair on other points, at least. Dad just hated losing. Maybe it was the military in him. Win or die trying.

Hmm. Maybe she could redraw the battle lines for him. A big shock might be enough to make him see the real problem.

"What if you offered a different trade?" Alexandria asked. "Say you'll take no child support if he gives you sole custody with no visitation."

Mom put down her fork. "Oh, honey, are you sure you want that?"

"He won't take it, Mom. If he thinks he'll lose us altogether, he'll agree to pay child support. He's not stupid. And if he balks, you can threaten to report ungentlemanly conduct."

Ian rolled his eyes but stuffed food into his mouth instead of commenting.

"Are you absolutely sure you want me to try this?" Mom asked.

Alexandria shoved the last bite of pancake into her mouth and nodded. It would work. She knew it would work. Faced with losing his kids, Dad would compromise. She grabbed her jacket and backpack and darted for the bus, Ian close behind.

For the rest of the week, she bubbled with hope, and by the time Ian's birthday arrived on Monday, she was dying of anticipation. School and Diplomacy Club seemed to take forever, especially since the asteroid had re-emerged from the asteroid belt.

Mr. Reynolds's planned lecture dissolved into chaos as the students speculated again about the possibility of aliens. It took both teacher-sponsors to get the crowd to focus long enough to grasp that the asteroid was in a totally normal orbit that would miss Earth by enough to make a safe-but-exciting show. Without aliens. And its trip through the asteroid belt had smashed it into less than one percent of its original size, which made it even harder to see and less interesting.

Finally, Alexandria and the boys left for home with Mrs. Moss.

"It's my birthday," Ian told Nikos. "Can you come for dinner?"

"Is that okay with the major?" Nikos cautiously asked.

Ian shrugged. "I haven't seen him lately, but we've always been allowed to invite friends on our birthday. Please?"

"Sure, buddy, I'd be happy to."

Smiling broadly, Ian pulled out his phone and texted Mom to pick up an extra pizza.

When they arrived home, Alexandria let them all into the house a little nervously, but it was quiet. The three of them set the table and then worked on their homework while they waited.

Mom arrived an hour later, arms full of pizza boxes and mail. Nikos sprang to help, and Ian hurried to fill the water glasses.

"Welcome, Nikos," Mom said. "I'm glad you made it." She pulled him in for a quick hug, then threw open the boxes. "Grab what you want. I tried to get everyone's favorites."

She'd even gotten Dad's favorite, but Dad never came home. Alexandria choked down her disappointment to avoid spoiling Ian's party. He deserved a better birthday than she'd had, and he preferred Dad's absence.

The pizza was soon demolished, and after ice cream and cake, Ian opened his presents. By now, his proficiency in his newest languages had progressed enough to read in them, and Mom had found used novels in German and Spanish, while Nikos provided a storybook in modern Greek.

Alexandria gave him a frisbee with "One Ring to Rule Them All" written in Elvish around the edge. "So you still get some exercise," she teased.

"Thanks, everyone!" Ian said.

The party broke up after that so Alexandria could finish homework and Nikos could work on his visa extension. Alexandria walked Nikos out, and Mom motioned for her and Ian to sit back down.

"I have to tell you something." Mom looked very serious, and all the joy of the celebration had disappeared.

Alexandria sank back in a kitchen chair. "What happened now?"

"Dad signed the divorce papers." Mom's voice was flat instead of excited.

Ian sneaked a peek inside one of his new books. Didn't he even care that Mom and Dad weren't getting back together?

"I told you my plan would work." Alexandria should have felt triumphant, but she only felt tired. She would rather have heard that Dad wanted to reconcile and Mom was laying down rules for that.

Mom winced. "No, honey, he signed the new papers. The ones you suggested. I get sole custody in exchange for no child support, no alimony, no share in the house, cars, or bank accounts. Nothing he bought for any of us. No financial assets of any kind. But I get both of you, with no input or visitation rights for him. And I didn't even have to threaten to report him."

Across the table, Ian straightened and closed his book.

Alexandria blinked at her, trying to process the sentence. Mom must have gotten it wrong somewhere. If Dad gave Mom sole custody, that would mean he didn't want his kids anymore. He couldn't have signed the new papers; they were only a ploy to bring him to his senses.

"I'm sorry, honey," Mom said. "I know this isn't what you wanted. It wasn't what I wanted, either."

Ian grimaced but said nothing.

Alexandria barely heard Mom. Dad gave up *all* custody? Without the worry of being reported? Didn't he love her anymore?

"I already turned in the papers to the court," Mom continued. "There's no point in giving him a chance to change his mind. Or in dragging out this torture any longer."

Dad had given her away. The world tilted sideways, as if gravity had stopped working. Alexandria clutched the table to keep her balance.

"Honey, are you okay?" Mom's voice sounded far away. "Ian, get water."

Ian pressed her water glass into her hand while Mom rubbed her back.

"Drink, Alexandria," Ian insisted.

Numbly, she obeyed. Once her vision cleared, Ian sat again.

"If Dad doesn't want us, we can't stay here," Ian said. "Where should we go?"

"He still won't let us move out until everything is final," Mom said. "But we should make a plan for when that happens, because I think we'll need to leave immediately. I'm afraid of what his temper will be like when there's no going back."

Ian cringed. "He has guns. Will he be mad enough to use his guns?"

"He wouldn't do that," Alexandria protested.

He wouldn't hurt them, would he? She glanced at Ian, who still cowered in his chair, and Mom, who had looked hopeless for the past year. Dad had already hurt both of them.

And though he didn't treat Alexandria the same way, he kept breaking his promises to her. She didn't even recognize him anymore. She'd been fooling herself that he would go back to being the Dad she remembered and loved. But that didn't mean she should let him hurt them more.

He probably wouldn't use his guns, but they couldn't take the chance he would do anything else, either. If he wasn't interested in saving the family, then she needed to save what was left. Yes, they needed a plan. Alexandria took a deep breath that sounded much too much like a sob and forced herself to think. How could she protect her mother and brother?

Mom buried her face in her hands. "Where will we go?"

"I don't know," Alexandria admitted. "We'll have to figure that out."

"Okay," Mom said, "*how* will we leave? I don't get to keep my car, and by the time I finish paying the lawyer, I can't afford a new one. After squeezing out enough for an apartment, it will take months to replace our clothes and dishes and other essentials." She frowned. "I really wish he would have at least let us keep our things, but he said if he paid for it, he's keeping it. I suppose it doesn't matter. You two are far more important than any possessions."

To Mom, perhaps, but not to Dad. Alexandria's heart cracked.

"What about my books?" Ian asked.

"I bought your birthday books from my salary," Mom said, "but anything that wasn't a gift from someone else, Dad's salary paid for. I'm sorry."

"The court won't actually go for that, will it?" Ian asked.

"Probably not if we argue," Mom said, "but if we take it to court, what do you think the chances are he'll still agree to sole custody?"

Alexandria crossed her arms. "If we can't take any of our stuff, then we don't need a moving van. That will save costs."

And what a real jerk move of Dad's. What did he need with their clothes, anyway? They wouldn't fit him. And he didn't even like her new Mars globe. She liked her stuff. All her stuff, even the cheap stuff. It was hers. She'd been collecting it for a lifetime, and every time they moved, she got rid of what she didn't want. Everything left was precious. What about her mementoes? Her space posters? Her solar system bedspread? Her laptop and phone? Well, they did have the secret phones, at least. But almost all her clothes would have to stay. Her dresser and bed. Her books, even though she had fewer than Ian. This was not fair.

She gasped. Her telescopes! She'd have to leave the one Dad bought, though she could at least take the 80 mm reflector Grandpa gave her. Actually, it was more expensive than Dad's, even though it was half the size. But it didn't see the stars very well, just the moon and planets. Her chest twinged, and she panted for breath.

Ian and Mom kept talking, sounding much more hopeful than she felt.

"Dad didn't buy all my bookcases," Ian said. "Grandma made the one for me."

"And our cedar chests," Mom added. "And we've gotten a few clothes from other family or friends. Yes, we should make a list of what we can still take."

Instantly, Ian bolted to his room and came back with a notebook and pen. He ripped out two pages for Mom and Alexandria and started scribbling. Alexandria bit the pen and stared at the paper, trying to forget about all her beloved things that would have to be abandoned. No time to mourn them now. What did they need to plan?

A timeline. Money. Resources. A car. Would anyone help them? It wasn't illegal to divorce, and Dad hadn't hit any of them. Yet. As much as she hated to admit it, his temper had gotten even more erratic lately.

She looked back at her first item. Time depended entirely on the court now, and they'd have to be ready at all times. Alexandria scribbled notes, though every drop of ink felt like it had been leeched from her veins. But if Dad no longer loved them, then there was no family left to save. No whole family, just the broken remnants.

Alexandria forced her pain into a corner of her mind. "We need more money. I'll quit judo and get a job."

"No," Mom blurted. "That's not fair to you. I don't want to ruin your life. Besides, aren't you trying to get a judo scholarship?"

"I'll quit judo *for now*," Alexandria emphasized. "Once we're resettled, I'll start again. If your job is paying for the lawyer, then we have to have some way to pay for everything else."

She looked at her list again. "We could rent a car for the move." That goal was more realistic for a couple of months of work.

"Oh, good idea," Mom said. "Then we can worry about buying what we need later."

"What about yard sales?" Ian asked.

"I don't think they sell cars at yard sales," Alexandria said.

He rolled his eyes. "No, for clothes and dishes and stuff."

"That's actually a good idea." Alexandria made another note. "But I think we should concentrate on the stuff we need just for the trip, not for later. The less we have to move, the more options we have for a rental car."

Mom made a note. "And summer clothes take less space than winter clothes, fortunately."

"What if the judge doesn't decide until winter?" Alexandria asked.

"Now that we've signed an agreement," Mom said, "I don't think it will take that long."

Ian grimaced. "My bookcase won't fit in a tiny car," he whispered. "Even with the shelves folded."

Grandma Ellison had anticipated them moving a lot for Dad's job, so the bookcase collapsed nearly flat, but it didn't get any smaller than the back panel.

"Neither will our cedar chests," Alexandria complained. "But they do lock, so at least we'll have somewhere to hide our stuff from Dad in the meantime. And maybe we can rent an SUV."

"We can also hide stuff in my closet." Ian's voice was quiet and sad. "Dad doesn't come in my room anymore."

Mom bit her lip. "I hate to ask this, Alexandria, but you're the only one he's still talking to. Can you bring yourself to listen to him for clues to his plans? Or danger signs."

Alexandria drew a savage line through "decide what to leave" on her list. Dad was the worst thing to leave behind. Being around Dad and pretending everything was fine would be torture. But what choice did she have? Dad had already abandoned her, but she couldn't abandon Mom and Ian.

"Yes, Mom." She would do what she had to do, because she had no choice.

Life had narrowed to just three things. Turn in all homework early and finish the school year with good grades. Get a job to pay for their escape. Prepare to run.

If something wouldn't help save her ruined family, it didn't matter.

She could cry later.

She wrote "spy on Dad" and ignored the ink blot that spread as a tear hit the page.

CHAPTER 21

IN WHICH THEY MUST ESCAPE

GIL AND ZAK were sharing their meal with Shar in the navigation training room when Miknon exploded out of the grille in the wall and plummeted toward their heads.

"They saw me!" she screamed. "They're looking for everyone with blue wings. They'll find me, and they'll kill me!"

The three boys jumped into action. Zak ran and locked the door while Shar double-checked that the spyhole in the floor was closed and covered.

Gil held out his arms to his sister. "Calm down and tell me what happened."

She landed on his hands, shuddering so hard her wings rustled. "Zaidu and his conspirator saw me spying on them. I told you this was a bad idea! They're going to use magic to question everyone with blue wings. And when they find out it was me, they'll kill me."

"I won't let them." Gil clenched his jaw.

Nobody would touch his sister! It had been his idea to have her spy, so if anybody was punished, it ought to be him.

Shar cleared his throat. "How will you stop them?" When Gil frowned at him, the prince shrugged. "Sorry, but it's true."

Sadly, it was. The lords had magic and guards and rank. Gil had nothing. If he stood between them and Miknon, they'd simply squish them both.

"They will find me," Miknon moaned. "No hiding place on the ship is good enough if they're actually looking for me."

"I'm hiding," Shar said.

"Nobody's looking for you," Miknon said. "They all saw your dead body ejected from the ship. *I* don't have a dead body for a decoy. And if you're discovered, you can defend yourself with magic or call on the people to defend you. Many people would."

"But not everyone," Shar said. "I'm trying to avoid a civil war."

"No war is good." A sudden idea struck Gil like lightning. "No hiding place *on* the ship. What if you left the ship? What if *we* left, because I'm not letting you go alone."

Ram was always nagging him about taking responsibility, and now was when it mattered.

"There's no air on the worldlet," Zak reminded them.

"There is on Ki," Gil said.

"Ki! How are we supposed to get to Ki?" Miknon asked. "I can't fly that far, even if we had air, which we don't."

"The dragons can fly there." His mind raced, trying to plan it all.

"The dragons are conditioned to only obey their driver," Shar said. "They're imprinted as soon as they're big enough to pull a barge. If you try to steal a dragon, the driver will just take control of their mind and bring them back to the ship."

"Azidaka is still too young for a barge," Gil said. "We'll take him."

"The baby?" Zak said. "Are you out of your mind? Are you planning to ride him bareback?"

"And suffocate?" Gil said. "Of course not. We'll take the message capsule."

Zak and Shar exchanged skeptical looks.

"Gil," Shar said, "you won't fit in the message capsule. Let's think of a really good hiding place for your sister." He grimaced. "We can try."

"Oh, I think I'll fit," Gil said. "And Miknon doesn't take much space."

They had to fit, because the alternative was death. "We don't need to take much with us. How long would it take to fly there?"

Zak folded his arms. "Seventy hours. You can skip food for a day and a half, but you can't go without water."

Frowning, Gil calculated. "We won't be moving around, so we can get by on less. Two meals plus one for when we land. We can find more on Ki as long as we're alive."

"What if we can't eat the food on Ki?" Miknon asked.

Gil raised his eyebrows. "If we can't eat the food, then everyone in the fleet is dead; we just haven't stopped moving yet. The seer said to come here, so if we trusted her before we left Kunisu, why shouldn't we trust her now? Besides, we have no choice. Ki is the only place we can go to save you."

"I think we'll die," Miknon protested.

"Well, do you want a chance of escape," Gil asked, "or do you want to stay here until the lords catch you and kill you slowly?"

"And how do you intend to make them stop looking for me?" Miknon asked. "Won't they guess we escaped on the dragon?"

"They stopped looking for me when they thought I was dead," Shar said. "Stage some kind of accident."

"Good idea," Gil said.

"Why can't we stage an accident and then hide?" Miknon asked.

Gil turned to Shar. "I'm actually hoping to accomplish two missions at once. I plan to ask Ki for sanctuary in exchange for information about our fleet."

With no expression on his face, but sadness in his voice, the prince asked, "Would you betray us all?"

Despite his bodice and flounced skirt, he looked like his father at his most kingly.

"No, Shar," Gil said. "I mean to seek a truce, if you will allow me to be your emissary. I will bargain for a new home for us, without a war. I know I'm not powerful in magic or rank, but I do care what happens to our people."

Shar flickered a smile. "You care about everyone, Gil. But how would you make a treaty with the enemy? You don't even speak their language."

Gil shrugged. "Honestly, I have no idea. But I'll look for a way. You do want peace, don't you?"

"Yes."

Gil nodded. "Then leaving the ship saves Miknon and gives us a chance at a treaty. Miknon, did you want to take any of your belongings?"

"Just my baby blanket," she said. "It's the last thing I have from my parents."

"I'll get it," Gil promised. "You work your way to the hold, and I'll meet you there. Hurry, we need to be ready before the next feeding time."

"I'll find food and water," Zak said, "and spells for air and shielding."

He unlocked the door and peered out for a moment before exiting.

Miknon flew to the maintenance tunnel. "I still think you're crazy."

Gil flashed her a smile. "But I'm your crazy."

She rolled her eyes and disappeared into the tunnel, closing the grille behind her.

Shar reached into his bodice and pulled out a ring. "Take my signet as a sign that you represent me, in case you find a way to talk to the natives."

"The king's signet!" Gil exclaimed. "Don't you want to keep that?"

Like everyone on the ship, the king had brought little that his son could inherit, and as an emblem of the royal authority, the signet was more than just a keepsake.

Shar shook his head. "I'd rather keep it out of the council's hands. Try to keep it in one piece and return it to me later, will you?" He forced the ring into Gil's hands. "I'll try to delay troop landings. Maybe sabotage the weapons, something to give you a little more time. If you do manage a truce, send the dragon back as a signal if you can't come yourself. We've already discussed terms, so you know what I would agree to. Do the best you can." He clasped Gil's shoulders tightly for a moment. "Now hurry, and be safe."

Gil removed his necklace and strung the ring next to his family emblem and the key to the zoo. Oh, yes, he'd have to leave that, too. Well, it would certainly identify his "body." With a final wave at the prince, he replaced his necklace and hurried from the auxiliary room to his assigned dormitory.

All the way down to the third deck, excitement and fear battled in his stomach. He was going to Ki — today. He would be the first of their people on the new world. Almost alone, without adequate supplies, without a mage, without speaking the language. And could he even walk on the heavier world? Miknon might have a point about him being crazy.

Having fun was lots better than this responsibility trouble. Maybe it was a good thing he hadn't finished his meal, or nausea might bring it back up again. He waved as he passed everyone, trying to act normal, but he didn't stop to chat.

Even though Miknon tended to sleep in the tunnels, she left her belongings with the rest of the family for safe-keeping. Gil snuck quietly through the always-full dormitory and found his family's usual bunk. From the storage cabinets in the corner, he collected Miknon's baby blanket, three standard passenger blankets, a bandage, and his only extra kilt.

After a moment of thought, he raided the bandages again and wrapped himself under his kilt like an infant, since he'd be three days without hygiene facilities. He unstrapped his leg weights and tucked them under the bed. If Ram found them, maybe he'd know Gil had a plan. Or maybe he'd just think Gil had been shirking his physical training. Ram wasn't impressed with his brother's fighting talents anymore than he was with his sense of duty. Too bad Gil couldn't tell him what he was doing now.

Before leaving, he pressed another blanket to his face. When Mother and Ram came to bed, they'd smell his scent. Whether or not it would make them feel better, he didn't know, but it was the only way he could say goodbye.

"I love you," he whispered, then crept quietly through the dark room and hurried to the very bottom of the ship.

At least everyone was used to him checking on the dragons and wouldn't alert the guards to his presence. As he entered the dragon's hold, Zak and Miknon slipped out of one of the barges. Miknon was still shaking so hard she could barely fly. Gil shut the hold doors and threw the latch. For this to work, they couldn't afford some random passenger wandering by at the wrong moment and catching them mid-escape.

"Hurry," Zak said.

He took Gil's armload of cloth and dumped it by the message pod in front of the hatch. While Gil unlocked the baby dragon, Zak folded two blankets to fit the tiny pod. He arranged Miknon's blanket as a pillow, then fastened several flasks and bags to the hooks along the inner sides that allowed packages to be strapped down. Miknon tugged on every parcel to make sure it would stay in place.

"Good Azidaka," Gil crooned. "Good boy. Come over here. Come here."

He led the little dragon, who was still the size of one of the freight barges, to the message pod and pressed on his haunches until he sat.

Due for another feeding, the dragon was sleepy and let his jeweled wings sag on the floor. At least he would get plenty of sunlight on the trip to Ki, more than enough for the flight.

Gil held the dragon's head and stared into his eyes. He pictured a world in his mind, half light and half dark, and added a small dragon swooping to the edge of the darkness.

"Land in the dark," he whispered. "Land just in the dark."

If the dragon could manage that, Gil and Miknon would land unseen and walk to the light side of the world before they starved. But Gil wasn't a dragon driver and couldn't speak mind-to-mind. Could the dragon read him, or would they land in a random place? Or fly between the stars until Gil and Miknon starved, or return to the ship?

Miknon was right. This was crazy. He clenched his fists, then flexed his fingers. Closing his eyes, he took a deep breath. Crazy it might be, but it was Miknon's only chance.

Azidaka licked his cheek, and Gil laughed. "Okay, I hope you under-stand and remember."

One on each side, Gil and Zak lifted the pod onto the dragon's back and buckled the harness in place. Gil left Zak and Miknon to check every fastening three times, and he hurried to move the adult dragons to feeding position in front of the great hatch. It would stay open for most of a shift to allow them to absorb enough sunlight, and no one could enter the hold until the hatch closed again. That was as long as they would have to make their escape.

"Have you thought about how to fake your death?" Zak asked.

"I think I'll be swept out when the hatch opens during feeding time," Gil said. "Got stuck and couldn't leave when the bell rang, idiot boy that I am. The baby dragon flew away because I hadn't gotten him chained yet."

As he locked the mother dragon's chains again, he deliberately caught the edge of his extra kilt inside the cuff. "Does that look like I accidentally snagged myself getting them ready?"

"I suppose," Miknon said, "but why didn't you just unlock it when you found out you were trapped?"

"Because I stupidly dropped the key." Gil suited action to words, and when the key hit the floor, he kicked it sideways to the closest barge. "See, it goes that far." He picked it up and wedged it just under the edge of the barge. "If it gets sucked out, Nik has another one, but I hope it stays to enforce my story. Make sure somebody takes care of the animals, please."

Zak frowned. "You could have left the kilt behind and run for safety."

"I did, of course," Gil said, "but I was too slow."

He drew his dagger and cut his palm. Once enough blood had welled up, he patted his hands together, then pressed his back against the hatch and grasped at the edge of the frame as if he were slipping off. The blood smeared in messy prints.

"Yuck," Miknon said.

"Yes, but the bloodworkers can test it to prove it's mine," he said. "And you tried to help me and were swept out with me."

Without warning, he yanked one of her smallest feathers and pressed it into the bloody smear. She yelped and examined her wing, but he had pulled on a loose one, minimizing the damage.

Zak stood on tiptoe to grab the bandage from the pod. "I thought this was just for emergencies, dimwit." He wrapped it around Gil's hand and tied it snugly. "Come get in, and I'll explain the supplies."

One-handed, Gil climbed up Azidaka's back and settled into the message pod. The blankets padded the bottom nicely, but the space was so narrow that once he lay down, his shoulders touched the walls. With his feet brushing the bottom, his head almost reached the top.

Zak shifted the packages so they rested on top of Gil instead of cramping his arms and sides even more, and Miknon tucked herself between his side and injured arm.

"You won't be using this one anyway," she muttered.

Gil reached across with his good hand and patted her. "I'll be fine."

They had much bigger worries than a simple cut, and she was right about him not using his hand for a few days. Fortunately, since it already ached. Stupid, stupid.

Zak tucked the last blanket over them both, then ran straps across Gil at shin, thigh, waist, and chest, tugging them firmly against the hooks.

"You have four flasks of water," he said, "including one for between landing and finding a stream. You'll need to refill them before your return journey. I put enough fruit in here for four meals, so you can eat again as soon as you land. I hooked the shielding spell into the lock mechanism so it will come on automatically."

He touched a glass ball near Gil's head. "This is the biggest air spell I could get. It has enough air for both of you for three days if you breathe slowly. Don't panic, or you won't have enough to get back. To use it, tap it once on or three times off." He pointed to a metal block near Gil's elbow. "This is your cold spell. Tap twice on or three times off."

"Don't we need heat instead of cold?" Miknon asked.

"No," Gil said, "Azidaka will get warm once the sunlight hits his wings, and we're right on top of him. We'll be plenty warm with the blanket."

"The cold is for when you pass through the world barrier," Zak said. "Don't forget, or the dragon will survive but you'll bake. It has two uses, one for each direction." He puckered a frown. "If you can come back."

"We'll be fine, Zak," Gil said.

Maybe they would, and maybe they wouldn't, but at least they'd have a chance. If they stayed here, he would lose his sister, and that was completely unacceptable. Why did Ram have to be right about growing up?

"It's almost time," Zak said. "May the stars light your path home." He lowered the lid slowly, then raised it a little and slid a hand inside to tap the latch. "Make sure you fasten it."

The lid thumped closed, and Gil smothered a chuckle. "Yes, Zak."

Obediently, he locked the pod in the darkness by feel. Without the light, the walls felt even closer. Gil twitched his feet and touched the wall. He lifted his head, banging into the lid. So close. No room to move. He took a breath and choked, suddenly desperate to get out.

The hold doors opened and shut again. Zak was on his way back to his tower, from which he would soon open the outer hatch.

"Gil, are you sure this will work?" Miknon's voice quavered in the dark.

"Yes." No. "Why wouldn't it?"

The list of things that could go wrong was as vast as the number of stars. His breathing grew tighter, and he stretched again, bumping into the walls. No room. Miknon shifted, a light tap sounded, and a breeze suddenly drifted across Gil's face.

"It helps to turn on the air spell," she said.

"Oh. Of course." He inhaled and tried to rest quietly.

Seventy hours or so to hope the dragon landed in a good spot. Seventy hours to wait in the dark, unable to move. Seventy hours to see if they lived or died.

After that, it would get trickier.

Chapter 22

Family

Nikos leaned against Alexandria's shoulder in a silent gesture of support. She had barely smiled in the last month, and he didn't know how much longer she could stay sane waiting to hear about her parents' divorce. Though the other students in Diplomacy Club listened attentively, she sat like a statue, unmoving and silent.

He was willing to bet her mind was racing a million kilometers an hour, though, planning and rehearsing. After all, he'd spent the last four Saturdays driving her to yard sales on her way to or from her new job at a local fast-food restaurant. They'd found most of the clothing on her list, but he knew she still needed sleeping bags and a few other items. More worrisome was the sheer uncertainty of her family's timeline. Did they still have time left to prepare, or would they come home and discover it was the day to flee?

"So," Mr. Reynolds continued his lecture, "part of problem-solving between people is finding common ground. What do you both want or need? What are you both willing to do?"

Nikos wasn't willing to help Alexandria's parents get back together, that was for sure. Oh, a few months ago, that might have worked, but the major had proven by now that he wasn't interested in being a good father or husband. So what could Nikos do for his friend, besides driving to yard sales? No mere spit on the ground would help this problem.

He glanced over his shoulder at Ian, sitting in the back of the cafeteria as usual, in the middle of students who needed language help. Both of the Fitch kids were doing their best to keep themselves together under the stress, but Ian had dark circles around his eyes, and his pencil trembled when he wrote. Alexandria had lost all her sparkle, and she barely talked to anyone except to answer a direct question.

"Sometimes it helps to define the problem more precisely," Mr. Reynolds said, "or in a different way. Instead of saying immigrants need houses, say they need housing. The slight difference in wording might trigger a different idea, like a tent or a dorm or a tiny house or a room in someone else's home."

Crete had a lot of immigration issues. Not that it mattered right now. Redefine. Alexandria needed a different father. Ha, can't help with that. She needed peace. He couldn't help with that, either, but he knew she found some in her church. Fortunately, the major hadn't changed his mind about letting his family attend, and Nikos had watched through the window every Sunday to make sure they got out the door all right. He hadn't needed to go with them again, though he would have if necessary. Even if the people at her church called him Brother. He rolled his eyes.

So peace was a work in progress, maybe. She had courage in plenty, pushing her forward through her fears. If his dad was as scary as hers, he didn't know if he could be so brave.

What else? Alexandria needed safety. Okay, what would make her safe?

Somewhere to go where her father couldn't find her. Jobs for her and her mother. Some kind of housing. Getting into a good college that offered the major she wanted. Being with her mother and brother, since they were the only family she had left.

Lucky him, to either have most of those or not need them. He would be going to his top college pick, and housing would be easy, as would a job. His visa and other paperwork had all been approved for college. He didn't need to avoid his father. In fact, he was looking forward to his parents' first visit in a few months. They emailed him and called every week when the time difference allowed, but it wasn't the same.

"What does one of you have that the other one could use?" Mr. Reynolds asked. "And then turn the question around and ask it the other direction."

Nikos grimaced. They sort of had the same problem, but not really. He had a family and a home but couldn't visit them. She was losing part of her family and all of her home and had nowhere to go. Both of them were alone, in a way. It was too bad they weren't really brother and sister, like her church members called everybody, because then neither of them would be alone.

He stiffened. Could they… No. But maybe… She didn't have to stay in Colorado once the divorce was final, so maybe.

For the rest of the hour, he ignored Mr. Reynolds and examined every bit of his idea for weaknesses. As soon as the club meeting ended, he followed Alexandria and Ian outside, still thinking furiously. Could this work? And would they say yes? His parents wouldn't mind.

Maybe it was lucky Mrs. Moss had a conflict today, so Mrs. Fitch was taking them home.

After holding the car door for Alexandria, he hopped into the back. "Excuse me, ma'am, do you have time to talk today? All of you? Could we go to a park or something?"

Mrs. Fitch glanced at him as she pulled out of the school parking lot. "I guess that would be fine. What's up?"

"Just need to talk," he said.

And Nikos stayed firmly silent no matter how Ian pestered him about the secret.

Once at their neighborhood park, they all found seats on the grass or benches. Three pairs of eyes stared at Nikos, and he cleared his throat several times, trying to decide how to approach this.

"I got into Lehigh University," he said, "in Pennsylvania."

"Yes," Mrs. Fitch said, "Alexandria told me. Congratulations!"

"Pennsylvania is a long way from here."

Ian gave him a puzzled look. "Yes, we know."

Nikos flushed, feeling idiotic. "Pennsylvania State U has an astronomy program and an extra campus not far away from Lehigh."

Alexandria shook herself and looked more alive than she had all day, even though it was irritation bringing back her color.

"I know that," she said. "Nikos, what is wrong with you? What are you trying to say?"

"Move to Pennsylvania with me," Nikos blurted, rushing through the idea as fast as possible. "Be my roommates. My name will make it harder for the major to find you. Alexandria will qualify for in-state tuition by the time she graduates high school. I know Penn State isn't her top college pick, but it is far away from her father."

"Your name?" Mrs. Fitch asked. "Nikos, I won't facilitate a marriage between you and my daughter. She's only sixteen, for one thing."

"Gross, Mom!" Alexandria said. "He's like my brother!"

Face burning hot, Nikos tried again. "Sorry, I just meant my name on the lease. Alexandria brings up exactly my point. I think of her as the little sister I never had. Ian feels like my brother. You guys are the closest thing I have to family in the States. You don't have anywhere to go, but I can make room for you. There should be plenty of houses available off-campus. The ladies will probably have to share a bedroom, and Ian can share with me." He raised his hands in innocence. "If I ever lay an inappropriate hand on any of you, you can shoot me." He winked at Alexandria. "Or throw me over your shoulder."

Ian threw his arms around Nikos. "I always wanted a big brother. Sisters aren't the same."

He and Alexandria stuck out their tongues at each other.

Mrs. Fitch started to speak, stopped, and tried again. "Nikos, that's very generous, but we can't saddle you with our problems."

"Oh, but I don't have siblings besides Ian and Alexandria," he protested. "My parents can't visit often, so I'm all alone. I'd have to have roommates at college, anyway, and I'd rather have your family than strangers."

Mrs. Fitch still looked skeptical.

Nikos kept talking. "We can split expenses, just like roommates. I can cover rent for a couple of months while you find a job, ma'am. I'll get a car that will fit all of us."

"Oh, come on, Mom," Ian pleaded. "I like Nikos."

"So do I," Mrs. Fitch said, "but this is a big deal. For one thing, a car is expensive."

Nikos shrugged. "I need to get a car, anyway. There's no reason we can't share it, at least until you can afford one of your own."

"I know you got your license," Alexandria said, "but are you sure you can buy a car?"

"My visa required proof of support for high school and my first year of college," Nikos said. "Didn't you ever wonder how much money my family has?"

"Nope," she said, "I never even thought about it. Though you do have a very nice suit." Her eyes shone with tears.

"I vote yes." Ian bounced on his knees and threw his arms around his mom.

"Maybe," Mrs. Fitch said. "Maaaaybe. I have serious doubts about several things and I wasn't planning to move out of state."

"Please," Nikos said. "This would make me really happy. I miss my family in Crete, and you feel like my second family. Living with you will be no problem for me, and I'll follow whatever rules you want. You'll all be safe with me, in every way. I've been worried about leaving you behind in trouble, and I think this would be better for all of us. Won't it be easier not having to worry about running into the major around town?" He took a deep breath. "Please, Mrs. Fitch, be my college family?"

Alexandria covered her face, and her shoulders shook. Was she happy at the idea? Sad at leaving her father? Laughing at Nikos?

Mrs. Fitch patted her daughter's knee. "I suppose I don't have any better ideas, Nikos. I think we will accept, tentatively, though you can expect a long list of rules. And I reserve the right to change my mind and allow you the same."

He let his breath whoosh out. "Anything you say."

"What if the divorce isn't final by the time you have to leave?" Mrs. Fitch asked. "We can't make you late for college."

Nikos shrugged. "I don't have to leave until August. If you aren't ready to leave by then, I'll go first and find an apartment. You'd have to rent a car to join me, but that's possible. And I can take some of your things with me, to make your move easier." He winked at Alexandria, who had finally raised her head, revealing tear tracks on her cheeks. "You can keep in touch with me with those secret phones of yours."

Alexandria blushed. "Oh, you saw those, did you?"

He tapped his head. "I'm not stupid, you know."

To his surprise and pleasure, she treated him just like she did Ian and stuck out her tongue at him.

"So, Mrs. Fitch, let's keep in touch, okay?" Nikos said. "We can coordinate our plans, and once school is out, I'll be sure to be ready anytime you need to go."

"Just one more thing right now," Mrs. Fitch said. "And this is very important."

"What's that?"

"I'm tired of being Mrs. Fitch or ma'am. To you and in general. Call me Helen," she said. "Or Mom, if you want."

She flashed him a smile that reminded him of Alexandria at her most charming, and for the first time, he could see past her weary heartbreak to the beautiful young woman she must have been once.

Her phone buzzed, and she checked the texts. "Oh, no, Troy got home early. Let's go."

Everyone bolted for the car, and they hurried the two blocks to home. Nikos waved as he went next door, and he entered the house with cheeks aching from a grin.

"Nice day, dear?" Mrs. Moss asked.

"Lovely day." But it must all stay top-secret so no rumors would drift back to the major. Only his parents could know, since they were too far away for gossip to matter. Nikos kissed her cheek and grabbed a bunch of grapes. "Lots of homework, so call me for dinner?"

She beamed. "Of course, dear."

He ran to his room and hurried through his homework to have time to make his own lists. Now that he would have a brother and sister with him at college, he wanted everything to be perfect. And he didn't want to disappoint Mama Helen.

ALL WEEK, Nikos made plans. He already had his clothes, unlike the poor Fitches, and all of them could get furniture in Pennsylvania instead of dragging it halfway across the country. Until he got his syllabi, he didn't know what books he'd need for school, and entertainment could wait. After all, he needed to leave some room in his car for his family's belongings.

His family. Every time he thought of the Fitches, a grin split his face. He'd always wanted siblings, and now he had two great ones.

On Saturday, Nikos drove Alexandria to yard sales in Mrs. Moss's car. Once she was safely home, he went into town and bought his own vehicle with the able assistance of Mr. Moss, whose mild face hid a bargaining guru. Once Nikos parked on the street by his house, he knocked on the Fitches' door.

"Hey, Alexandria," he said when she opened it, "want to see my new truck?"

Ian popped his head around his sister. "I do!"

Both of his new siblings followed him outside.

"It's a Ford F-150," he said. "Crew cab, so we can all ride inside, but there's still room for Ian's bookcase in the back."

"Smart," Alexandria said.

He unlocked the doors and let the others explore. Alexandria played with all the controls, and Ian dug the owner's manual out of the glove box. Perfectly content, Nikos leaned through the window of the open door and watched them.

Eventually, they finished examining his truck and hopped out.

"I saved the best for last," Nikos said.

"What, the sapphire blue color?" Alexandria teased.

"Nope." Nikos reached into the back seat, pulled out his bonus gift, and unfolded it by the passenger seat. "The seller included this step for the short girlfriend he was sure I had." He looked up into Alexandria's eyes and let his chuckle escape. "I didn't tell him my *sister* is taller than I am."

Alexandria rolled her eyes. "I guess you'll have to save it for Ian."

"Hey," Ian protested, climbing in and out of the truck with no difficulty, "save it for Mom."

Helen leaned out of the house and waved her hands. "Alexandria, NASA is on the news!"

Alexandria bolted for the house. With a laugh, Ian stuffed the folding step back into the truck. Nikos locked and closed the doors before following.

Inside, Helen and Ian lounged on the couch, while Alexandria perched on the edge.

The announcer said, "We are discussing the new asteroid discovered near Jupiter nine months ago that recently reappeared from the asteroid belt. The Minor Planet Center tracked an orbit that would take it past the far side of the moon. NASA announced it has now crashed on the moon."

Alexandria muted the television. "Well," she said, "it's too bad there are no moon landings planned soon. The geologists would have a field day."

Ian shrugged. "It's just a rock."

Helen laughed. "Do you suppose Troy will stop worrying about it now?"

"Ha," Alexandria said. "He likes thinking it was aliens. I'm sure he'll say it landed, not crashed."

Ian sniffed. "You're no fun. Aliens are more exciting than a rock. Hey, if it was really aliens, do you suppose Dad will try to go fight it and get killed? Then we wouldn't have to move."

"Cruel boy," Nikos scolded. "Wishing death on your father."

Ian gave him a withering look.

"Well, then," Nikos said, "wishing me back to a lonely existence." He made sad eyes at Ian, exaggerating for effect, even though he did feel crushed at the thought of losing his new siblings.

Ian pondered that for a minute. "Okay, Dad can live, if he wants. I'll keep you."

Alexandria reached for the remote. "Why don't you boys go help Mom with dinner. I want to watch the rest of it."

And so Nikos and Ian did, sure their sister would tell them more than they wanted to know after dinner. Science lectures or not, Nikos was happier than he'd ever been.

Chapter 23

In Which They Sneak Away

THE DARKNESS WAS NEARLY ABSOLUTE, and even the glow of the air spell was too faint to illuminate the inside of their escape craft. Only the feel of her brother's warm skin next to her kept Miknon from panicking. Air blew softly across her face, but she could touch the lid of the message pod above her. Heat from the young dragon seeped upward.

They were trapped in a coffin. This was a bad idea.

A grinding noise echoed through the pod, and she jerked.

"The hatch is opening," Gil whispered. "It's almost time."

When the grinding stopped, the dragon moved, rocking their prison from side to side. Miknon clutched the safety harness and wiggled a little lower until it crossed her chest instead of her belly. The dragon paused, leaned forward, and jerked.

"Fly for the dark side," Gil whispered as if the dragonet could hear him. "Land in the dark."

Miknon gripped the harness and his arm and held her breath.

The dragon dipped and rose and dipped again. Weight pressed them against the base of the pod as the little beast struggled to escape the pull of the worldlet.

"Come on," Gil said. "You can do it."

And what if it couldn't? They would crash.

"We'll die," she said numbly.

"We won't die," he said.

The dragonet jerked. It wasn't strong enough for the flight. They would die. They should have stayed on the ship. She could have tried to hide for a conjunction or two, until the lords and warriors left for Ki. And even if she was caught, at least Gil would have lived. Now they would both die.

The dragonet kept rising and dipping, obviously struggling. It would get lost, or crash, or fail to pass the world barrier. Or land on the light side of Ki where the natives could tear all three of them apart.

Gil put his hand over her. "Breathe. We'll be fine."

She tried to absorb his optimism. They had food and water until they landed. All they had to do was survive until then.

And then make their way through a foreign world of strangers with unknown powers.

No, his optimism was ridiculous. How could he be so hopeful? Her stomach churned.

The dragon jerked again, and then the motion stopped. Weight vanished, and Miknon floated up against the safety harness.

"Well done, Azidaka," Gil said, even though the dragon couldn't hear them. "We're past the worldlet. Now we just wait."

Just wait. Wait to land in enemy territory. Wait to live or die.

His breathing slowed and deepened, and then he began to snore as if he wasn't at all worried.

Miknon's heart raced, and the back of her neck tingled. Breathing slowly to settle her nausea, she stared into the darkness for a long time until she also fell asleep.

When she woke and stirred, Gil spoke.

"Hey, sleepy, are you hungry?"

"No," she lied. "We should wait. But I am thirsty."

With his help, she drank a little from a flask, then heard him swallow. With no light to distract and no exterior sounds, every movement they made was audible in the small space. Even the dragon's breathing echoed softly.

"This was a bad idea," Miknon said. "We should have stayed."

Gil grunted. "Not a chance. I won't let them find you."

"Then I should have come alone."

"We have a better chance together," Gil said. "Hush, and save your energy."

"For what?"

"Then save your air." He squirmed a little, then took a slow breath and held still. "I'm going back to sleep."

With no better ideas, she did the same.

The next time they woke, the air spell had fallen about a sixth, so they ate a little and drank again. The dragon's warmth radiated into the message pod, though the blanket was still helpful and so was Gil's warmth. With no better options, she crawled — bounced — to the foot of the pod and relieved herself in the far corner, pressing against the blanket to make sure the liquid was absorbed instead of floating around.

"Gil? Are you — Do you need—" He couldn't even move, so what could he do?

"No, I prepared already."

He didn't offer more details, so she crawled back to her place and wiggled under the blanket and the safety strap.

For a while, she watched the air spell gradually shrink, until she realized she was panting. This wasn't helping. She closed her eyes and concentrated on breathing slowly until she fell asleep again.

After each nap, they drank, and each time they thought long enough had passed, they ate a little. Always hungry, always thirsty, not daring to slake themselves. They rarely spoke, though Gil frequently rested his hand over her, and she clutched his fingers for comfort.

By the time the air spell reached the halfway mark, the food and water were almost gone and the pod stank of urine and sweat.

"Soon," Gil whispered.

He tugged on every strap, flask, and bag he could reach, making sure they were tight. And yet, the dragon kept flying smoothly, with long, slow wing beats and no dive.

After a long time in the quiet darkness, Gil spoke again. "Very soon."

Unless they were lost in the expanse between stars or the dragonet had run away with them.

Preferring to miss her own death, Miknon went back to sleep.

Eventually, her aching belly woke her anyway. The air spell was now two-thirds empty.

As soon as she stirred, Gil spoke. "We can't return to the ship."

Miknon shrugged, knowing he would feel her shoulders move against his arm. What difference did it make if they died on Ki or in the middle of nowhere?

"We'd better save the last of the food for when we land," he said. "But you might as well have some water."

He held the flask for her, then took a few swallows himself.

She took a deep breath and dared her burning question. "Gil, do you honestly think we'll survive?"

"We aren't dead yet."

She glanced at the diminishing air spell and rolled her eyes. Not yet.

An hour or two later, their pod tipped, and they slid until Gil's head smacked into the wall. He tugged on the straps again and put his good hand over her.

"This might be it," he said. "Are you ready?"

"Ready to get out of here." Not a bit ready for anything else.

"I hope Azidaka can get through the world barrier." Gil's voice finally sounded worried. "He's never done it by himself before. He was only a wee baby when we left Kunisu."

"Mmm," Miknon murmured.

If they didn't make it, at least they'd die fast. At least her stomach was empty, with nothing to vomit if the flight got rough. Or if her nerves got worse.

The pod tipped even farther, until they were nearly upside down. Weight returned and then doubled. The walls of the pod got warmer, then hotter, then very hot. Miknon shifted away from the burning as much as the straps allowed. Gil tapped the cold spell twice, and the pod gradually cooled to merely uncomfortable instead of burning.

Their weight doubled again, pressing them into the blankets until she couldn't even move. Miknon took quick, shallow breaths, trying to always keep air in her lungs. If they emptied entirely, she might not have enough strength to inflate them again. Beside her, Gil likewise panted.

Their weight doubled yet again, and the cold spell whined with effort. Miknon gasped for breath, but her lungs were too squashed to move. The dragonet jerked and bounced, throwing them from side to side in the pod, but they couldn't move enough to protect themselves.

And then their weight decreased, though it didn't disappear. The jostling continued more softly, and she could yet again breathe.

"I think we made it through the barrier," Gil said cheerfully.

"Oh, good," Miknon croaked.

Her head and arms ached where they had slammed against the pod, and the strap had cut into her waist. The dragon's flight evened out for a while, then jerked again. They fell, yanking against the safety straps, then smashed into the sides of the pod as the dragon suddenly stopped.

Gil tapped off the cold spell, hand hovering over it in case the heat rose again. The dragon was motionless beneath them.

After a few minutes, Gil inhaled deeply. "I think we're here."

He fumbled for the closest straps, freeing Miknon and allowing him to sit up. He reached past her to open the latch, moving slowly.

She didn't blame him. Moving was agony, and her arms shook with effort just pushing herself to her knees. She must weigh at least twice as much as she ever had on the ship, and much more than she had in the ship while parked on the worldlet. Flying was out of the question until she strengthened her wings. She couldn't even flap without pain.

Gil groaned and shoved on the lid of the pod. It gave an inch, then stopped. Grunting, he lifted his shoulders and threw the strength of his entire upper body into the effort. The lid rose higher, and Gil forced himself to a sitting position, giving the lid one last push. It clanked onto the dragonet's back, startling a jump from it. Gil and Miknon clutched the safety straps again.

"Sorry, Azidaka," Gil said.

He tapped off the air spell, and they both took deep breaths. If the air was toxic, better to find out quickly. But it filled her lungs painlessly, so she took another breath.

Near-darkness surrounded them, so the little dragon had remembered to land on the dark side of the world. Above her, stars twinkled. She had expected that from the stories of the old world the elders told. She hadn't expected to be able to see the worldlet, much less that it would shine so brightly that the darkness was incomplete. Though no color was visible, she could see the bulk of the dragon beneath her.

She also hadn't expected the lower lights in the near distance. Were they that close to the light side, then? The dragon had done very well indeed, to land so close to the border. Perhaps they had a chance to survive.

"What are all those smells?" Gil inhaled deeply and sighed.

Well, he could sniff if he wanted, but she had other things on her mind, including getting out of this stinking tub. Once the dragon settled again, Miknon slid over the edge and down the dragon's side until she reached the ground.

The light was only enough to see shadows beneath her feet. To the touch, the ground was tickly and poky, not the hard, dead ground she expected, but it didn't matter. Limbs shaking with the effort, she crawled a short distance away and emptied her bladder. Her head spun, and she couldn't seem to tell which way was up.

"Which way did you go?" Gil's shadow rose above the dragon, as if he was sitting on the edge of the pod.

"Left of his head."

A soggy squelch came from above, then a wet splat to the right side of the dragon. Gil must have thrown out the disgusting blanket that had covered them. He shuffled in the darkness, and another splat followed. The padding blankets. His clothing rustled, and something else hit the ground with a mild splash.

"Here's the food and water," Gil said. "We'll need to find a stream soon."

She crawled the few steps back to the dragon and waited until he lowered a single flask and the last bag of food. Instead of carrying them, she merely guided them to the prickly ground and waited.

Gil's clothing rustled again, and then something clinked inside the pod. He grunted, then the shadow of the lid hid him before it swung down with a clang.

"I'm leaving everything else inside," he said wearily. "If we have to run, we can grab onto the harness, but Azidaka can't move with the lid banging into him."

"Good plan." Miknon fumbled with the ties on the food bag while she waited for him to descend.

In a minute, his foot brushed her wings. Gil moved a little to the side and sank down, bare skin warm against her arm. He was nothing but a shadow in the darkness with a glint at his neck. He still wore his family emblem and the king's signet, so the clink in the pod must have been his dagger.

"It's so hot here," he said. "I expected the dark side to be cold. Do you suppose our entrance heated the air that much?"

"I don't know," she said. "Maybe it's always so hot."

"This world makes no sense," he grumbled.

She shoved the water flask until it bumped into him. "We'd better eat and drink."

He groaned. "My head is spinning, and my arms weigh as much as a troll." But he fumbled for the water and took a drink, then held it for her. "How much food do we have?"

She peeked inside the bag. "One meal."

"Then I can only shift once before we find more to eat," he said. "Ugh, my bones already ache. Well, it's easier to walk on four legs, anyway. Spreads out the weight."

But would it make enough difference, or would his bones snap under his own weight? What choice did they have?

"What do you think is edible here?" she asked. "And how far will we have to walk?"

"The lights don't look that far," he said. "I hope we'll find plants that look a little familiar. Otherwise, we'll have to pick something random and hope for the best."

Hope. She didn't remember what that felt like, but she would keep going for his sake.

They divided the food and ate silently, forcing each bite upward with heavy, aching limbs, then drained the water flask. For a while, they rested against the warm sides of the dragon.

Finally, Gil groaned and moved. Obviously, he felt as miserable as she did. He scooted a short distance away and shifted slowly. With his heavy fur coat, he'd be even warmer, but there was no help for it.

When he was four-legged, he lay on the ground for a few more minutes, panting with exhaustion.

If he couldn't even move, how would they find food? This whole idea was stupid.

Gil rolled over enough to touch her. "Is it getting darker?"

"Maybe?"

They stared at the sky as the stars twinkled brighter.

"Yes, a little darker," Miknon decided.

"Are you ready to move?" he asked.

"No," she groaned, but she crawled to him so she could ride on his back.

A horrible roar cracked the darkness. The dragon bolted and disappeared. Either it didn't feel the pull of the world as much as they did, or sheer panic was driving it. Though it surely couldn't run far even with the strength of fear, it didn't respond when Gil shouted after it.

Miknon dove under Gil and clung to his chest fur as he rolled over to put his feet beneath him. As if he could run, when he hadn't even managed to stand yet.

They had no way to escape. They were dead. As soon as the monster caught them, they were dead.

The roar went on and on, impossibly long. Then it coughed and stopped, and a light sprang up. Metal clanged, and voices drifted through the air.

Was it a tame monster, then? Miknon froze, hardly breathing. If they didn't make a sound, maybe it wouldn't notice them.

Footsteps approached, rustling the scratchy groundcover. A shadow stopped nearby, and Miknon held her breath. Metal rasped softly, then water pattered gently onto the ground. An all-too familiar reek struck her nose. Oh, the monster wasn't chasing them after all.

Miknon let out her breath, and Gil chuckled softly.

The shadow froze. Metal rasped again, and the shadow turned slowly in a circle.

Gil ducked his head, but it was too late. The shadow approached on quiet feet. It had two legs and two arms and was shorter than Gil in his other form. As it got within a few steps of them, the light from the worldlet shone on its face.

Gil raised his head, and Miknon gaped from beneath him.

It looked like a highborn, a little, though its hair was between the silver and gold most common for the lords, and its ears were round. More surprising, it looked younger than Gil. Its eyes widened, and it crept forward, falling on its knees by Gil, who tried to scoot backward but yelped in pain.

The monster — not-monster? — put a gentle hand on Gil and turned its head to call behind it. Her idiot brother licked the monster's cheek.

Miknon's heart pounded. She could let go of Gil and escape by herself, but where would she go? And Gil was in trouble because he had tried to save her. She couldn't abandon him now.

She tightened her grip on her brother's fur. Whatever happened, they would endure it together.

CHAPTER 24

ESCAPE TIME

June 14, 2022, Colorado Springs

ALEXANDRIA SQUINTED in the bright sun. "Hurry, Mom! We'll be late."

She waved at Ian as he went into Nikos's house. She had gotten her driver's license and a full-time job right after school ended three weeks ago, so the boys hung out together.

Mom dashed out the door. "I need to grab the mail."

Alexandria backed up the car to the end of the driveway where Mom stood reading a letter. "Mom, just grab it, and let's go."

"Go," Mom whispered. She stuffed the papers back into the envelope with trembling hands. "It's time."

"Yeah, I know," Alexandria said. "Will you get in the car already?"

"No, not time for work," Mom said. "The divorce is final. Troy will get his copy at work, so we need to leave before he gets home."

Alexandria turned off the engine and stared at Mom in shock. Today? Didn't she get even one more day with Dad? Ha. Dad hadn't spent any time with her for weeks. Months. The warm sunshine suddenly felt cold on her skin, and her chest ached. She pressed her arms over her stomach to combat nausea.

"What about work?" she asked.

"We'll text them." Mom slapped the car on her way past. "Come on, Alexandria, get moving."

Right. Alexandria parked, then pounded on the Moss's door. Nikos opened it, one eyebrow already raised in a question.

"It's time." Alexandria leaned against the doorjamb and closed her eyes.

A warm hand gripped her arm, and Nikos shook her gently. "Are you okay?"

She took a breath and opened her eyes. "Yep, awesome."

Just stick to the plan and pray. With Dad's job dragging them all over the world, she knew how to adjust to a new place and make new friends. This was more of the same. Except without Dad.

"Okay," Nikos said. "I'll send Ian right over. Can you guys be ready to leave in an hour?"

She gulped. "Let's see if we can beat that." She forced some kind of smile and ran home.

By the time she reached her bedroom in the back, the front door slammed. Must be Ian. Her cedar chest was already packed with clothes and the few books and mementoes she could keep. A small duffle bag held clothes and toiletries for the trip, and a used backpack carried her notebook, a card game, and several maps and lists.

She yanked off her work uniform and changed from the skin out. Like Dad insisted, she was taking nothing he bought. Space posters gleamed with color above her galaxy bedspread, like the universe surrounded her. Her telescope from Dad leaned in the corner, and she tucked it into the closet to block out her old life. Nothing mattered now except the remnants of her family.

But a tear still crept down her cheek.

After texting work to quit, effective immediately, she left her old phone and made sure her new one was in her pocket.

Mom tapped on her door. "Are you dressed?"

Alexandria wiped her eyes and opened the door. "Yeah. Almost ready."

Mom, also in a new outfit, squeezed her quickly and headed for the back door.

Alexandria grabbed her backpack, duffle bag, and Grandpa's telescope. "Goodbye, Dad," she whispered.

She hurried out the back door, passing Ian and Mom headed back in. After dropping her armload over the waist-high fence into the Mosses' back yard, she hurried back inside, yet again passing her family.

A quick look into Ian's closet showed all the small stuff was gone, so she went to her room and started dragging her cedar chest. Mom returned, and they carried it to the back yard, then fetched Mom's chest. Ian managed his folding bookcase by himself.

As they dropped Mom's chest by the fence, Nikos exited his back door with three suitcases. He set his luggage by his truck at the back of the long driveway and gave Ian a hand to climb over the chain-link.

"Can you ladies lift the chest to the top of the fence?"

They hoisted the first one up. He shoved it into the back of his truck, then returned for the second one. Meanwhile, Ian stuffed their three backpacks into the rear seat of the truck. Ian's bookcase slid down the side of the truck bed, with one of Nikos's suitcases protecting it from the chests.

Nikos helped Mom climb over the fence while Alexandria clambered over by herself. Nikos ran a bungee cord in front of the chests, then added his other suitcases. Alexandria nestled her precious telescope between the sleeping bags while Nikos threw in the cooler, duffles, an empty crate, and Ian's book boxes. Together, they covered the back with a tarp.

Alexandria started for Nikos's back door. "I should go say goodbye to Mrs. Moss and tell her thank you for everything."

"She went shopping, but you can email later." Nikos opened the front passenger door for Alexandria.

Once everyone buckled, Mom prayed for safety and a smooth journey, and after a pause, she prayed for Dad's heart and mind to heal.

Nikos started the truck. As he reached the end of the driveway, Dad's car screeched down the street and parked in front of them, blocking their escape. He jumped out of his car and reached for his gun.

Mom burst into tears and lowered her head to her knees. Ian wrapped an arm around her and glared at Dad. Neighbors turned off lawn mowers or rose from their gardening pads, reaching for cell phones.

Dad dropped his gun inside his car and slammed the door. The neighbors lowered their phones but didn't put them away. Some aimed them subtly toward the driveway and tapped the screen, as if they were recording the drama. So much for sneaking away. Though with Dad here, that was meaningless, anyway.

Dad stomped toward the truck, and Nikos flexed his hands on the wheel.

"The doors are locked," he said calmly. "Just stay put."

Alexandria bit her quivering lip. "Now what?"

If he didn't want them, why couldn't he let them go in peace? Or had he decided to fight for them at last? Relief fought with frustration at his poor timing. He should have said something before signing away custody.

Dad pounded on the window. "You can't sneak off," he bellowed. "Where are you going?"

He didn't want them to stay, just to disclose their destination? Why? So he could ruin their lives even more?

Alexandria unfastened her seatbelt. "I'll talk to him."

Nikos grabbed her arm. "Don't risk it. Look how angry he is."

"Yeah, well, I'm angry, too!" She clamped her lips together and blinked away the tears burning her eyes.

"I'll talk to him," Mom choked out between sobs.

"He's madder at you than at me." Probably. "I'll do it. If he tries to do anything, just run over him, Nikos."

Nikos reached for his phone. "If 911 doesn't get here in time, I'll keep that in mind."

With a deep breath, Alexandria stepped out. Dad darted around the truck and screeched to a halt three feet away. His face blazed red, and his hands clenched and unclenched. The neighbors held fingers poised over their phone screens, and Nikos rolled down the passenger window a couple of inches and aimed his phone camera at Dad.

"Where—" Dad yelled. He held his breath, then lowered his voice. "Where are you going?"

"I'm not telling you."

"You're my daughter!"

Alexandria hissed, "You should have remembered that earlier."

Dad's face turned darker. "I don't like you leaving with that boy."

"Then you should have done your job, Dad." Alexandria tried to make the title sound like an insult, enjoying the way he flinched.

Dad flung his arms wide. "I gave you everything! This house, driving lessons in my new car, judo, nice clothes, a *second* telescope, a good school, free college tuition, entry to a great career. Why don't you realize how good you had it?"

Alexandria whispered, "I wanted you." She squared her shoulders. "But you stopped being you. You broke your promises, stopped caring about my activities, just stopped being my dad. I don't know you anymore. And you belittled Ian for his headaches and discounted his brilliant language ability. You didn't even want us. Why did you give up shared custody if you love us so much?"

With half her support gone, it was like balancing on one leg, and she couldn't stop wobbling.

Dad scowled through the truck window at Mom. "I thought it was a ploy from your mother. You know, give me a deal so bad I'd be willing to pay alimony."

Alexandria winced. That had been the idea, only it was hers, not Mom's.

"I thought she'd come back with a more reasonable deal," Dad continued. "Or come back entirely. Everything was good enough if your mother would try to understand me a little better."

"Good enough?" Alexandria blurted. "Is that what you think? You seriously need therapy."

After another look at the neighbors, Dad mumbled, "I've been going to my PTSD therapy. Not that it's any of your business."

"I meant family therapy," she said. "If you had only tried, we would have stuck with you. You are our business, Dad. We love you."

"Your mother doesn't."

Alexandria glanced over her shoulder. Nikos, Ian, and Mom watched in horrified fascination, and Nikos held the door latch, ready to jump to the rescue.

"Mom's been crying for months," she said. "Not just for the way you treat her, but from missing you. A minute ago, she was praying for you to be healed. She loves you — loved you."

With wishful thinking and happy memories blinding her, Alexandria had taken far too long to realize where the real problem lay.

Dad's shoulders sagged. "But now I'm just an engineer and not a pilot, and this house is as fancy as we're getting. And the PTSD…"

Alexandria's heart cracked. "Oh, Dad. Mom doesn't care about any of that. She loved *you*. But you stopped treating her like your wife and started acting like she was in your army."

"Air Force," Dad corrected, then winced.

"Under your orders," she amended. "Not a partner. You lost your kindness and your loyalty and your sense of humor. And you threatened your own children. Mom had to protect us."

"I did not threaten you," he protested, squaring his shoulders.

Alexandria raised her eyebrows. "You told us we had to join the military, like it or not. You said you'd put Ian in military boarding school."

"I just want what's best for you," he said. "If aliens are coming from that thing on the moon, the military is the best way to protect yourself."

Alexandria sighed. "Dad, if aliens were coming from a crashed space rock, they would already be here, long before we made it into the military. And we don't want military careers. You pushed us away because you wouldn't listen."

"I still want you," he argued. "We could appeal to the judge. You're old enough for that to make a difference."

She could stay with her father. Same school, same friends except for Nikos, same house. Keep all her stuff, including her telescope. She could email Mom and Ian, and visit. Maybe they could settle nearby. She could tell the judge she wanted shared custody, even if Ian didn't, and split her time between Mom and Dad.

She had gone along with the escape to Pennsylvania because she didn't have a choice, but now she could have everything. All she had to do was say yes to Dad. Yes to staying, yes to family, yes to her old life. Every nerve tingled, and she could picture it all.

"Alexandria?" Nikos said.

She glanced over her shoulder at him, then at Mom and Ian. They were all watching her, eyes wide.

Alexandria turned back to Dad. "And I could go to any college I like and study astronomy?"

Dad beamed at her. "We can talk about it. Just stay with me." He held out his arms.

Pain struck her chest like a steam roller. *We can talk about it.* He still thought his ideas were best. If she stayed, how long would it take before he ordered her around like he did Mom? How long until he started breaking promises again?

Alexandria closed her eyes and looked for her inner zen. With her world turning upside down, she'd better find her own balance, or life would throw her like the best judo opponent.

What bout could she actually win? Not the one with Dad. Her heart crumbled, and tears choked her throat. If she couldn't depend on Dad, she'd have to take care of herself. And Mom and Ian. And Nikos.

"I'm going with Mom," she whispered.

And they might as well stick with the plan and go with Nikos. Dad could have lots of space to fix himself, and maybe Ian would heal with some distance.

Dad grabbed her arms. "I don't think that's a good idea."

Nikos opened the truck door and jumped out.

"Everyone is watching you, Dad," Alexandria said. "They'll show the videos to the police when they arrive, and you'll never be allowed to see us again." And Nikos might flatten him, military physique or not.

After a quick look around, Dad's shoulders sagged, and he let go, flexing his fingers. "What about letters or emails? Can I come to your college graduation? Your wedding? Will I ever see you again?"

Alexandria rubbed her aching forehead. "Until I'm eighteen, I'll stay with Mom and Ian. If you commit to getting the help you need, and stop thinking it makes you weak, I'll consider contacting you then. Prove yourself first, then you can tell Mrs. Moss you're ready to talk to me."

"Mrs. Moss knows where you're going?" He narrowed his eyes at the house next door.

"She only knows how to contact Nikos, who will know how to reach me. If you threaten her in any way, this deal is void, Dad."

Her old dad wouldn't have needed the clarification, but he was gone, and she didn't know if the major could find him again.

"Two years?" Dad protested. "What about Ian?"

Alexandria shook her head. "Ian will make his own choices; I'm only dealing for myself. Yes or no, Dad?"

He gulped. "Yes." He held out his hand for her to shake.

This was her last chance. She ducked inside Dad's reach and threw her arms around him.

"I love you, Dad," she whispered.

Slowly, his arms closed around her. "I love you, Alex — Alexandria."

She let go and backed up. Maybe he did love her, if he knew what love was. Time would show.

He stood for a minute, arms still spread, then let them fall. "I'll contact you in two years."

He pressed his hand against the back window, and Mom copied him from the other side of the glass. After nodding at Ian, Dad glared at Nikos and drove away.

The neighbors let out a collective sigh and put away their phones. No 911 calls, thank goodness, but embarrassing videos might show up online.

Alexandria climbed back into the truck. "Bank's next."

Nikos examined her face for a long minute, then spit on the ground. He hopped in the truck and turned the key. "Bank it is."

As they drove through the neighborhood, he waved at all the neighbors. Some waved back, and some gave various gestures of triumph.

Alexandria went into the bank alone and emptied all but a few dollars to keep the account open until their last paychecks were deposited. Back in the truck, she handed the receipt to Mom.

"Two thousand should get us through the trip," Alexandria said.

"Three days of hotels, yes." Mom's head creased with worry wrinkles. "But what about restaurants? And how long will it take to find an apartment once we arrive? What about furniture?"

Alexandria winked at her. "Nikos, go to Walmart next. I have a plan."

"Why would I ever think you didn't?" But he headed north obediently.

Alexandria rummaged through her backpack for a list. "Buying food each day will be cheaper, and the cooler is big enough for milk and sandwich fixings."

"I suddenly understand the empty crate," Nikos said.

She grinned and tore her list into fourths, handing two backwards. "I've divided what we need by store area. You'll get exactly the same things every day or two on the trip. Mom, two loaves of bread and pick some fruits and veggies."

"Thanks for trusting my judgment," Mom said dryly.

Alexandria wrinkled her nose at Mom. "We haven't died of malnutrition yet. Ian, get cereal, granola bars, and pudding cups. You can pick flavors, okay? Nikos, the milk and deli stuff weighs less than four hundred pounds." She stuffed his list into his chest pocket, ignoring his snickers. "I'll get peanut butter, jam, and mayo. Be at the front in five minutes."

When Nikos parked, all four of them streamed into the store, grabbing small baskets on the way. Alexandria was the first one to make it to the checkout counter, though Ian arrived seconds later, grinning from ear to ear. Mom and Nikos were only a minute behind.

"Apples and carrots," Mom said triumphantly.

Nikos merely waved a jug of milk with one hand and cheese and meat with the other.

Working together, they grabbed ice, got through self-checkout, and had the cooler and crate packed in minutes. Forty dollars, ouch, but fast food would have cost almost that much for one meal.

Once back in the car, Nikos pulled up their route on his GPS, and they headed east.

"If all goes well, we'll make Kansas City in less than nine hours," he said.

"Yay," Ian cheered.

He was smiling harder than anytime in the past year. Maybe this whole disaster would be worth it eventually, if her little brother could be happy.

"If you're okay driving, I'll take a nap." Mom leaned her head against the window and closed her eyes. In the mirror, Alexandria could see quiet tears running down her face.

Alexandria bit her lip. She wouldn't cry. She didn't have time to cry.

"Things will get better now," Nikos said. "You'll see." He kept his gaze on the road, but he patted her hand for a second. "We'll make a good family, and you can be an astronomer like you want."

But I wanted astronomy and Dad, her heart wailed. She nodded anyway. If Dad put his life back together, she might have a chance in two years. And if not, she'd have to learn to do without him. Somehow.

After a couple of hours, Nikos pulled off at a city park. They ate peanut-butter-and-jam sandwiches and apples, then switched drivers. Nikos climbed into the back seat, took some migraine pills, and shoved his sunglasses up his nose.

Alexandria pulled back onto the highway with Mom riding shotgun because of her brand-new driver's license. The cars zipped by like comets burning down the road, and she clutched the steering wheel with white knuckles.

Mom said, "Speed limit's seventy-five. Set the cruise control."

"How about sixty-five?" Alexandria bargained.

"The trip will take too long," Nikos said.

"Seventy?"

"Seventy-five," Mom repeated.

Alexandria swore internally every time Mom or Nikos caught her turning off the cruise control and going slower. When Mom took her turn after a couple of hours, Alexandria collapsed in the back seat, only waking when the truck stopped again. Nikos waited for her to sit up from off his shoulder, then swapped places with Mom.

In Kansas, they gobbled ham-and-cheese sandwiches, with pudding for dessert. Then it was her turn to drive again, with Mom and Nikos constantly reminding her to speed up. She gritted her teeth and pressed harder on the gas pedal, only to discover a few minutes later that she had slowed again.

When Mom took over, Alexandria nearly cried in relief.

At nine p.m. they reached Junction City, still two hours from their intended destination. Ian was fast asleep in the back seat when Mom pulled off for gas.

"I don't think we'll make it to Kansas City." Diplomatically, Mom didn't mention Alexandria's slower driving. "Should we look for a hotel here or push another hour to Topeka? It will be dark soon."

"I'm still wide awake," Nikos said. "I can drive some more, and Ian won't care. That means it's up to you ladies."

"Alexandria," Mom asked, "are you okay for another hour?"

"Yeah, I got a nap, remember?" Alexandria winked at Mom.

As they drove, the sun sank to the horizon in the rearview mirror, and the light slowly faded.

Half an hour after they pulled out, Ian stirred, then jerked awake. "I gotta use the bathroom!"

"We'll be at our hotel in about half an hour," Mom said.

"Right now," Ian squeaked. "Sorry."

Nikos pulled off an exit to the middle of nowhere. As soon as the truck stopped, Ian bolted into the field. Within a few steps, the darkness had swallowed him, but they could still hear his footsteps.

"Seriously," Alexandria said, "tomorrow we need to wake him up at every rest stop."

Nikos laughed. "No worries. He'll see this as an adventure."

Alexandria rolled her eyes. "Boys!"

"Mom, Mom," Ian called in a high voice.

Oh, no, had he run into a skunk or a patch of nettles or something?

Mom grabbed a flashlight and ran after him, with Nikos and Alexandria on her heels. They found Ian on his knees, bent over something dark. He turned to look at them, and other eyes shone in the flashlight's beam. Dark fur gleamed under Ian's hand.

"I found a dog," Ian said. "Can I keep him, Mom? Please?"

"No." Alexandria turned to go. The hotels would protest, and they couldn't afford a pet.

"Oh, please, Mom. He's a great dog."

Alexandria stopped, back to Ian, and folded her arms. They needed to get going.

"Honey, we can't take care of a dog," Mom said. "Come on, we've got to go."

"But he's hurt. We can't just leave him here. He'll die, Mom. Come on, Nikos, he can go in the back of your truck."

"Injured animals can be dangerous," Nikos said. "Stray dogs wander Crete's countryside, and they aren't afraid to attack humans."

"I'm not leaving him."

Alexandria turned, and Ian had thrown himself on top of the dog, hugging him tightly. Oh for—

Nikos groaned and threw his arms in the air. "Okay, we'll drop him at the animal shelter tomorrow morning. Best we can do."

"Yay!" Ian hopped to his feet and pumped his fist.

Nikos slowly approached the dog and scooped him up. The dog filled his arms and then some. While he couldn't weigh four hundred pounds, he was the biggest dog she'd ever seen.

"Alexandria," he said, "please lower the tailgate for me."

"This is a bad idea," Alexandria predicted, but she rearranged the truck bed to make room.

Nikos settled the huge black dog. "I'm not sure he's injured," he said, "but I can feel his ribs."

Alexandria groaned and tossed the dog the last of the luncheon meat. "You're not keeping him, Ian."

Ian patted the dog as Nikos fastened the tarp with a gap. "He's a good dog. You'll see."

Alexandria dragged Ian to the back seat and buckled him in. "No dog, Ian."

But her brother immediately started trying to persuade Mom to keep the stupid dog.

The last thing they needed was a dog. Nothing would make their situation harder than having to take care of a dumb animal.

EPILOGUE

IN WHICH THEY FIND ALLIES—
OR ARE TRAPPED BY ENEMIES

157 CONJUNCTIONS AFTER DEPARTURE, SOMEWHERE IN THE DARK, SURFACE of Ki

THE ALIEN WAGON hummed under Gil's feet like a monster. The aliens had climbed inside it and started it with their magic, though Gil hadn't understood their spells. Neither the magic nor the wagon surprised him after the scrying, but he hadn't expected any people to live on the dark side of Ki unless they were ice monsters. Then again, Mother had told him the dark side of Old Kunisu was unbearably cold, and the dark side here was very warm.

They were trapped, and he couldn't get out. Miknon crawled up his chest and hugged his neck. But she had managed to stay with him, unlike the terrified dragon. Poor Azidaka, alone in the dark. At least he had eaten plenty on the way down, and when he got hungry again, he could fly to the light side.

Gil blinked in the darkness as lights flew past him. Why so many lights on the uninhabited side of the world? Perhaps these aliens had so much magic that they could spend enough to make the dark side a livable place. If they had that much power, they wouldn't fear his people, and his offer of information for refuge would be wasted. Had he placed himself and Miknon in danger with no chance of salvation?

Between the impossibly hot air and the even hotter wagon carrying him, Gil was baking. He wished he still had his knife, but at least he wouldn't miss his clothing. He hung out his tongue and panted.

Beneath his chin, Miknon clutched his necklace and shivered. She couldn't be cold, but he didn't blame her for being scared. By the time they could tell if they were in the hands of potential allies or trapped by enemies, it would be too late. But they had given them food. That had to be a good sign.

Shar was right about this being a bad idea, but how could he leave Miknon to face the wrath of the lords? For that matter, he still didn't like the council's plan to conquer this world by force. He wanted to take any chance to make allies.

The magic wagon picked up speed until the air whistled past. This magical beast wasn't as fast as a dragon, but it was much faster than a kelpie. An even larger wagon flew past, and then another, and the air of their passing sucked fiercely at him. Miknon clutched his necklace, and Gil ducked below the edge to keep her safely inside.

First things first. Strength, then assessment of their choices.

He sniffed the food the alien had given him. What was it? If he ate it, would it help him or make him sick? He licked the thin slices. They tasted fine. And sooner or later, they'd have to discover if they could eat the food. He set aside half of it for Miknon and gobbled the rest.

While he waited to see what would happen to him, he squirmed around to face the window to the navigation part of the wagon and raised his head. As they rushed past each light, he could briefly see the silhouettes of all four aliens talking and gesturing. Arguing, assuming their body language meant the same as the fae, but they looked so similar he couldn't help applying the same rules.

The smaller one in the back talked the most, waving its hands and tilting its head in a pleading way. It wanted something. That was the one that had found him and touched his fur so gently. From the way it had smiled and bounced when the wide one picked up Gil, it had wanted *him*. Since he hadn't been hurt, he counted the little one as a tentative ally, but he wasn't sure about the others.

The two in the front, the darker-haired ones that were tallest or broadest, talked the least, but their tight shoulders and frowns told him they disagreed with whatever the little one was saying.

The big one in the back, whose pale hair matched the little one, rubbed its forehead and shook its head at the little one's pleas. Definitely no agreement. If the little one was asking to help Gil, the pale big one was no ally. But would they simply let him and Miknon go, or imprison them?

Or kill them?

Assuming their food didn't poison him before then. But it had been a few minutes since eating the sliced stuff, and he still felt fine.

"Go ahead and eat, Miknon. I'll shift now."

The more he could strengthen his bones, the better their chances of escape if things went badly. And hands would allow him to hunt around the wagon, because he thought he smelled more food right behind him.

He hated to steal from possible allies, especially if they might also be starving, but he had to be strong enough to protect his sister. Once he could explain, he would make it up to them.

Gil sniffed around the strange crates until he identified the two that smelled like probably-food, then shifted. Immediately hungry again, he forced his too-heavy arms to pry open the sealed crate that ought to guard the best food. It was full of bottles and strange packages that were hard to open, especially with his injured hand. When he finally got access, most of the food was too strange to eat, but the thin slices were edible and the creamy liquid was delicious. He returned the jars and pushed down the lid.

An open crate held apples and carrots and crunchy-chewy bars of grain. Saving one each for Miknon, he ate everything else. Stomach full, he ripped open the rest of the packages, except the impenetrable cup things, then shifted again. Already his bones felt less creaky.

Once again hungry, he gobbled the squishy white slices and the tiny crunchy circles. With his claws, he slashed open the tops of the cups and licked out the sweet, creamy insides. He had eaten enough to shift one more time, but then he'd only be hungry again, and all the food was gone.

And with the aliens locked inside the wagon-monster, he couldn't talk to them. Any apologies or tries at alliance would have to wait until they stopped traveling. He checked through the window again, and none of the aliens were still talking. The little one leaned against the big pale one, who stroked its hair slowly, soothingly.

Gil's heartbeat slowed with the rhythmic motions. Moving on this heavy world was exhausting. He could talk to the aliens after they emerged from the belly of the magic wagon. Miknon was already asleep, curled up between his front paws.

He yawned and closed his eyes. Later, then. For now, he needed to gather his strength. Later, he would ask them for refuge and alliance. Shar was wrong; these aliens would see the value of new friends. They had to, to save his people and their world.

Wait a second, dear author! Did you just end the book in the middle of the escape?

Sure did! Exciting, huh?

But are Gil and Miknon safe or not? What will the Fitches do when they discover the truth about the dog? Er, werewolf!

Find out in The Peril of the Fae. Turn the page for a sneak peek!

THE PERIL OF THE FAE

The fae are real...

Gil and his sister escaped their spaceship with two goals: save her from murdering lords, and forge an alliance with Earth before the same lords try to conquer it. The fae have magic, while Earth has tech and greater numbers. But in a battle, which would win?

And they are here...

Alexandria and her family are fleeing her parents' toxic divorce, seeking peace and safety. But when they accidentally make first contact with the refugees, their troubles suddenly become global. If they can't make a treaty, the fae will attack Earth, and both sides might die.

But Earth doesn't even believe in the fae...

*The Peril of the Fae is a new first-contact novel where fae from space don't match Earth's mythology, and a found family holds the world's destiny in their hands. It is the second book in the **Return of the Fae** series of clean YA contemporary fantasy with a dash of sci-fi & mythology, from the author of **Unexpected Heroes**, and is best read in order for the most enjoyment.*

Still want more? Get free stories by joining my newsletter. Every two weeks, I chat about my current writing or my life & offer book news and deals. And did I mention free stories?

Sign up at MCLeeBooks.com.

Free story #1: Spotting the Fae

Zak is considered too young to navigate the spaceship, even though he's the best among the fae.

On Earth, Gaby loves math and helping her astronomer Mama with her data.

When Mama spots a new asteroid heading toward Earth...

Everything will change.

*The author of **Unexpected Heroes** returns with a startlingly plausible blend of sci-fi, mythology, and the modern world. **Return of the Fae** is a clean YA contemporary fantasy series where fae from space don't match Earth's legends.*

Free Story #2: The Cat's Fortune

On another world, so long ago that truth has faded into legend, a cat and a boy seek their fortune together. You think you know the story, but do you?

Orphaned and homeless, young Aktar travels to the city of Rapata for a better life.

But it seems the rumors of gold-paved streets are false. Can he find a home and a job before he starves? Maybe with the help of a foundling kitten.

*A retelling of Puss in Boots and Dick Whittington, with timeless themes of belonging, courage, and self-discovery, set on the fantasy world of Kaiatan, home of the **Unexpected Heroes**.*

Please leave an honest review on any retailer or reader site. Seriously, it would really help me. :)

If you found a typo, you're welcome to report it at mcleebooks.com/report-a-typo/

CHARACTER LIST

Humans
Nikolaos Antonakis: "Nikos," 17-year-old exchange student from Greece
Ms. Blackwell: trig teacher
Alexandria Fitch: 15-year-old future astronomer
Helen Fitch: Alexandria & Ian's mother
Ian Fitch: Alexandria's 12-year-old brother
Troy Fitch: Alexandria & Ian's father
Forest McConnell: high school football player
Edgar & Patti Moss: Nikos's host parents
Mr. Reynolds: history teacher

Fae
Arishaka: king of the fae
Ashur: dryad, Gil's friend
Azidaka: baby dragon
Dagan: chief guard, Gil's Grandsire
Gil: shifter, youngest fae on ship
Izdu: gremlin, chief navigator, Zak's father
Kishar: fae lord, Arishaka's cousin
Maia: shifter, Gil's mother
Merodach: fae healer
Miknon: pixie, Gil's adopted sister
Nik: pukel, king's secretary
Ram, shifter, Gil's twin
Shalla: sirin, king's housekeeper
Sharrukin: prince of the fae
Zaidu: fae lord
Zak: gremlin, youngest navigator

Places

Ki: the intended new home of the fae; Earth

Kunisu: the old home of the fae

New Kunisu: the flagship of the fae fleet

Acknowledgments

Thanks to my critique group for their usual spot-on comments: Carol Malone, Donna Gonzales, Gail Porter.

Also thank you to my fabulous alpha and beta readers: Bart Denison, Breanna Cypers, Laura Drake, Lea Carter, Melanie Ansley, Molly Morrison, Robin Cranney, & Virginia Cummings.

Special thanks to Joe Jensen at Utah Valley University for his science knowledge, Ioanna Papadopoulou for help with Nikos, & Robin Cranney for military info. If there are still mistakes, they are my own.

About the Author

Marty C. Lee told stories for most of her life, but never took them seriously until her daughter asked her to write one for her. Between writing and spending time with her family, she reads, embroiders, paints-by-number, and gardens.

She has lived in five states (including Colorado), seven cities, and eleven houses so far. She knows bits of two extra languages, but some days can't even speak her native tongue fluently. She isn't any kind of athlete but does have sneaky ninja (or fairy) feet. Though not an extrovert, she does have friends besides her books. You are welcome to write to her as a new friend. :)

You can find her at MCLeeBooks.com and on Facebook and book sites.